GLINDA'S
Ruby Slippers

A NOVEL

MIKE RADICE

KENILWORTH, NEW JERSEY

© 2025

This is a work of fiction. Names, characters, businesses, places, events, locales, and incidents are either the products of the author's imagination or used in a fictitious manner. Any resemblance to actual persons, living or dead, or actual events is purely coincidental.

CIP available upon request

Cover design by: Gram L. Telen
Interior design by: Gram L. Telen
WWW.FIVERR.COM/GRAMTELEN

Chapter One

LOS ANGELES

FEBRUARY 1939

Victor Fleming banged his fist on the wall and yelled, "Cut." He'd never punched a wall before during filming, at least not that Billie knew about. But then again, *The Wizard of Oz* was a whole new experiment to direct. Color. Delicate sets. Delicate people. Delicate budget. Pieces that only sometimes seemed to fit together.

Would there ever be an end? Some people had been working six days a week.

Billie stood on a platform playing Glinda the Good Witch, wand in hand, holding her breath. Sweat formed on her brow and pushed through the thick makeup, the kind that would make a fifty-four-year-old woman look thirty-five. Hopefully, this "accident" wasn't her fault. She'd been an actress for forty years and knew enough to avoid mistakes, but with a hoop skirt this wide, who knows what she may have banged into, especially since she was on the border of being lost in the scene? Filming had been stop-and-go, stop-and-go. She'd lost her place once, something a professional never did, something *she* never did, or at least not since she was in her twenties.

Victor swung his arms and paced. He was a thick-muscled man in his late forties, calm when things were calm, a tornado when they weren't.

The room was silent as if everyone in it had been caught in mid-breath, but then a clipboard fell on the floor, startling Billie and making her heart race. The klieg lights clicked as if tapping their toes, waiting.

Victor ran his hand through graying hair and barked, "In ten."

Billie felt the collective sigh and was glad she wasn't to blame. If she were, Victor would have said something by now. *Oz* had already been delayed twice, and was now three months behind schedule and two hundred thousand dollars over budget. Billie could buy a Bel Air estate with that amount of money. She could also buy back Burkeley Crest and restore it. Her energy dropped as sadness crept in over the loss of her home. She shook her head and took a deep breath. She was a professional, doggone it. If she thought about her former home, she'd cry. But she was Glinda the matriarch now, and Glinda never cried.

Assistants scurried about checking and fixing things. Billie touched her wig. Good. It was in place.

She used the break to get back into character. Thinking about the past always sunk her, making it take longer to find her way back. She relaxed her shoulders and became one with a set that looked like a page from the Brothers Grimm. One hundred thirty dwarfed people dressed in colorful clothing were about, talking to one another. Most of them weren't professional actors. They were just interesting folks bused in from circuses and vaudevilles across the country. Here, they were *Oz*'s villagers, her subjects as Glinda the Good Witch. They were her children. Her responsibility. It was time to turn on "the mother."

She closed her eyes to slide back into Glinda, but someone tapped her shoulder. She tensed. Was she partly to blame for the delay after all? It wasn't that studio head L. B. Mayer kept score, but Billie knew she was viewed as less valuable to the studio at her age, so she needed to be careful. She opened her eyes and saw Judy Garland before her, the girl playing the lead role in the movie. Judy stood in her cute gingham dress, hair braided, with Terry the dog in her arms. Judy played twelve, but she was actually sixteen, her bosom strapped tight to her chest. Billie had been there. Most actresses had, and thinking of it made her breath quicken. The poor girl was locked up like Spam in a Hormel can.

Billie smiled. "Yes, dear?" She rubbed the terrier's chin. "Sweet Toto," she said. It was the dog's character name, and she wanted to help keep him in character, too.

"Do I look okay?" Judy asked.

Billie motioned. "Turn around." She held onto her wand with her right hand and lightly touched Judy's shoulders with her left to give her a gentle steering.

Judy made a slow turn as Billie inspected her. Stops these days worried professionals on the set, and Judy had caused more than her share. It was forgivable, Billie believed. The girl was so young in many ways, though she acted younger than Billie's daughter had at the same age. When Patty was around Judy's age, Billie and her husband, Flo, had lost everything—the theater, the house, Billie's Broadway career. Patty had handled it all so maturely that Billie worried about what was really happening inside. But now, at twenty-three, Patty still seemed fine.

"I don't see anything," Billie said, shaking her head.

Judy's shoulders relaxed. Her brown eyes asked: When will this end?

"Maybe this will be the last time," Billie said.

Judy frowned and shook her head. "I doubt it." She adjusted Terry's position in her arms. "This dog is heavy, and I can't let him down. I need to keep him out of the way of things."

Billie wanted to hold the dog, but she was still working to stay in character. She also wanted to keep her dress clean.

"Two minutes," Victor called out through a megaphone.

Judy turned. "Excuse me for a minute," she said. "I'm going out in the hall to the fountain."

"You don't have time," Billie said.

Judy left with the dog. They'd better not have to wait for her.

"In one," Victor yelled.

The townspeople, called "Munchkins," hurried into place as the klieg lights flashed and clicked.

Victor looked left and right, then his face turned apple-red. "Where's Miss Garland?" he bellowed.

Billie shook her head. That girl had been responsible for almost half the stops so far. Billie had been on the stage since age twelve, and never had she been so careless.

"Here, here," Judy called, running onto the set, the dog squirming in her arms.

Victor's chin dropped. "Good grief."

Judy took her place in front of Billie. "Sorry," she said as she set the dog on the floor.

"Thirty seconds," he said as he scanned the room.

Heads shook, but everyone seemed to be in place.

"Action," Victor said. He turned and walked to the director's chair.

The cameras purred like giant cats. The lights clicked rhythmically to the heatwave.

Judy, the Kansas girl, turned to Glinda.

Glinda tilted her head and asked, "Are you a good witch or a bad witch?"

"Who, me?" Dorothy raised her eyebrows and stepped back. "Why, I'm not a witch at all. I'm Dorothy Gale from Kansas."

Glinda pointed her wand at the dog. "Is that the witch?" she said in a lilting voice.

"Who, Toto? Toto's my dog."

Three Munchkins pranced up to Dorothy with "put 'em up" swaggers and thumbs in their pockets. "We wish to welcome you to Munchkinland," they sang, rocking back and forth.

Billie held her wand in front of her chest and smiled.

"We welcome you to Munchkinland," they continued. "Tra la la la la la. Tra la la tra la la. Tra la la la la la la."

The top-hatted Mayor stepped up. "From now on, you'll be history."

"You'll be hist—, you'll be hist—, you'll be history," sang the hundred-plus Munchkins.

A cloud of red smoke puffed up through the floor, followed by a flash of fire. The sulfur smell reached Billie's nose. She tasted mineral oil, which made her stomach curl. She swallowed to keep her insides down.

The Munchkins screamed and scattered, hiding behind buildings and plants. The leaves quivered.

The cameras rolled as vomit surged up from Billie's stomach. She swallowed again to force it down. There was something suspicious about the smell. It was more pungent than usual. Judy stood in front of her, facing the cameras. Billie gently pulled the girl toward her to protect them both and backed up a step. The move didn't help. She backed up again, and her hoop skirt hit a plant behind her. The leaves on those plants were Egyptian fan-size, and she thought she heard one hit the floor. Hopefully, the camera (and Victor) hadn't noticed.

"Goddamn it," Victor yelled. "Cut."

Billie let Judy go, closed her eyes, and dropped her chin to her chest. Film was so different from theater. On stage, you continued in front of an audience even when something unexpected happened. You figured out how to work around the problem and then you just did it. You kept going. In film, however, they spliced the scenes together in a lab. What appeared in the theaters was nothing like what had been filmed. The pieces were assembled like a puzzle. Billie had learned to suspend her character through a stop, using intention and holding on to the last memory. Doing so was becoming increasingly complex with *Oz*, though. It was like having a conversation with someone only to be stopped mid-sentence and then, twenty minutes later, being asked to pick up where you left as if nothing had happened.

She opened her eyes, half-expecting to see an assistant or someone patiently standing before her with hands folded in front of his heart, waiting. But nobody was there. She sighed in relief, turned to look at the plant, and saw that the leaf was intact.

Oh, thank God, she thought.

Victor unbuttoned his vest and looked up. "Miss Garland," he said in a measured voice, making Billie think an explosion was coming. "I need you to move closer to the smoke ring. Just a foot." He held his hands up to show the distance, then pointed to the smoke ring. It was about six feet away from Judy.

Judy stepped forward, and Billie's hands twitched to grab her from behind. She wanted to say, "No, don't." Fires on the set were dangerous. She'd known a few actors over the years who had been burned. Earlier in the day, a fire had burst through the ring prematurely, and everyone had jumped. If that happened once, it could happen again. The odor and taste from the ring were stronger today. Something was wrong.

Billie grabbed her wand with two hands and squeezed. This was Judy's issue, and Judy wasn't Billie's child. If Judy were her daughter, Billie would grab her from behind, pull her away from danger, and give Victor a piece of her mind. But Judy had to learn to defend herself. How she would do that was another question. Judy was a sixteen-year-old with a child's heart; she was completely controlled by the studio as if she had no mind of her own.

Judy and Billie were coworkers, and this wasn't Billie's problem. She had to let it go.

"Miss Burke," Victor said. "I need you to move closer to the fire ring, too."

Billie stiffened.

Victor motioned for her to move. "Miss Burke."

Billie dug her feet into the floor and remembered Martha Moore. Martha had been one of her husband's dancers who got her start in his *Ziegfeld Follies*. She later went into silent film and died because of a situation like this.

"We repaired the ring," Victor said. "You don't have to worry."

Billie let go of Glinda. "I'm sorry, but I can't," she said, shaking her head and trying to sound soft and sweet but rock-firm. If she got burned, she'd be scarred. If she were scarred, she'd never work again, and she had to work. Victor might tell her to get out if she refused, but who would replace her at this point? Nobody. He'd have to refilm all the prior scenes in which she'd played a role. He wasn't going to do that, for sure. That would cost even more money and create additional delays.

Victor crossed his arms over his chest and spoke through his teeth. "Miss Burke. I'm going to ask you one more time."

She shoved her hands on her hips. No man was going to push her around. "No," she said sharply.

His jaw tensed. He motioned for her to step forward. "Just a foot," he said in a kinder voice, almost like a question.

Judy bit her lip.

Billie squeezed the frame of her skirt. "No," she said, more forcefully this time. "You can hire a stunt double if you want." The Wicked Witch had a double.

"You have to step forward. It's in your contract."

That wasn't entirely true. There was no mention of fire in the contract, only obedience, but compliance didn't mean risking her life for the work. Victor's contract had an obedience clause, too, but if a producer told him to stand before a firing squad and be shot and killed, Billie knew perfectly well he'd refuse. There are fundamental human limits that exist beyond the signed dotted lines.

Judy looked away.

"Now, step forward," Victor said. "They repaired it, and you won't get hurt."

Billie's shoulders tensed. She pointed to the floor. "I'm not moving from this spot." She owed this to herself. She owed it to women in film. She understood Victor's pressure, but it had nothing to do with her. Would he pay the bills after MGM fired her because she wasn't attractive enough? No, he wouldn't. If it had been a woman directing *Oz*, she'd have understood.

Time was money. What was Victor going to do? Billie didn't want to embarrass him or deflate his authority, yet she also wasn't going to move.

A cloud of silence filled the studio like the still before a tornado.

Victor's eyes narrowed. "We'll deal with this later," he muttered.

Nervous coughs poked through the crowd on set, and Billie felt her shoulders relax.

Victor jotted a note on a pad of paper, ripped off the page, and handed it to an assistant. The young man carried the note off the set.

Billie froze. Was the note about her? Was Victor complaining to the producer? She shook the idea from her head. She was thinking like a schoolgirl. It was time to re-become Glinda. She closed her eyes and remembered where she'd left off—what she felt, what she said, what she was thinking, and how she wanted to protect her Munchkin townspeople.

"Places," Victor shouted.

Judy looked at Victor and then at Billie. Her face seemed to ask if everything was going to be all right. Billie pulled Judy toward her for a protective light hug.

"In one," Victor snapped.

This was what Glinda would have done: stand down anyone who threatened her people. It set a good example for Judy, who needed to learn to stick up for herself. Billie straightened her skirt, softened her insides, and searched for her first line. She couldn't remember it. What was it, "This is the Wicked Witch of the West?" or "Bring the carriage around?" or "That's your sister under that house, and I'm glad she's dead?"

The cameras groaned. The lights clicked on.

Victor called out, "Action."

What was that line? It had something to do with the witch. It would come to her. If not, she'd make up something that worked that could be even better than the original.

She could make something up if she didn't remember. That's what you did in theater. So what if film was more scripted?

A ring of red smoke puffed through the floor. Her stomach churned at the smell, so she swallowed, hoping it would help.

The actress playing the Wicked Witch, Maggie Hamilton, appeared from below on a rising platform amid a red cloud of smoke. The smoke quickly dissipated, revealing an angry, beaked woman in a Southern widow's black dress and coal-black coned hat, her face and hands emerald green.

The witch spun around, broom in hand, her skirt swinging wide.

The Munchkins screamed and scattered.

Maggie made the perfect witch. She'd turned this role into a child's game and had thrown herself into it. She was quite scary, even to the actors who knew better. Offstage, she was one of the sweetest, smartest, and kindest people Billie had ever met. She was also easy to work with, yet she knew when to say no like a long-term veteran. Billie had been on stage for over forty years, and Maggie for about ten.

The Munchkins hid behind the plants as the witch growled and stomped toward the prairie house on the set. Protruding from underneath the house was a pair of striped-stockinged legs topped with ruby slippers. The house had fallen from the sky in a tornado storm.

The witch distracted Billie, and she'd lost her hunt for her first line. She had to start over. What was that line?

The Kansas girl quivered. "I thought you said she was dead," she told Glinda.

The line. The line.

The witch mourned her sister, whose legs protruded from the house.

It was time for a line. "That was her sister, the Wicked Witch of the East," Glinda said, pointing her wand at the ruby slippers. "This is the Wicked Witch of the West, and she's worse than the other one was."

The line was correct and had come from out of nowhere. Thank goodness. Glinda was back up and running.

The witch turned and walked toward Glinda and the Kansas girl, pointing a crooked finger at the girl. "Who killed my sister?" she snarled. "Who killed the Witch of the East? Was it you?"

"Cut," Victor said.

Billie dropped her wand to the side. Who had made a mistake this time?

Victor continued: "Freeze in place. Shoes."

Well, at least it wasn't a mistake.

A dresser removed the ruby slippers and slipped them onto Judy's feet.

"Roll," Victor said.

The Wicked Witch moved closer to the house and cackled, "The ruby slippers. What have you done with them? Give them back to me, or I'll—"

"It's too late," Glinda said, pointing at the slippers with her hand. "There they are, and there they'll stay."

"Give me back my slippers," the witch insisted. "I'm the only one who knows how to use them. They're of no use to you."

"Keep tight inside of them," Glinda said to the Kansas girl. "Their magic must be very powerful, or she wouldn't want them so badly."

Judy's pigtails shook, and Billie's insides froze. This wasn't the shake of fear; it was the shake of a loss of control. It was going to start. She just knew it.

Judy leaked a giggle, then a series of them, and then a big laugh. Billie closed her eyes and shook her head.

Victor dropped his chin. "Cut. God damn it. *Cut!*"

Judy put her hand over her mouth as her face reddened. It was no use. It was too late.

The air leaked out of Billie as if from a punctured tire. This was the third time Judy had broken character this week, and it was only Thursday. This was a movie set with a meter running on its cost. Billie fought back the urge to lecture. The girl needed to learn discipline, the driver's license of life. But who was going to teach her?

Yes, Billie had had a laughing fit once as a young girl. It happened during a stage rehearsal for a musical in London. She'd been given the job of rowing a canoe on stage and singing a song. However, there was something funny about it to Billie, almost like a sneezing fit when a dust speck goes up your nose. Her mother (her professional manager) had been in the theater seats, watching. It wasn't funny to her mother, who walked up to Billie at the first break with arms across her chest and a stern look. That's all it took. Billie never laughed during a scene again. She wasn't sure how she had managed to control herself all these years, but she had.

Judy, on the other hand, seemed unable to control her giggles, and her mother wasn't here to give her a stern look. This was an indoor movie set; nobody was allowed inside except actors and crew. The studio gossip was that Judy's mother was detached about her acting, letting the studio control the girl. Judy was left alone to straighten herself, and if she didn't, MGM would send her back to the music hall where she had been discovered. *Oz* would be the end of the road for her.

Victor walked toward Judy, who was still standing in front of Billie. His face showed an eerie calm, and he walked with a measured gait, stopping a foot away. The room went still: one hundred–plus Munchkins, crew, actors. No sound.

Billie stepped back, anticipating the lecture the girl needed and glad she didn't have to deliver it.

Judy dropped her hand. The smile was gone, the face apologetic.

Victor clasped his thick hands together. "Now, darling, this is important."

"I'm sorry, Mr. Fleming. It won't happen again." Judy sounded sincere.

"You bet it won't," he said, then raised his right arm and slapped the girl across the face.

The room gasped. Some people shrieked. Billie stepped back reflexively.

Judy dropped her jaw, and her cheek turned pink. She put her hand on the spot, but she didn't cry.

Yes, Judy's behavior was inappropriate, but only parents had the right to slap their daughter. Even then, they shouldn't do it. Neither Billie nor Flo had ever slapped Patty. Worse than that, a man slapping a young woman was wrong. Billie wanted to say something to Victor, and she would have if she had been the girl's mother. As it was, she wished she could comfort the girl, but feared it might rile Victor. Instead, she just wrung her hands.

Over the forty-some years of her career, Billie had seen shouting, objects thrown, rants, and meltdowns. Creative types could be emotional. She'd even seen two male actors fall to blows, but she'd never seen a grown man hit a girl. At least a man could have punched him back, but a girl was defenseless.

Victor showed no remorse.

Billie understood Victor's frustration: The producer was upset with the delays, and Victor needed to finish the film, but turning to violence was crossing a line. Billie reached out to pull Judy toward her, but the girl shrugged her off.

"See everyone back here tomorrow, six a.m. sharp," Victor snapped. He looked at Billie and pointed to her. "Closer to the fire next time," he said.

After that slap, it was easier for her to scoff at him inside. She felt disgusted.

Judy raced for the exit, her pigtails flopping.

Chapter Two

Forty-five minutes later, Billie was wearing a blue summer dress, relaxing in her studio bungalow. Curled up in the corner of a pink chaise-longue, she sipped a cup of chamomile tea. On a nearby table sat an unopened envelope from her mailbox. She pulled her legs up under her tighter. The handwriting on the outside belonged to L. B. Mayer's executive secretary. She was the one who ran the studio. Notes from The Mount—the nickname given to Ida Koverman because she was impossible to get around—often carried bad news.

Billie stared at the writing as she counted to ten, swearing she'd open the envelope on eleven. When eleven arrived, she lengthened the count to twenty-five and slowed her pace.

At twenty-four, she set the teacup on the table and closed her eyes. At twenty-five, she changed the count to fifty. At fifty-three, she opened her eyes, shook her head to clear it, and said out loud, "Good grief, just do it."

She picked up her pearl-handled letter opener, sliced through the envelope, and pulled out the note. She took a deep breath, unfolded it, and read, "Please call me to set up an appointment with Mr. Mayer." It was signed, "Mrs. Koverman."

Billie's breath quickened. News of her refusal to move closer to the fire ring must have reached L. B. already. She closed her eyes and crumpled the note in her hands. What was he going to do with her? Fire her permanently? Yank her top-billing status? Force her into "B" films? Relegate her to fishwife roles?

She readied for a fight, which wouldn't be her first. But she couldn't help wondering: Would she win this time? How many times could she defend herself before Mayer grew tired of it? The older she got, the less valuable she was to him. Her fan base was aging and dying, and the younger generation—the moviegoers—were more interested in actors like Judy Garland and Mickey Rooney. Billie's daughter, at age twenty-three, was older than both.

Billie straightened the note in her lap and stiffened her spine. After all, she'd earned her spot in the galaxy of stars, and MGM benefited from her presence. Once a star fell, her lights went out, but she wouldn't let that happen. She was going stand up to Mayer.

She reached for the phone and dialed with determination. The phone rang once before The Mount answered: "Mr. Mayer's office."

She sounded calm and professional. Then again, Billie thought, you could drop a bomb before The Mount, and she'd still sound the same. Billie wished she had nerves like that.

Billie cleared her throat, and the two women shared pleasantries. The actress inside Billie turned on the calm. "He wanted to talk to me?"

"Yes, he does," The Mount said. "Can you come to his office tomorrow after filming at four-thirty?"

Billie wanted to end this. If she had to wait until tomorrow, she'd lose sleep. "Is he available now?"

"He's here. I'll ask."

Billie took several slow deep breaths. Thoughts jumped around in her head like popcorn on the stove.

"Yes, you can come over now," The Mount said. "Are you out of costume? Can you be here in fifteen minutes? He has another meeting in an hour."

Was she ready for this? "Yes, and yes," Billie said through vibrating teeth. "Is it bad news?"

"I don't know what the news is," The Mount said.

Oh, yes, she did. The Mount knew more about this place than L. B. did. She was dodging the question. That meant it *was* bad news. If it were good news, she'd have said something.

"I'll be there," Billie said.

"Splendid. We'll see you in fifteen minutes." The phone clicked off. Billie grabbed her purse and hustled out the door to the reckoning.

Walking quickly down MGM's Main Street toward the Thayer Administration Building, Billie passed newsstands, the diner, and a costume shop as people called out, "Miss Burke, how are ya?" and "Miss Burke, slow down, you're going too fast." She ignored them, focusing only on the white marble building ahead.

When she reached the front of the commissary, Bert Lahr blurted, "Billie." He was in his *Oz* lion costume talking to a ginger-haired young man she didn't recognize. His eyes bulged with a clear signal: "Help."

She hesitated for the flash of a second, but then kept going. Fifteen minutes wasn't long enough for a stop; she'd apologize to Bert later. A few steps further, she heard a young man's squeaky voice from behind: "Miss Burke, wait. May I talk to you?"

She rushed ahead, shaking her head and muttering, "Good grief."

"Miss Burke, wait," the voice called from behind. It seemed closer, almost on top of her. Her heart raced. She stepped off the sidewalk and hurried along in the street.

A motorized cart honked from behind her, then its brakes squealed.

She stepped to the side, looked, and shook her head. "I'm so sorry." She'd raised her daughter never to run into the street, and now look at what she had done.

"You wanna get killed?" the driver snarled.

She nodded in apology and stepped back onto the sidewalk.

"Miss Burke," the young voice said from directly behind her.

She lost her focus and bumped into an actor dressed as a monk who was standing next to a Civil War soldier.

The monk snapped, "Well, I never! How rude. You should be more careful." His eyes suddenly opened wide, and his jaw dropped. "Oh, my stars. It's Billie Burke." His face signaled an apology.

"It was my fault," she said. "I'm so sorry."

He waved her along.

"Thank you," she said with a smile as she resumed walking quickly, ignoring the persistent boy behind her. The stairs to the building were only about twenty feet ahead. She was almost there.

The ginger-haired boy—a young man, actually—jumped in front of her, removed his hat, bowed, and combed his hair back with his pinkish hand. He wasn't wearing a wedding band. His blue eyes looked imploring.

She dug her nails into her palms and stopped. The young man's leprechaun face seemed harmless, but he was certainly persistent ... and annoying. "Excuse me," she said through her teeth and then stepped to the right.

He stepped in front of her.

She looked around for security, but didn't see anyone. The guards were supposed to protect the talent from intruders like this. How had this young man gotten here in the first place? The guards at the gate were usually quite thorough.

"I'm sorry to bother you," he said. His breath smelled like root beer.

"I'm in a hurry. I have an appointment." She pointed at the building.

"It will only take a second."

"I don't mean to be rude, but I have to go. If you'll excuse me." She stepped to the left, but he raised his hands to stop her. She scanned the area again for security. "If you'll excuse me," she repeated, more insistently this time, as she tried to push past him.

He stepped in front of her again.

Her pulse raced, then slowed when two men in suits she didn't recognize approached in an electric car. She sighed in relief and waved at them, hoping they'd see her gesture as a signal to help her. They returned her wave and kept going.

"Good grief," she snapped.

"Miss Burke," the young man said. "I don't mean to startle you, and I won't harm you. Just thirty seconds." He held up his hand. "Then I'll let you go."

She looked at her watch. She had seven minutes left for a four-minute journey. "Very well, then. Thirty seconds." She folded her arms across her chest. It was the only way she'd get rid of this tenacious young man.

He took a deep breath, holding his hat in front of him. "Gosh, it's swell to meet you. May I ask a question?"

She held up a finger. "One."

He took a deep breath. "Thank you. I'm Tom O'Donough. I'm a publicist. My office is at Vine and Hollywood." He pulled a calling card from his jacket.

She raised her eyebrows. "You're too young to be a publicist." He seemed to be about Patty's age, which meant he was nothing more than a child to Billie.

"I know what you're thinking," he said. "But your husband was my age when he got started."

"My husband was a producer, not a publicist, and at your age, he made many mistakes."

"True, but he was also his own publicist."

She nodded. Tom's respect for Flo warmed her toward the young man. Flo Ziegfeld had been a Broadway producer. He'd had a publicist, but he also liked to tease the press himself, and he was good at it. He'd occasionally throw out a false story and watch the press run with it, like the time he made up a tale about Billie's jewelry being stolen from a Chicago hotel. The story was in the news for days.

"Continue," she said to Tom.

"I want to represent you. I could do a lot for you."

She threw her head back and laughed. "Is that what you tried to sell Bert Lahr?"

"That's what I'm selling to any star who will listen."

"MGM handles my publicity, so I'm afraid I don't need you. Now, if you'll excuse me." She took a step forward, but he didn't budge.

"Are they getting the job done?" he asked.

Of course not, the answer was, and it was a sore point for her. But she said, "Yes, they are, and your thirty seconds are up." It was MGM that promoted her films, not Billie herself. She'd asked them to do more, and they'd made promises, but nothing happened. Regardless, she wasn't going to hire a mere boy to handle her public relations. She looked at her watch. She had five minutes to reach Mayer's office.

"Now, please move out of my way," she said. She eyed two security guards in gray suits who were approaching from the left. Her shoulders relaxed. Finally, she thought.

Tom stepped back. "You haven't heard what I can do for you."

Her jaw stiffened. "If you'll excuse me."

The boxer-shaped guards stepped behind Tom and gripped the boy's arms. "Come with us," one of them said.

Tom's blue eyes bulged. Sweat formed on his brow.

Billie was relieved but also worried. "Please be gentle with him. He didn't hurt me." The boy seemed frail in their grasp. "He was only asking questions. It's okay."

"He's trespassing," said the strong-armed guard on the right. "The security office has had three complaints in ten minutes."

Tom's hat fell to the ground, so Billie picked it up and handed it to one of the guards. The young man shoved his card into Billie's hands as the men dragged him away. She took it.

"Call me," Tom said.

* * *

Billie hustled up the stairs to the building's entrance, jogged inside, and found an available elevator. She took deep breaths to calm her pounding chest. Once she reached the elevator door, she pulled a mirror from her purse and checked her hair, playing with the curls a bit. She looked fine.

Moments later, she stepped out of the elevator on the fifth floor and stood in front of L. B.'s office door. After a few more deep breaths, she was ready. She turned the knob, pushed open the door to reception, and stepped in. The clock on the wall read four-thirty-one, and she hoped it was fast. She checked her watch: four-thirty. She was on time.

The Mount was behind her desk with every white curl on her head in place. She looked up from behind a pair of horn-rimmed bifocals.

"I'm sorry if I'm late," Billie said. "I got here as quickly as I could. I was stopped on the lot by an intruder."

"Don't worry," said The Mount with a slight smile. Her smiles were always slight. "He's running late."

Billie sighed inside in relief.

The Mount motioned to a white cushioned chair along the wall. "Please, Miss Burke. Have a seat." She resumed writing in a ledger.

Billie sat like a schoolgirl anticipating punishment from the headmaster. She looked around the room to see if anything had changed, a way of keeping her mind occupied. She hadn't been in this office for six months, maybe longer, and had forgotten how white and bright the place was. Everything was white—the tile floor, the plaster walls, the leather furniture. Polar bears had more color. Billie would have gotten a headache if it hadn't been for The Mount's eggplant-colored dress. Why wasn't the woman wearing sunglasses?

The decor had been L. B.'s decision, a ploy to make himself and MGM seem pure because white was the color of virginity. Of course, he was far from pure himself. He'd had so many affairs with women, he'd run out of toes and fingers to count them on. Flo had had his share, too, but Flo had been different. He had a tremendous passion inside him, and he had always loved his family above all.

The Mount grunted. A letter was in her hand.

"Something funny?" Billie asked, appreciating the distraction from her thoughts of men's improprieties.

"Just the opposite," The Mount said with a blank face.

"Oh? Somebody is in trouble besides me?"

The Mount scoffed. "Everybody's in trouble around here. You know that."

Billie bit her lip. "*Am* I in trouble?"

"I don't know, Miss Burke. He didn't tell me."

Well, Billie had tried. She crossed her legs and rubbed her thumb along the edge of her purse.

The Mount opened another ledger on her desk, licked her finger, and turned the page, making a flicking sound.

Billie tapped her foot. The clock on the wall read four-forty-one. How much longer would this be?

Her contract was clear that she had to obey, but she couldn't do what Victor was asking with the fire for safety reasons. She could lay out exactly why she had been right to refuse: If she became disfigured, she'd be useless to the studio. After all, her films made money, and she did have a fan base, even if they were a little on the older side.

If that argument didn't work, she'd suggest a stunt double. Plenty of actors had them. Choosing one this late would delay filming a day or so, but that wasn't so bad. And they didn't need more costumes: There were several Glinda costumes on the rack. Of course, they'd have to choose someone who was a good physical match, which could be difficult.

If that route didn't work either, Billie would use her biggest weapon: She'd threaten to deny the studio access to Flo's shows. L. B. loved making films from them because they made money. Billie had heard that L. B. wanted to produce a *Ziegfeld Girl* film using Flo's work. He'd have to go through her to get the rights to use them. She'd sold the rights to the Lemberg brothers to pay off debt, and the brothers would only give them to L. B. if she asked on his behalf. The brothers—who were still producing on Broadway—hated L. B. Most people hated L. B., although they masked their feelings for professional reasons.

Billie felt a smile leak onto her lips. She straightened her skirt and held her head up high. At last, she had a lever that she knew would work. She was ready. "Rabbits, rabbits, rabbits," she said in her head. It was her mother's Welsh saying for good luck. Sometimes it worked, sometimes it didn't, but it never hurt to try.

The intercom on The Mount's desk buzzed. Billie jumped.

L. B.'s tenor voice scratched through the speaker. She couldn't understand what he said but she was glad to hear it. She wanted to get in there and get this over with.

The Mount stood. "You may go in now, Miss Burke."

Billie clutched her purse under her arm, held up her chin, and stepped into his office.

L. B. rose from his crescent-shaped desk, and a smile spread across his face. His face seemed to honestly say, "Dear old friend, it's been too long."

Billie turned off the queen inside her and relaxed. This was going to be fine. It wasn't about the fire on set. It was about something else. Something good. "It's nice to see you," she said.

L. B.'s black hair was a touch grayer than the last time she'd seen him.

"I'm sorry I'm late, but I had to take a call." His voice was friendly.

"That's all right," Billie said. "I—" She stopped, catching herself before she could add, "I was late, too."

He motioned to a captain's chair across his desk and returned to his own seat.

She sat, covered her knees with her skirt, and straightened her purse on her lap. "How's your mother doing?" she asked. L. B. believed the mother of every family was its heart and the medicine to cure the world's problems. He appreciated it if you asked about her, so everyone did.

"She loves the Jewish Home," he said, folding his hands on his desk. "But she complains I don't visit her enough."

"Mothers are like that." Billie's stomach twinged. She missed her mother. Mother had lived with her, and she'd seen her every day except when she was on tour.

"Mine insists I show up every day, but I can't. I aim for once a week."

Billie took a slow breath. "I'm glad to hear she's well. If there's anything I can do, let me know." She sat back and crossed her legs.

"Thank you." His smile twitched and then faded. "I'm sorry to rush this, but I have another appointment in a few minutes, and I'm behind."

She nodded for him to continue, but she had a queasiness in her stomach. His face was oddly still, his eyes flat and dull. She squeezed her knees together.

"Billie, I love running this studio," he said. "You know that, don't you?"

She nodded. "Yes, I do."

He swung his arms wide. "We make the best films here, and I want to keep it that way. I love this job. I love this place."

"Yes. You've done an astonishing job," she said, squeezing the life from her purse, wondering where this was going.

He locked his brown eyes onto hers. "Well, I have some news."

"Good or bad?"

He looked to the side. "I had to make a decision. I didn't want to, but I had to."

Okay, bad news. "Oh?"

"I called you here about your contract. I'm sorry to say that we can't renew it in May."

Billie looked at the Navajo pattern in the rug; it seemed to swirl and jiggle. This couldn't be happening. She couldn't lose this job. Thanks to Flo, she was fifty-four years old and still four hundred thousand dollars in debt. Acting was all she knew, and nobody else would hire her at her age. She had to do something. She told herself to be rational, work this through, find a compromise. She took a calming breath. She remembered Flo's rights.

"You want the rights to do *Ziegfeld Girl*, don't you?" she said, clutching her purse upright on her lap, her back stiff.

"I have them already."

"What?! How?"

"Money. I offered a good deal, and they took it."

She felt like she'd lost the last thread holding things together. Now, she didn't even have courtesy control over Flo's (and her own) creations. Everything was gone. She had to think of something fast, but no levers emerged.

She caught herself looking down, so she raised her chin and looked L. B. in the eye. "I don't understand. I've been here seven years. My reviews are excellent, all of them. In fact, they're fantastic, and my films make money. This makes no sense." Tears formed, but she fought them back. She couldn't cry now. She had to be tough.

"You have two more films scheduled through June," he said. "You'll be with us until then." He looked away and shook his head with fake sympathy. He was a terrible actor.

She drew a sharp breath. "What is this really about?" Her lower lip quivered. She stiffened her spine to regain her self-control.

He jabbed a finger at her and his eyes turned flinty. "I warned you."

Her power switch turned on. "Warned me about what?"

"Two words: *Dorothy Arzner*."

Billie's face turned hot. "What?! What about her?" How dare he bring up Dorothy? Her best friend. They had resolved that issue years ago. Yes, Dorothy was a lesbian, but she was committed to another woman. And no, Billie wasn't a lesbian—there was nothing wrong with that, of course. Dorothy was her friend. It wasn't as if they'd had sex, which they would never do. Yes, they'd been to social events together, and L. B. had told Billie four years ago to stay away from "that woman," as he called her. But he'd said nothing since. Billie had thought it was over.

His eyes narrowed. "You were filmed holding hands with her."

She gasped. That was on film? It had no meaning—certainly not *that* meaning. Women held hands. It's what they did. Billie and Dorothy had been on the lot at RKO walking from one location to another. When Billie saw the camera, she instinctively ran off, knowing that the handholding could be misunderstood. It was a stupid thing to do. If she hadn't darted off, she wouldn't be sitting here having this conversation now.

"The newsreel goes out next week with *Gunga Din*," he continued, jabbing a stubby finger at her. "I can't have my Good Witch on a screen with a known . . . well . . . you-know-what. It'll deflate the box office, and you know how expensive this film has become. I'm sure Victor told you by now."

"It was nothing," she said.

He leaned back in his chair and put his hands behind his head. "It won't happen again," he said.

Her heart raced. She hated being ordered around, and she wanted to tell him so, but she pressed her lips shut. If she said something, this would only escalate, and he might call security. Those men were known for roughing up the talent. Right now, she wanted to find that cameraman who'd filmed them and tell him what she thought. She shook her head. It had happened so quickly.

L. B. reached under his desk, pulled out a scarf, and dropped it on his desk. "Yours?" The question was an accusation.

Her heart slugged against her ribs. That scarf had fallen off mid-run. She hadn't stopped to pick it up, afraid the camera would focus on her. The fact that L. B. had the scarf indicated how the industry worked. He was the king around here, and everyone was loyal to him, even at other studios. There was nothing he didn't know about or control.

She turned her head to the side and took a deep breath. She'd done nothing wrong. "The public doesn't care about it."

L. B. shook his head. "Miss Burke, this is the second time, and you know what I told you the first time."

"You have no right to pick my friends for me."

He tapped a manila folder on his desk. "Here's your contract. It says I do."

She leaned forward. "But I didn't violate it."

"That's not how I see it. The terms state that you cannot act outside any moral convention."

She clenched her teeth. "Women hold hands all the time. It isn't immoral. It's a sign of friendship."

"Since you made the first film with that woman, lesbian rumors have circled."

She'd met Dorothy in 1933 when MGM had loaned her to RKO for a role in the film *Christopher Strong*.

Dorothy was the director, and it had been the first time Billie was directed by a woman. It was a whole other kind of experience, and she had loved it. They had bonded during the film.

"Nobody believes that rumor," Billie said. "Nobody believes that the widow Ziegfeld would do something like that."

"I can't risk it." L. B. shook his head. "And I'm finished arguing. Howard Strickling will do damage control." Howard was the studio publicist. "He'll clean this up." L. B. dropped his arms, then pointed at her. "And you'll do whatever he says."

Why should she do what he said if she was going to be fired anyway? Or did L. B. mean that Howard's effective cleanup might still save her job? Maybe L. B. hadn't meant to fire her. Perhaps he'd just meant to change her behavior. That's what he usually did with stars. Dorothy was her friend, and Billie would find a way to keep both her job and her friend. In this business, real friends were rare. She wasn't ready to give one up.

Then again, how could her friendship with Dorothy be the reason L. B. was firing her? It seemed so petty. He was a businessman, and Billie's work made money. She studied his face, looking for the real reason, but his faint smile gave nothing away. The glisten in his eyes told her he was enjoying making her squirm. It also made her wonder.

"What is this really about?" she asked.

He drummed the desk blotter. "I had to make choices. New York is pressuring me to drop expenses. Everybody is cutting back. You read the papers, yes?"

She gave him a poisoned glare. "Of course." Every star read them, looking for news about themselves. If they said, "I don't read those things," they were lying.

He continued. "Twentieth Century Fox let five stars go. Five. I had to pick five to drop, too, and you're one of them. This is a business, and I have to operate it like one. So, yes, there was another reason. I wasn't sure what to do with you until I saw the newsreel. It was the deciding factor."

"So, if I weren't in the reel, I'd have my job?"

"I hate it when people don't do what I tell them to do."

"Dorothy and I are just friends," she repeated—a line she knew wouldn't work, yet what else could she say?

"Cuts had to be made."

Her hands balled into fists. She could give him a long list of ways to make cuts, like closing the executive bungalows, getting rid of the lazy actors, and not firing people who made money for him. She had a long list.

"I waffled about what to do with you at first." He lifted his left palm. "On the one hand, older audiences love you, and you're a big name." He lifted the other palm. "On the other hand, I need to bring in younger talent, and I don't have the money to keep everyone. The bucket, so to speak, is full." He set his hands on the desk. "Most ticket buyers are under thirty, and they want to see younger faces."

Her teeth rattled. There it was. This was about her age, not about Dorothy. She pointed to a poster of *Topper* on the wall with her picture on it. "There I am. See how important I am to this place?"

"That poster's up because of Constance Bennett." Constance's picture was on it, too, as the female lead. But Billie had been in the business for over forty years, and she'd paid her dues. She was talented, motivated, a hard worker, and a draw. She wasn't "old," and she wouldn't back down. She'd earned her place here, and she was determined to keep it.

She rose quickly and thrust a finger at him.

He sat there like a boulder.

"This isn't over!" she said. "You can't do this to me."

He pyramided his fingers slowly and put his thumbs to his chin. "Miss Burke, you've been informed. I'm a businessman. It was a business decision."

"You haven't heard the end of this."

His mud-colored eyes dulled with anger. His face told her to take it or leave it.

She turned and headed for the door.

"Don't forget to do what Howard says," he said.

She spun around and glared. "Over my dead body." She walked out and slammed the door behind her.

The Mount called out in an unknowing tone. "Miss Burke, I need to speak with you."

Billie ignored her, stormed into the hall, and hustled down the stairs.

Chapter Three

Billie was behind the wheel of her Buick Thirty-eight, racing north on Benedict Canyon Road. She made a hard turn on Tower Road toward the house and leaned right as momentum pushed her against the door. Once in the driveway, she stopped the car. An ache formed in her chest, an ache for her daughter, an ache for a place called "home." This place was lovely, but it was a rental. How could she afford a house when she was four hundred thousand in debt? Home was Burkeley Crest. Home was New York. She longed for home. She wanted to go home, feel at home, be comforted by home.

She didn't want to enter the house, and couldn't seem to get out of the car. She wanted to back out of the driveway and head for the East Coast.

Billie had only had a "home" for twenty of her fifty-four years. As a child, her father had worked as a singing circus clown. "Home" had been a tent on the road or a cold-water flat where they landed for the off-season. In 1907, when she was twenty-three, she'd finally become a Broadway leading lady and earned enough money for a real home. She named it Burkeley Crest—a three-acre-plus estate in Hastings-on-Hudson. She'd assumed she'd live there to the end, but here she was, on a dry suburban lot in Beverly Hills. She appreciated the house, of course, but it was nothing like what she'd had back east. She missed the forest, the seventeen-room stone house, the flower gardens, the horses, the barns, the proximity to the Hudson River. She also missed the zoo she and Flo had put together, populating it with rescued circus and stage animals.

She let out a sob, but took a deep breath to stop another.

She couldn't afford to buy a house, and probably never would. The debt was like an anchor around her life. Of course, there were things she was thankful for: her daughter, her friends, her work. This house certainly beat those old cold-water flats. Yet good grief. When would the drama end?

Then, she thought of her career and the meeting with L. B., and she pounded the steering wheel. Falling movie stars quickly lost the support of their fans. To the fans, the definition of a movie star was someone rich with full access to whatever they wanted: luxury, love, happiness, and health. When a star fell—or even tripped—fan loyalty vanished, and your career was over.

If fans only knew how fragile an actor's life and work could be. The movie stars couldn't tell them; the truth would damage the image. That's why studios spent so much money and effort keeping stars elevated. To moguls, it was a bottom-line thing. Nothing personal. Sometimes, Billie was grateful for their help. She had especially appreciated it when MGM offered her the contract after Flo had died. Today, though, she felt differently. This "We aren't renewing your contract thing" was all about turning off the light on a falling star before the fans could douse it out themselves. She understood that, but didn't she deserve a safety net after all she'd done for the studio?

A horn honked from the street, and she turned to look. It was just a passing car, enough to wake her up and jolt her back into the now. She lifted her chin and went into the house.

Patty's baby-blue jacket hung on the coat tree in the mudroom. Billie paused to straighten it, pulling on the sleeves, centering the coat on the hook, and smoothing its back. The girl was in New York on an apprenticeship with WCCD radio for three months, which Billie had arranged when the girl's writing career stalled. Patty needed a career to fall back on, just in case. Billie had learned that lesson after the stock market crash. In '29, Flo's theater and production company had fallen apart, and Billie had returned to full-time stage work to support the family. Thank goodness she'd built an acting career before the disaster. Without it, they would have been on the streets. Every woman needed a career, Billie believed, and Patty needed to learn that, just like Billie had done.

Still, the girl seemed disinterested in developing her career. Billie had paid for two years of college at the University of California branch in Westwood. She assumed sending Patty there would help sort things out. Patty wanted to be a writer, so she majored in English. But what the girl really wanted was to be a wife and mother.

"That's fine," Billie had told her. "I did, too. But first, put something underneath you to fall back on. You never know what might happen, and you need to be prepared. You don't have a husband on the horizon right now, and hopefully, you won't have one for a while. You have time."

Billie had married Flo when she was thirty years old. Before that, she had plenty of "down on the knee" proposals, but she had turned them down while building her career. She hoped Patty would do the same.

Billie pushed Patty partly because her own mother had pushed her. With Billie's mother, however, it had been more like a constant shove: Billie was to become a famous actress, period. Her mother had constantly scraped together her pennies for elocution and music lessons. Billie was forced to be on stage whenever she wasn't in a lesson: in pubs, music halls, vaudeville theaters. Her mother had never given up; the pressure had been constant and exhausting. Billie's body tensed now just thinking about it.

Everything had eventually worked out, but Billie wanted to use a softer touch with Patty, partly because she didn't want her daughter to feel the same pressure she'd faced and partly because the world itself had changed. Nowadays, children didn't automatically obey their parents—and Billie didn't want to risk damaging her relationship with her daughter.

Yet the girl needed something to build on, and Billie was her mother. She couldn't simply do nothing. At least she was letting her daughter make choices. Billie's mother had made the choices for her.

This was the first time they'd been away from each other for more than a few days. They talked on the phone once a week, but it was different. Billie never felt the girl's spirit over the phone, and the tinny sound of the connection made it hard to know what Patty meant when she talked. Conversations were telegraphic.

"How are things at the station?" Billie would ask.

"Fine," Patty would answer.

Billie would twist the phone cord around her wrist. "What's fine?"

"Everything."

Billie's head would drop. This kind of exchange disabled her motherly intuition, the glue of effective parenting. She needed to hear sentences, paragraphs, and rants. She hoped Patty would be more forthcoming on the next call.

At least Billie had her dogs. They were here, real, and she could hear them loud and clear. Ziggy and Pippin, her white Cairn Terriers, were scratching on the inside of the kitchen door down the hall as Billie entered the house.

She smiled. The sadness drained away as she listened to their excited barks.

"Coming," she called. She walked down the hall and opened the door to two knee-high dogs jumping at her skirt, tails wagging like windshield wipers. She stroked their warm, soft backs and scratched them behind their ears. This normalized everything, making her feel grounded.

"Oh, you're so lovely," she said in a lilting voice. "How were my children today? My little whoopsies tootsies."

Pippin sneezed. Ziggy smiled and panted.

She opened a cupboard by the kitchen sink, pulled out a box of Spratt's Puppy Biscuits, and rattled it.

The dogs plopped at her feet, licking their lips. She pulled out two bone-shaped biscuits, held them up high, and dropped them with a smile. The dogs caught the treats in midair and pranced away. She was grateful. She loved those two creatures, but right now, she needed a few minutes to herself.

She made a cup of tea, sat at the kitchen table, opened the *Los Angeles Times*, and saw an article about the Nazis demonizing the Jews in Germany and an American group, the German American Bund, supporting them. The Bund was planning support rallies in the United States.

Reading this soured her mood. She should have opened the paper to the Garden section.

She'd never given Jews much thought before moving here. In New York, Lee Shubert, a New York theater producer, had been Jewish, and she'd worked for him on Broadway, but the term *Jewish* had simply been an interesting fact to her, more like thinking of someone as being Russian or from New England. Her own parents were from Ohio, but that didn't define them or Billie. She sorted people by how they treated her and others, and even that was a light sort.

After moving to Los Angeles, she became more aware of the Jewish identity; after all, most studio heads (and many directors) were Jewish. She cultivated relationships with them by attending their fundraisers—the Jewish Home, the Jewish Women's Foreign Relief, and the Jewish Orphan's Home. But with Hitler abusing Jews in Europe and the studio moguls worried about their families, she wanted to do something more to help. Thank goodness she had no family in Europe, but that didn't matter. She still felt the angst.

It was hard to feel empathy for L. B., however. She had her limits.

Billie needed to call Dorothy, no matter what L. B. had to say about it. Billie needed to get this off her mind and find support. She made herself another cup of green tea, carried it upstairs to her home office, and set it down on a stack of fan mail. She plopped down onto the cushion yet found herself fidgeting. Not even her favorite comfy chair could relax her today.

Dorothy's phone rang three times. Marion, her partner-in-life, answered.

"She's in the pool," Marion said, sounding breathless. "Can she return the call? She won't last long out there. You know what it's like here when the sun goes down. Brrr."

Billie pulled her free arm around herself. "Um." She tried to say yes, but it wouldn't come out.

"Wait. I'll go tell her," Marion said. "You may have to wait a minute."

Billie relaxed into the chair and put her head back. "If she can't come to the phone, I can call back. It's fine."

"Hold on."

Billie was glad Marion was home to answer. Often, when Billie called, nobody was there. Both were busy working. Marion was a dancer/choreographer with her own company.

"Billie?" Dorothy said when she got to the phone. "What's on your mind?"

A mix of sadness and relief surged through Billie. "It's good to hear your voice."

"Marion said it sounded important."

Billie explained what L. B. had said and took a deep breath.

"You must be devastated," Dorothy said, her voice soft and gentle.

"I'm trying."

"It's the emotional equivalent of having a tooth pulled."

"Yes, it is."

"And my teeth are chattering right now," Dorothy said.

Billie felt a chill. "Oh, I'm so sorry, dear. Perhaps we should talk later."

"No. Marion wrapped a blanket around me. I'll warm up."

Billie bit her lip. "Well, if you want to hang up, I'd understand."

"He is a fool for tossing you aside."

Billie pulled off her right earring and crossed her legs on the ottoman. "He's an ass, is what he is. I'm hoping you have some ideas."

"That's strong language for you."

"You haven't heard me at my worst." Whenever Flo had an affair, and Billie confronted him, her word choices—and volume—had been limitless.

"I don't think I want to," Dorothy said. "As for my ideas, you normally don't like them."

"That's not true."

"You're right. I'm freezing to death, and this blanket isn't helping."

"I'm sorry. I should call back later."

"Don't worry about it. I'd be freezing, regardless. Marion and I are heading to Palm Springs for the weekend, and we have to get ready. It's the first chance we've had to get away in a year. How about this? We can do breakfast at RKO on Monday, and I'll prepare some ideas. You'll love them, I guarantee it."

Tears rolled down Billie's cheeks. She had no words. She knew she would be happy just listening to Dorothy for a while.

"Seven-thirty," Dorothy said. "You're off in the morning, right?"

"Yes, on Monday."

"Okay, good. Now, take a hot bath and call Patty."

Chapter Four

A bronze elephant the size of a coffee cup sat on her bedstand and triggered a memory. Flo had collected elephant figurines from around the world, and she'd kept a few after he died. In '29, he'd lost everything in the stock market crash, forcing her to act in films to support the family and her career. If the crash hadn't happened, she'd still have Burkeley Crest, Flo, and her stage roles. She certainly wouldn't have fallen into a faceoff with L. B. over her future.

In October of 1929, and Billie had been home in Hastings-on-Hudson at Burkeley Crest. She and Flo had just returned from a European vacation tour, and she was in her bedroom's walk-in closet hanging up three new gowns she'd bought in Paris. Twelve-year-old Patty was in her bedroom playing with the dogs.

"Billie," Flo said from behind her.

She jumped and put her hand to her heart. "I wish you'd stop startling me like that."

"Sorry." The whites of his eyes were red, his broad shoulders slumped, his face pale. His graying temples looked grayer.

"Are you okay?" She squeezed the pink chiffon gown she was holding to her chest.

"I need to talk to you about something," he said, shoving his hands into his pockets. "Can we go to my office?"

Conversations about serious things happened in his office. They'd long ago decided that bedrooms were for sleeping, not places to argue or discuss business.

"Certainly," she said. She hung up the dress, straightened its floating cape, and gave it a little room among the others so it could breathe. She'd bought the gown to wear to the annual New York's Eve Ball at the Astor. She and Flo had met at the ball years ago, and they'd attended every year since.

She followed him down the hall. His gait seemed shuffling, and she wondered if perhaps he was sick. He hadn't gone to the doctor in months. Perhaps she'd suggest it.

They entered his oak-paneled office, and she gently closed the door behind her so Patty couldn't hear. The girl's bedroom was two doors down, and her ears seemed to pick up everything. Flo motioned to a chair by the window.

Was he leaving her for someone else? Flo, the grand showman, was rarely serious. The last time he'd done this kind of thing, he had met another woman—Olive

Thomas—and the news had hit the press. He'd called Billie into his home office to "explain." That talk had resulted in her smashing a vase at his feet, one he'd bought in Greece and had particularly loved. She'd reminded him that he was also obligated to his daughter, and that seemed to end the affair. Since then, he'd had several other affairs, but the number had decreased as he aged. He was sixty-three now, but that didn't stop younger women from chasing him for the money and fame. Fortunately, he seemed less interested than he used to be.

Billie approached the chair and saw her reflection in the window glass. Her hair was out of place and needed brushing. This wasn't a good time to look bad. She straightened it with shaking fingers.

"Sit, please," he said.

Her heart raced. She sat, crossed her legs, and pressed her hands into a ball.

He unbuttoned his jacket, sat in a nearby leather chair, and leaned forward. "I'll get right to the point."

"That's a good idea."

He sat up straight and took a deep breath. "It's all gone."

"What's gone?"

He looked away. "My money."

She opened her hands and sat back. This wasn't great news, but he wasn't leaving her. Besides, she had her own money, and the house was hers.

Flo had always been a gambler, often making a lot of money and then losing it. Billie called it the "Ziegfeld

Cycle." He was apologetic every time it happened, and promised to get it all back soon, and he did. The last time, she'd threatened to take Patty and leave him. That seemed to cure it—until now, at least. She had a sinking sense that things were different this time, though she couldn't pinpoint why.

"Did Chance Shot lose at the Belmont racetrack again?" she asked.

He shook his head.

"Poker?"

"No."

"Then what?"

He looked out the window across the room, the window with a new English vase in front of it. "I invested in railroad stock," he mumbled. "I have nothing left."

She sat back and uncrossed her legs. "What do you mean by nothing, dear?"

His big shiny brown eyes were slits. She couldn't see inside of him.

"Bill," he said. "The entire economy has shut down."

She knew the economy was struggling, but it had teetered before. "What do you mean 'shut down'?"

He sat up straight. "Didn't you hear?"

"No, I've been trying to get things in order since we returned from Paris. I've had a lot to do."

"The stock market crashed. The banks are closing. It's the railroads: They overbuilt, and now they're going out of business, many of them. I put all my money on Kissel."

51

"What's Kissel?"

"Kissel Motor Cars. It's gone. There's nothing left."

Flo had recently invested in stocks, something new for him. Billie had never been an investor because she thought it was too risky, but the market had been strong, so why not? It was his money, anyway.

He dropped his head into his hands and spoke softly. "I can't open *Bitter Sweet* next month."

She turned her head to the side. Why did he look so worried? He'd been in this spot a hundred times. "Borrow the money, then. That's what you always do."

He looked her in the eye. "Nobody's lending," he snapped. "Didn't you hear what I just said?"

"Don't talk to me like that!"

"I'm sorry." He ran his fingers through his hair. "The stock market has crashed. Stocks aren't worth anything, and people are racing to the banks to withdraw their funds. Bank doors are closed everywhere, and long lines of people are waiting along the sidewalk. The banks are closing to stave off runs. The show opens in a couple of weeks, but I don't have the money to open it, and there's nowhere to borrow it."

Billie's own money was with Chase National Bank, and she felt sure it was safe. The bank had opened its doors in 1877, which was partly why she chose it. If Chase could last that long, it would be around for the long haul. So what if the bank closed its doors for a couple of days? She'd already paid the household staff for the month, and they had plenty of cash in the house. This was just a financial hurricane: Here for the day, gone, do the cleanup, and then life would return to normal.

Then again, Flo was telling her that this was unusual. She usually didn't discuss the business side of things with him, just the creative. If she learned something on the business end, it was usually from a casual conversation, a newspaper article, or party gossip. He'd never sat her down to explain things before.

She bit her lip and straightened in her chair. "Why are you telling me this?"

He paused and looked away. Tears welled in his eyes. He rarely shed a tear. The last time he did was when Patty had been born. Billie reached out and touched his knee.

He moved in his chair, dislodging her hand. He took a deep breath, stood, and started to pace, something he never did. Billie was the pacer in this family.

"I borrowed from Dutch Schultz to open the last show," he said. "I have nothing to pay him back with."

She leaped up, clenched her jaw, and eyed the vase across the room. She wanted to throw it at him.

"What the hell were you thinking?" she growled, then threw her hands into the air. "You endangered your family!"

Dutch was a gangster, often in the papers for killing double-crossers. She walked to the window across the room and looked down at the gravel driveway. It was dark outside, and she couldn't see much. Was Dutch waiting out there right now in a car with the lights off, his men pointing guns at them?

She closed the drapes.

"Don't be silly. He isn't going to hurt us," Flo said in a condescending tone.

She glared at him and tucked her arms across her chest. "How much did you borrow?" she asked, her teeth clenched.

"Ten thousand dollars," he said.

She looked up at the ceiling and rolled her eyes. They'd paid that much for their Canadian vacation home.

"I'm sorry," he said.

She thrust her hands on her hips. "So, what are you going to do about it?"

"I don't know."

She moved toward the vase by the window. It was a large one, about three feet tall. Blue. Thick. It would take two hands to lift and then drop it, but it would make a loud, satisfying sound.

"I've spoken with every lender," he said, "including other producers. Every dime is frozen."

Billie paced hard and fast in a circle and couldn't stop. She couldn't talk either. She wanted to storm out, grab Patty, and drive away, but she knew she couldn't.

Over the next couple of years, Billie used her savings to pay off Dutch and support Flo's subsequent failed productions, things she'd vowed never to do. She and Flo had had a prenuptial agreement: What was hers stayed hers; what was his stayed his. But she had to keep her family safe. Doing this had drained every dime, forcing her into being owned by MGM. She'd spent the past seven years rebuilding to a point of a safety only to have them dump her.

Chapter Five

On Monday morning, Billie was in her Buick pulling up in front of RKO Pictures for her breakfast with Dorothy. Dorothy was always full of ideas. Billie didn't always agree with them, but having them was better than having nothing.

She pulled up to the security booth and rolled down the window. Inside the booth was a wiry young guard wearing a cobalt-blue uniform. Dandruff dusted his shoulders, and his fist covered a yawn big enough to crack his jaw. He seemed engrossed in an edition of *Life* magazine open on the counter.

She cleared her throat.

He jounced and then closed the magazine.

"Mornin'," he said, through an embarrassed smile. "May I help you?"

She put her arm on the car's windowsill and nodded. He couldn't be a day over eighteen, maybe even younger. "I'm here for a breakfast meeting."

He pointed to the magazine. Dirt was under his nail. "I'm awful sorry, ma'am. I shoulda been payin' attention, but I can't seem to leave it alone." He shoved the magazine under the counter, pulled out a clipboard, and tipped his hat, revealing wheat-colored hair flattened to his head. He was a thin boy. Even his scalp looked thin.

"Name, please?" he said.

She stuck her head out the window. "Miss Billie Burke."

"Who?"

She leaned out farther. "Miss Billie Burke," she said louder. The booth smelled like sausage.

The boy scanned the list, flipping the pages, and scrunching his face. After the fourth flip, he looked up. "I'm gosh awful sorry, ma'am. Could ya spell that, please?" He returned to page one.

She wasn't surprised that he didn't recognize her name. At his age, he would certainly be more interested in younger actresses, like Jane Bryan, Margaret Lindsay, or Joan Blondell. These days, Billie played people's mothers. She was no longer the ingenue.

She squeezed the car windowsill and stiffened her jaw. "B-U-R-K-E," she said, spitting out each letter, trying to hold in her frustration.

He turned the page. "I got two Burkes, ma'am. Tony an' Gretta. Tell me your first name agin?"

She had to be on the list. Dorothy was meticulous about these kinds of things. Billie strained her neck to lean farther out the window. "Billie. B-I-L-L-I-E. I'm here for breakfast with Miss Dorothy Arzner. She's a film director here."

He rubbed the back of his neck. "I'm awful sorry, but they'll fire me if I let ya in." He tapped the list. "Ya hafta be here. I'm sorry."

Two cars behind her were waiting, and the dashboard clock read 7:21. She had nine minutes before she had to meet Dorothy and still needed to park the car. She put her hand out the window and asked, "May I see the list?"

His brow wrinkled. "Sorry, ma'am. Can't do that."

She shoved her hand out farther. "I'm not going to run off with it. I promise."

He pulled the list to his flat chest.

The situation wasn't his fault, and she didn't want to escalate things, but she had to get to the commissary.

"Perhaps you should call your supervisor for help," she said. His boss was probably older and would recognize Billie's name.

His eyes opened wide. "Oh, no," he said, fumbling with the clipboard. "He'd have a conniption. I'm in trouble with him already cuz of my nails. I work on cars at night and can't keep 'em clean."

She wanted to suggest that he wear gloves, but she kept her mouth shut. She just wanted in. She took a deep breath. "What's your name?" she said in a calmer voice.

"Peter, ma'am. Peter Rapp, but don't tell my boss. Cain't help it." He pointed to the list.

"I have to meet with Miss Arzner in less than nine minutes. Please call him. He'll know me. I promise that you won't get into trouble. I'll vouch for you."

"You an actress or somethin'?"

She threw her head back and laughed. Her last RKO picture had been *Becky Sharp* four years ago, and not a film for a fourteen-year-old like this boy would have been. "I try to be. I've made several films here, but probably none you've seen. Did you see *The Young in Heart*? It appealed to boys your age. It was released in November."

His face lit up. "For cryin' out loud. That was funny. You was the crazy lady. Ya tried to con the old lady outta her money."

"Yes, that was me. The crazy lady," she said with a sigh. Well, at least he recognized her.

The car's clock showed five minutes left. She squeezed the wheel.

"If that don't beat all," he said. "You was a pistol." His brow furrowed. "You peoples seem different in real life."

If he only knew. She motioned to the list. "You hold the clipboard, and we'll look together."

"Okay," he said, and he shared the list.

The names were in alphabetical order, and he was correct; there was no Billie Burke. But on the last page at the end was "Ziegfeld, Mrs. Billie." Whew. She pointed to the name. "That's me. That's my married name."

"Bless Patsy," he said. He removed his cap and bowed. "It's an honor, ma'am. I'm standing here with Mrs. Ziegfeld. You is famous."

Flo's last name still carried some weight. Even today, he remained better known than Rudolph Valentino, Charlie Chaplin, and Mary Pickford combined. Dorothy had likely listed Billie under her married name to make her easier to find. Billie was embarrassed she hadn't thought of it.

The boy checked her off. "Ya know where you's goin'?"

"I certainly do." She waved good-bye and drove inside.

Billie parked the car in the guest lot, tucked her purse under her arm, and hustled toward the windowless, stucco building that held the commissary. Dorothy stood outside, waving, her Jean Després silver bracelet jangling on her wrist.

Billie stopped and smiled with a bit of pride. Thanks to Billie's prodding, Dorothy was wearing something feminine for a change. It was an olive-colored dress with a lacy white collar. Billie had tried (for years) to get Dorothy to wear dresses. They didn't have to be frilly, just fashionable. Billie had to admit Dorothy looked cute in this outfit. She usually wore a tweed skirt with a man's white shirt and a dark tie. Despite the clothes, Dorothy's hair was still in that Humphrey Bogart style and color.

They hugged. Dorothy smelled like lavender.

"I have happy news," Dorothy said, stepping back.

"I'm ready for some."

"You'll have to wait until we sit," Dorothy said.

Billie rolled her eyes. "May I at least have a clue?"

Dorothy gave a chiding look.

"A seven-year contract with RKO at a higher salary?" Billie asked, only half-kidding. RKO was a step down from MGM, but she'd take it. Work was work. Bills were bills.

"Later," Dorothy said. She opened the door and waved Billie inside.

Billie felt the tingle and the warmth of home. There was a mingling sound of clanging forks, announcing cooks, ringing cash registers, and murmuring employees. And then there were the smells of sugared donuts, sizzling bacon, and fried potatoes. Billie didn't eat those things for fear of gaining weight, but it didn't matter. This place smelled and sounded like a home, and that relaxed her. It was where everyone could go and feel like they had both feet in the real world. No fans. No press.

A cigarette girl many condescendingly called a "Sugar" approached with a wooden tray suspended from her neck. She wore a red, saloon-style skirt hemmed three inches above the knee with a neckline revealing the top of her milk-colored breasts. These girls dressed to please the moguls, hoping for a bit part. Most only made it as far as the mogul's couch. It was so sad.

Smokes, candy, and gum filled the girl's tray. Billie rubbed the back of her neck, feeling the vicarious strain of the strap.

"Cigarettes? Luster-Mints? Zagnuts?" the girl said with an Alabama drawl.

The girl would never get a part with that voice. She needed elocution lessons. Hopefully, somebody would tell her.

"Billie. Do you want anything?" Dorothy said.

"No, thank you, dear."

"Well, I do. A pack of Wrigley's, please."

Dorothy and the girl exchanged money and gum.

"Thank you," the girl said.

"What's your name?" Dorothy asked.

"Thelma."

"Would you like an audition?"

Billie smiled. Thank goodness for the gesture, although she had no idea how Dorothy would use her. Dorothy's casts were small.

Thelma made a twisted face. "Audition for what?"

Dorothy folded her hands in front. "I'm a film director. I'm Dorothy Arzner."

Thelma thrust her hands to her lips. "I've never heard of you, and I've worked here for a year. Besides, there are no women film directors."

Billie laughed aloud. "Oh, yes, there are. There is this one. The only one." She pointed at Dorothy.

Thelma's eyes narrowed. "What movies have you made?"

"*Christopher Strong, Craig's Wife, The Bride Wore Red?*"

"She's done eighteen films," Billie said proudly.

"Sixteen, really," Dorothy said.

"Haven't heard of them," the girl said.

"She's directing *Dance, Girl, Dance* right now," Billie said.

"Who's in it?"

Billie continued: "Maureen O'Hara. Lucille Hayward."

Thelma shook her head.

"Louis Hayward?"

Thelma dropped her jaw. "He's a dream."

"Yes, he is," Dorothy said with obvious reservation. He was handsome, but Billie knew he caught on slowly.

"I've been taking acting lessons at the Bliss-Hayden School," Thelma said. "Can you give me some advice?"

Thank goodness, Billie thought. They'd give her elocution lessons.

"That's a great school, and I know the founder, Lela Bliss," Dorothy said. "I've hired a few extras from there. Have you been in a film yet?"

"No, but I've been auditioning. I'd sure like to work for you."

Dorothy put a finger to her chin. "Stop by my office and have my secretary schedule a screen test." She handed Thelma her business card.

Brandy bounced and squealed. The candy in the box jostled. "Oh, thank you!"

Dorothy and Thelma exchanged hand squeezes. Billie and Thelma did the same.

"You're welcome, Miss Thelma..." Dorothy said.

"Willis. Thelma Willis," Thelma said. "I'm pleased to meet you." She looked at Billie. "I'm sorry, but I don't know who you are."

Billie chuckled. "I'm nobody." She certainly was feeling like a nobody today.

Dorothy scoffed. "You have got to be kidding. You're one of the biggest talents of the twentieth century." She turned to Thelma. "This is Billie Burke Ziegfeld, an MGM star."

Thelma blushed. "Mrs. Ziegfeld? You mean the Ziegfeld of the *Follies*?"

"My husband owned the *Follies*, but I never danced with them. I've had my own stage and film career."

"I'm sorry, but I've never heard of you." Thelma bit her lip. "Stupid me. I don't mean to be rude."

"Did you see *The Young in Heart*?" Dorothy asked.

Thelma looked to the side, then back, and smiled. "Now I know who you are. You were downright evil in that film but redeemed yourself in the end. You were good. It's a pleasure to meet you."

"Thank you," Billie said.

"What a lovely suit," Thelma said to Billie. "I love that color."

It was a blush-pink summer dress. "My favorite color," she said.

"I like your dress, too, Miss Arzner," the girl said, sounding too polite. Dorothy's dress was plain at best.

"Thank you," Dorothy said.

Thelma pulled out a Wrigley's Spearmint Gum pack and handed it to Dorothy. "Here," she said. "A gift."

Dorothy gave Thelma a nickel.

"No," Thelma said as she tried to return the coin.

Dorothy put her hands into her pockets. The dress had pockets? Well, maybe it was a compromise, but it was a dress.

* * *

Dorothy picked up a food tray to share with Billie and slid it along the aluminum ledge of the buffet line. The aroma of scrambled eggs, fried potatoes, pancakes, sausage, and scrapple stirred Billie's stomach and challenged her willpower as they moved through the buffet, but she refused to touch any of it. She knew perfectly well that most of it would give her hippo hips. She'd eaten breakfast at home to defend her stomach: a cup of yak's milk, a bowl of cut strawberries, and a chunk of cheese. She'd hold out for the green tea at the far end of the line.

When they reached the pastries, Dorothy selected a glazed donut the size of a man's fist, but Billie kept going, all the while forced by the gods of fatty foods to inhale the scents of fried dough, butter, and powdered sugar. She could even smell the cinnamon. Her stomach growled, but she told herself she didn't need it. She pushed herself to keep moving.

At the far end of the buffet, she poured herself a cup of hot water and placed a tea ball into it. While waiting in line behind Dorothy, she opened her purse to dig for change to pay.

"Put that away," Dorothy said.

"But you paid the last time."

"Yes, and the world did not end. Now put it away."

"I'm going to catch up at some point," Billie said as she dropped the coins back into her purse. She saw an Amazonite pendant around the cashier's neck when she looked up. Its milky-green color almost matched the pretty young girl's eyes.

"Dear," Billie asked the cashier, "where did you get that lovely necklace?"

"My mother makes them," the cashier said.

"Don't you have enough jewelry?" Dorothy said to Billie.

It was true; Billie had a cabinet full of treasure chest jewelry boxes. But she couldn't help it. She loved stones. She glared at Dorothy. "Do you have enough golf balls?" Dorothy golfed at least once a week. She had a collection of balls in her garage stuffed into an old wooden crate collected from courses in Europe and the United States, wherever women were allowed to play.

"Never."

"Well, then?"

"I have them because I sometimes lose them or one of my irons gashes them. It's different. You don't lose your jewelry; it never seems to break."

Billie ignored the comment. "It's for Patty, not me. That's the kind of jewelry she likes. It's quite modern." She addressed the cashier: "How can I order one from your mother?" She pointed to Dorothy. "My friend can pick it up for me. She works here."

"I'll bring you one next Monday. It'll be five dollars."

That price was reasonable, the equivalent of dinner for two at the Brown Derby restaurant. Billie had expected closer to ten dollars. She paid the cashier, who tucked the money into her pocket.

Dorothy paid for the food, and they headed for an empty booth along the wall, passing monks forking syruped pancakes, fishwives spooning oatmeal, and circus clowns sipping coffee.

Billie looked at her watch as they sat. "We have forty-five minutes," she said, "until you have to be on the set, and I have to head to the studio. You present your idea, and I'll present mine."

"Did you call Sam Goldwyn in New York?"

"The studio may be called Metro-Goldwyn-Mayer, but Sam has nothing to do with it anymore, despite the rumors that he helped me get the job."

Dorothy dumped four sugar cubes into her coffee and cut her donut into six pieces. "That's too bad." She paused to stir, then said, "Now, I'll tell you my news." She set the utensils down and cleared her throat. "I spoke to Pan this morning." Pan Berman was an RKO producer. "He has something for you."

Billie blew on the hot water. "What is it?"

"He wants to make a film about Flo, and he wants you to consult on it." Dorothy sipped her coffee as she waited for Billie to respond.

"You know the answer to that. I need the money, but I'm unwilling to prostitute my husband."

Dorothy set her cup down. "Just hear me out."

Billie pressed her lips together, then said, "When they made *The Great Ziegfeld*, the whole film was full of lies. It made Flo look weak and me even weaker."

"This one is different, and it's good money. Pan's on the edge of the idea, and you could shove him over to the truth."

"What makes you think it'll be different?"

"You'd have more control. That's what you wanted on the last one. Control. And how much control did you have? None. So here we are: finally, somebody making a movie about Flo that could be authentic."

Billie scoffed. Money ruled this business, not truth. She crossed her arms over her chest and leaned back against the booth.

"This time," Dorothy continued, "you could ensure they got it right. Besides, this isn't MGM. It's Pan at RKO, and you respect him. He's no Hunt."

Hunt Stromberg had produced *The Great Ziegfeld*, and L. B. had controlled him. It was true that RKO was better at producing more artful and serious films, and part of Billie would love to have a say in Pan's project. Flo deserved a film that was true to his work and spirit. She trusted Pan, but she didn't trust studio bosses. This business was about money. Studios were factories, period.

She unraveled her arms. "The answer is still no."

Dorothy's brown eyes cajoled. "It's twelve thousand dollars. It could take four months to earn that much. You could make it in a month."

Billie hid a smile behind a sip of tea. Dorothy was right. That was good money. But would they really listen to her?

Dorothy gave her a wry smile. "I see you thinking about it."

Billie trusted Dorothy; she was the only one in this business Billie did trust. But Dorothy wasn't in charge of the film.

"Thank you for letting me know," Billie said. "I hope you didn't go to a lot of trouble, but I simply can't do it. I ... I just can't."

"I—"

Billie held up her hands to stop Dorothy from saying anything more. "No. You mean well, but I won't risk being a part of another film that damages Flo's reputation or mine. Besides, my contract won't allow it, and I don't want to upset L. B. I still have a couple of months left at MGM."

Dorothy threw her hands in the air. "He's dumping you. What do you care?"

"Maybe not. And besides, this business operates like a small town. If I anger him, nobody else will hire me."

"What do you mean maybe not? He's *not* dumping you?"

"Not if I can help it." She squeezed her teacup. "I want to stay at MGM, and I'm comfortable there. Besides, what if this whole thing is just a ploy to get me to take less money on the next contract? Or what if he realizes he made a mistake and changes his mind? If I upset him, he won't be able to find his way back. You know how he is."

Dorothy softened her voice. "Sometimes, you are like a passenger in your own boat instead of the captain. Look, I know it hurts, but he's letting you go, and you have got to move on. There's no life jacket on an MGM boat. You either drive or drown."

"Isn't that why we're here? To give me a life preserver."

"I just did, and you said no."

"How about just a few swimming lessons?"

Dorothy groaned, nodded, and stabbed a donut piece with a fork. "You think about it. In the meantime, I'll listen to you. You said you had some ideas." She put the piece into her mouth and chewed.

"I'm going to make L. B. want to keep me. I'm going to make myself indispensable."

Dorothy swallowed. "How in the world are you going to do that? Rob a bank and invest millions in the company?"

"I don't know, but I need a lozenge right now."

"Sore throat?"

"Bitter tea." She dug around in her purse but had trouble locating the lozenge she wanted. She pulled out her keys, a ballpoint pen, a hair clip. Tom's business card fell out onto the table with a handkerchief.

Dorothy picked it up and read it. Billie realized that she hadn't bothered to read the card herself and wondered what Dorothy might see that Billie had missed.

"Why do you have this?" Dorothy asked.

"Some boy ran up to me on the lot and wants me to hire him." Billie shook her head. "But I'm not going to do it."

"I've never heard of him," Dorothy said as she returned the card. "Do you know who his clients are?"

"No. I don't know a thing about him except that he's young and he managed to get past MGM security."

"If he could figure that out, maybe you *should* hire him."

"Whatever for?"

"Flo was creative at publicity; studio press offices aren't. You haven't been happy with what Howard puts together."

Billie snorted. "He doesn't put anything together."

"That's my point. You talk about how creative Flo was. Maybe you should get creative and hire this guy. You say he's young and got onto the most secure film lot on Earth. He'll be cheap, I suspect."

"But he could also make a huge disaster."

Billie picked up the card and read it. The boy's office was on Sunset Boulevard at the heart of the entertainment district. The strip had cleaned up a bit recently—fewer gangsters, more office buildings, and some upscale clubs. Perhaps the kid was legitimate, after all. She'd imagined him working out of a dusty, third-floor Edendale walk-up near the old Keystone Studios, probably the same block where Laurel and Hardy had pushed the piano down the stairs in *The Music Box*.

She drummed the card against her palm.

"You're savvy about those things," Dorothy said. "Make him get approval from you before he does anything. That should take care of it."

Billie pinched her lips. "I don't know."

"Maybe he could help you connect to a younger audience," Dorothy prodded. "He'll understand what they want."

Billie smiled. "The boy at the gate didn't know who I was when I got here."

"My point, exactly. Work out a deal with this kid. He sounds hungry. Maybe a thirty-day free trial and see what happens."

Billie reread the business card. "I suppose it wouldn't hurt to talk to him."

"That's all you need to do. Talk to him. It won't cost you anything, and it could be a first step toward getting out of MGM."

"Or staying there."

"What I mean is, you'll be taking charge of your own career, not leaving it in MGM's hands."

"I suppose."

Dorothy put another donut chunk in her mouth and chewed.

Billie could taste the soft dough and sugar. There were four more chunks on the plate. Dorothy put two on a napkin and pushed the plate across the table.

Billie licked her lips but shoved the plate back.

Dorothy slid it back again. "One piece won't hurt you."

"Oh, yes, it will."

"Your face says you want it."

"I've learned to ignore those cravings."

Dorothy rolled her eyes. "Come on, you'll be doing me a favor." She pointed to the pastry. "My body doesn't need all that."

"Neither does mine."

Dorothy's eyes showed wicked amusement. "Ha! You could afford to gain a few."

Billie felt like she couldn't afford to gain a speck of dust, but she wanted that donut, and there was an urge, a rush inside her, telling her to eat it. She stabbed it with Dorothy's fork and stuffed it into her mouth. It was soft, light, fluffy, and sweet.

She ate the other piece, too.

Chapter Six

Three days later, Billie was on Sunset Boulevard, standing in front of a Colonial-style building that reminded her of upstate New York. It was a rare two-story clapboard in a city of stucco, and it made her smile.

She opened the door, entered the foyer, and found Tom's name on the listings: Suite 221. She took the elevator to the second floor. When she walked into his office, she expected a reception area. Instead, she found herself standing directly in front of Tom's cluttered desk.

He looked up at her, chewing. The balance of his sandwich sat on its wrapping paper in the middle of the desk. She smelled sauerkraut.

"Oh, I'm so sorry," she said. "I didn't mean to interrupt. I should have knocked." She pointed to the door behind her. "I thought . . ."

Tom swallowed. "It's fine." He licked his fingers. "It was the only chance I had to stop the hunger pains; I've been so busy."

Billie suddenly felt hungry herself, but she also had second thoughts, and part of her wanted to turn and leave. Tom was too young, inexperienced, and naive. She saw it all over his face. She was used to walking into offices with well-dressed receptionists, art on the wall, and invitations to sit while the busy person she was visiting finished a previous appointment. Most of the professionals she'd worked with were her age or older.

Yes, she wanted to turn around and leave, but she didn't want to be rude. She shouldn't have listened to Dorothy.

She took a breath and tightened her arm around her purse. She was here, this meeting wouldn't last long, and it wouldn't cost her anything. She'd be kind and cheerful.

"Sorry, Miss Burke," Tom said as he finished swallowing, smiled, and stood. "I lost track of time. You sure are punctual."

"It's fine. I do try to be on time."

"Let me clean this up." He dropped the wax paper from the sandwich into a desk drawer and took a swig of Bireley's orange soda. His ears were red. "Sit, please." He motioned to a chair. "Would like a pop? I have another in the drawer. Two, actually. Big Red? Royal Crown?"

"No, thank you, " Billie said. "I'm a tea person." She sat and pulled off her gloves.

Tom sat back down in his own chair behind the desk. "You look lovely today," he told her.

"Thank you." She'd worn a robin's-egg-blue rayon suit with a white silk blouse and a matching Florentine hat, a new outfit she'd found at Bullock's.

Tom straightened his lapel and folded his hands on his desk.

Billie glanced at the wall, spotting something that showed intelligence: Tom's college diploma. "Miami University, Mr. O'Donough?" she asked, pointing to the framed evidence.

"Yes. Graduated two years ago. I'm glad I don't have to go through that again. And you can call me Tom."

"You're from Ohio?"

"Cincinnata."

Billie felt a slow smile spread across her face. "Where in Cincinnati? My mother was from Marietta, and my father was born in Waterford."

"O'Bryonville."

She straightened in her chair. "Irish. Me, too. My daddy, anyway. You can tell by my hair." She pointed to it.

"You know, we Irish need to stick together."

"Yes, we do."

"I know you're busy, so I don't want to take up too much of your time. Would you like to hear my ideas?" His face brightened like a schoolboy's.

"Yes, but first, may I ask a question?" She'd prepared a few and might as well ask them, even though she had no intention of hiring Tom. She liked him. He seemed sweet. But that was no reason to entrust her career to him.

He motioned for her to continue.

She folded her hands on her lap. "How did you get into this business?" It was, she knew, a fair question. He'd only recently graduated from college, and his degree wasn't from a place like Washington Square College in New York or the University of Southern California in Los Angeles, where you might expect someone to have gone to school if he was interested in the film industry.

"I love the movies," he replied. "I've seen one weekly since I was a boy, but I'm no actor."

"Neither is my daughter. She's about your age, I suspect."

He didn't have a wedding band on his finger.

"You sound disappointed that she didn't take the stage," he said.

"I'm still trying to get over it."

"To answer your question, I came out here after graduation, then worked in the Paramount press office for a while. But I wanted to get out on my own, figuring I could do better. No offense to Paramount. It does great work."

He had some experience, at least. "Yes," Billie agreed. "Paramount is quite good at what it does. Who are your clients?"

He looked down briefly. "I don't have any yet. I've been doing this for a month. Several have come in, just like you, though."

"Who else have you approached besides Bert Lahr on the lot?"

He bit his lip. "I'm sorry. I can't say."

"I understand," she said. "I wouldn't want you telling people I was here, either." She sat back and lifted her chin a bit. "So, Tom, why do you want to represent me?"

He leaned forward and folded his hands on the desk. "I'm a big fan," he said.

She smirked. "Of me? I didn't think anyone under forty even knew I existed."

"I sure do, and I want to help rebuild your career."

Her shoulders tensed. "Rebuild? What do you mean?"

He pulled on his collar. "I'm sorry. I meant that I'd like to get your name out there."

She felt herself relax a little. "What are your plans for me if I hire you?"

"I was hoping you'd ask that question," he said with a jaunty smile.

She thought of Flo, and a touch of sadness crept in. Flo had been the Shakespeare of public relations. Nobody crafted stories as effectively as her husband had done. Flo had once told the papers she took milk baths to soften her skin. She'd never done that, of course. She couldn't even imagine doing it. Milk was something you wiped off a baby's chin or something that curdled if you left it out too long. But ticket sales surged for her play when the lie hit the papers, as did milk sales—those poor cows.

"You're obviously talented, and you have an established career. You're an international name. You come with many assets," Tom said, emphasizing the last word.

"You make me sound like a bank."

"I mean, you have a long list of accomplishments."

"Thank you. But what, specifically, would you do?"

He sat back and paused. The corners of his mouth drooped. "I can help you with your, um, problem."

"My problem?" She felt her neck tighten.

He put a finger to his lips. "With . . . you know, the situation with Miss Arzner."

Her insides raced. "How do you know about that?" The newsreel hadn't hit the screens yet. The only people who were supposed to know about it were L. B., Dorothy, Howard, and The Mount, and they wouldn't have said anything.

"I was at the *Gunga Din* preview," he said, "and I heard Mr. Mayer talking."

"How did you get into the premiere?"

"Same way I got into MGM."

"And what way was that?"

"In the trunk of a friend's car."

She laughed aloud, then put a hand to her mouth to stop herself. "Oh, my God."

"At the theater, I slid in through a side door, just like I did as a kid."

She was amused, but her heart was racing. This conversation was getting too personal. If he knew the rumors about her and Dorothy, who else knew?

"Miss Burke, may I be frank with you?"

She froze. She wasn't sure she wanted to hear anymore. Then again, what could it hurt? She nodded for him to go on.

"When the press sees that reel, boy, there could be trouble," he said.

"I must be going," she said, fumbling for her purse. "Thank you for your time, but I won't need your services." She pushed up from the chair.

"I have some solutions."

She stopped. She wanted to hear his ideas, but at the same time, she didn't. She assumed they wouldn't be as creative as Flo's, and that she'd be wasting her time.

"You came all this way and paid for parking," he said. "Please, let me present one idea. If you don't like it, so be it. If you do like it but still don't want to hire me, the idea is yours to take elsewhere."

She sat back down. "All right, then. One idea." She put her hands on the arms of the chair, ready to push up again as soon as necessary.

Tom smiled. "Mr. Ziegfeld had one of the best minds for public relations."

"Yes, he did."

"I studied him thoroughly at Paramount. He's well respected there."

"I'm not surprised."

"I have a record idea for you," he said.

"As in record-breaking or a musical disk?"

"Musical disk. MGM contracts state that the studio gets a percentage of record sales, correct?"

"Yes, although I can't remember how much."

"I have an idea for one. A record, that is."

"I'm not a professional singer. I sing well enough for stage work, but I don't have a jazz sound if that's what you need."

"No, I'm thinking more like a record of you reading children's stories."

She tilted her head and smiled. "Children's stories?"

"Books for children are popular these days, but many parents don't have time to read them to their children. You could record them, and the parents could put the record on and do other things while their children listen. There isn't anything like it anywhere. You'd be the first. You're a storyteller by trade. This would just be a new kind of story."

She relaxed in her chair. "Original stories? Or stories like *Grimm's Fairy Tales*?"

"All kinds of stories. If you'd like, I could contact Columbia Records and see about getting you an appointment. We'd do a public relations plan with pre-release announcements, appearances at stores where you signed the record cover—you know, things like that."

She loved the idea, but realized that she'd have to hire him to do it. She wasn't ready to do that, and wondered if she could do the record independently. "What is your fee, Mr. O'Donough?"

A muscle moved in his cheek as if he were struggling to find the right thing to say to keep her. "It's low."

"How much?"

"Thirty dollars a month." It was a statement, but it sounded more like a question.

That seemed like a lot of money, and Billie was curious if she'd get enough out of him for the amount. Thirty dollars was the cost of a new walnut radio table.

"It's a lovely idea, but I'm facing a contract renewal in the next few months. I need immediate press. Do you have an idea for that?"

"I was at Max Factor's picking up some lipstick for my sister," Tom said.

"He has cosmetics for men, too, you know."

"Yes, I know, but it wasn't for me. My sister was visiting from Ohio. Mr. Factor—Junior, that is—invited me to a party at the Tropicana. I'd never been there before. It was swell. I met someone named Lydia Lane. She wants you to endorse a product."

Billie smiled and perked up. Lydia was the beauty columnist for the *Los Angeles Times* and had featured Billie's skin-care advice from time to time. Billie hadn't done a beauty endorsement in ten years. Margarine, yes. Cigarettes, yes. Soda, yes—things that damaged your skin. She realized she was tingling all over. She wanted this endorsement.

"A beauty product, I hope?"

"Yes, of some sort. I don't understand those things."

She pointed back and forth between them. "How did she know you and I were connected?"

"I told her you were coming in today. She mentioned she knew of new skin treatment for older women."

Billie bristled. "Older?"

"You know what I mean. Anyway, someone was bringing it to Los Angeles for the stars. I thought of you."

She squeezed her purse. "I'm not old."

"I'm sorry. You know what I mean. Maybe a better phrase is 'more experienced.'"

"How old do you think I am?"

"Your MGM bio says you're fifty-two, but you look much younger."

She loosened her grip. "Thank you." MGM had shaved two years off her age for press purposes, which was okay with her. Four years off would have been better.

"A beauty endorsement would help you," Tom said. "I told Lydia you were coming here today, and I suggested you endorse her product. For a fee, of course. She loved the idea. She said the woman who did the treatments was Rachel-something."

"Rachel Johnson?"

He snapped his fingers. "That's it. Miss Johnson wants to build a client base here and has a new facial treatment that takes the years away, something she learned to do in

Paris from the best doctors. She'll pay you, and I won't take a percentage. It'd be covered in the monthly fee."

"How much will she pay?"

"Two hundred dollars."

Billie nodded. If Lydia was involved, this was legitimate. "What's the treatment?"

"I'm a man," Tom said with a grin. "I haven't got a clue."

Usually, treatments come in the form of chemical peels or surgeries. The chemicals could scar, and surgeries often caused deformities. If Rachel Johnson had something new, it could be a natural treatment, like an exotic oil or reindeer milk. Billie had read about such things in women's magazines. She'd never tried them, but if the treatment was something of that sort—and it worked—the endorsement would be worth it. L. B. was letting her go because he thought she was too old. The endorsement would wash that excuse out to sea.

"Can I set up an appointment with them?" Tom asked.

Billie paused. She didn't want to pay this boy thirty dollars, but if she got the endorsement, she'd net a hundred and seventy, which wasn't bad.

"It's perfect for you," he coaxed.

"She didn't explain the treatment to you?" she asked.

"No, and even if she had, I wouldn't understand it. Besides, it's just a meeting at this point. You don't have to agree to anything. Let me set it up. Lydia suggested doing it over dinner since you're busy during the day. The three of you would meet."

"Why is Lydia involved?"

"She seems to be serving as Miss Johnson's agent, someone local to make the connections. I'm guessing she's getting a cut."

Billie thought about it for a minute. It was Tom's fee that bothered her. What if this didn't work out?

"You might not get another chance like this," he prodded.

"I suppose a meeting wouldn't hurt," she said. If it was a natural treatment, and if it flew off the shelves, she'd get the credit. Still, she wanted to wait to pay Tom thirty dollars. "Let's do this as a trial," she offered. "How about if I pay you in increments? We can start at ten dollars a month. If I contract with Miss Johnson, I'll pay you an additional ten dollars a month, which means twenty per month. If things go well after two months, and you have more good ideas, I'll start paying thirty dollars a month. I will also want to retain the right to drop you at any time."

"Ten dollars isn't very much, Miss Burke."

She wanted to keep the endorsement, but she also wanted to commit to nothing more than something short-term. If the endorsement didn't work, she'd be out thirty dollars with nothing to show for it. She studied Tom's face and saw desperation. She felt bad for him, but she had to stay firm.

"Ten dollars should pay half the rent for the month," she said.

"There's more involved than that," he said. "I'd negotiate the deal for you."

"I prefer to do that myself and have my barrister review it."

His eyes begged. "How about fifteen dollars for the endorsement and my full fee if you do more?"

"What would stop me from going to Miss Lane directly?" she said, trying to keep her voice steady. She would never go to Lydia directly. Billie had ethics, but he didn't need to know that.

"Nothing, but I don't think you'll do it. From what I heard, you're not like that."

She felt a tinge of regret over trying to get him cheap. On the other hand, he owned a business, and she needed money, too. Besides, he wouldn't spend much time on the project. All he'd be doing was connecting people.

"I'm not coming up in price," she said, crossing her legs under the chair. "I'll sign an agreement with you if that makes you feel better, and I'll pass your business cards around the lot."

"I . . . I can't do it."

"Very well, " she said as she rose, hoping he'd stop her. "If you change your mind, you know where to find me."

He pursed his lips and paused.

She turned toward the door, hoping he'd agree to her terms and stop her before she left.

"Okay," he blurted out as she reached for the doorknob. As she turned back to face him, he pulled out a small white box of business cards.

Chapter Seven

Billie walked into Howard Strickling's office with her stomach tied up in knots. She'd been called in to discuss "how to solve the problem of the reel." She was told the problem had to be solved before *Oz* was released. She still couldn't imagine what it showed that was so horrible. She and Dorothy had held hands. They'd dropped hands. Billie had left. It all seemed harmless.

Howard was known (behind his back) as "The Remover," a title earned because he miraculously "removed" any kind of stain an actor publicly faced, guilty or not. If the rumor was homosexuality, he paired the "offender" with an opposite-sex mate and forced the "questionable" relationship to break up. Some refused to ditch those they loved. Bill Haines had been one of those. His refusal banned him not only from MGM, but from every studio in the country. He became an interior designer instead.

Billie shook her head as she thought about it. All those smiles on screen? Many were the result of great acting jobs. What was going inside the actors was something entirely different.

Billie had decided that the answer would be no if Howard tried to pair her up with a man. She'd been married once, and that was enough. The public knew her as Flo Ziegfeld's wife, which was the core of her identity and a part of her status. She wasn't going to give that up.

"You may go in now," Howard's secretary said.

Billie held up her chin, took a deep breath, turned the doorknob, and walked in.

Howard rose from his desk with a slight smile—quite a good sign from a man who rarely smiled. He was a square-shouldered gent with farmer's hands, trimmed black hair, and buckeye-brown eyes. "Miss Burke. Good to see you."

Taking care to moderate her tone, she replied, "It's good to see you as well."

Howard's office looked the same as the last time Billie was here. It looked like someone had thoughtfully decorated an important man's office at the onset, but after years of hard work and no maintenance, the shine had rubbed off, and the knickknacks needed dusting. She wanted to clean, straighten, and polish everything back to its original splendor.

Another man was in the office, but she didn't recognize him. He was sitting in a chair across from Howard's desk. The man rose, bowed slightly, and said, "Miss Burke."

He was a young, slender man with delicate fingers. Billie guessed he must be a new person in Howard's office. There seemed to be a few new people coming into her life—first Tom, now this stranger. The public relations business was getting younger and younger. Everything about the movie business was getting younger.

"This is Francis Strong," Howard told Billie, nodding at the young man. "He's a classical pianist with a three-film contract."

As much as she loved listening to classical music, Billie couldn't help wondering why this musician was here. Clearly, she wasn't being paired with him. He was entirely too young for her, maybe around thirty years old. Indeed, she was old enough to be his mother.

Howard gestured to the chair next to Strong. "Miss Burke, please, take a seat."

Sitting beside Strong, Billie noticed he was a pretty young man with aqua-blue eyes and corn-silk hair, and he was wearing a navy-blue suit over a sinewy frame. He appeared crisp and pressed. He turned to her, offered his hand, then kissed the top of hers. He reminded her of a courtier. She felt a sudden twitch in her stomach.

"Miss Burke," Strong said. His voice was as smooth as olive oil. "My pleasure. My father loves your films."

Internally, she rolled her eyes. She was still trying to get used to phrases like "My grandmother thinks you're the best" or "My mother named her dog after you." Nobody under the age of thirty-five ever said, "Wow, I love your work!" She longed to hear those words again.

Howard folded his hands on his desk. "I might as well get to the point. Francis here has the same problem you do."

"Problem?" she said. Beside her, Strong knotted his fingers.

"Well, you know. Your problem is the reel." Howard pointed to Strong. "He's in the same category."

She was surprised. Strong looked like a twilight: pretty, effeminate, soft, groomed. Perhaps, despite the age difference, they were being paired in a romantic comedy. She had to admit: She wouldn't mind having him court her on the screen. It would certainly improve her reputation.

"Miss Burke, I'm going to tell you something you might not like, so please bear with me," Howard said.

She pulled her arms across her chest and squeezed.

"I'm putting the two of you together for an event."

"What do you mean 'putting us together'?" she asked. An event wasn't a film. It was a photo opportunity for the fan magazines.

"It's just one event," Howard said.

"In what way are we being put together, exactly?" If they attended an event together, that would be fine, but she wouldn't put on a false show of having a romantic relationship with this person over the long term.

"It's for the Jewish Home benefit at Mary Pickford's estate. All I need are some photos of the two of you together. Just a hint of a coupling."

It was the year's social event for movie-world types, and ordinarily, Billie would love to go, but not like this. She squeezed the arms of her chair and shook her head. "Coupling? No. Absolutely not."

"It's not a Cary Grant/Virginia Cherrill type of thing. One shot will do it."

She looked at Strong, who was looking in the other direction. His hands were in his lap, together. His knuckles were white.

"If you want to send us to this thing, that's fine, provided there is no hint that we are anything more than friends," Billie said.

"We're going to hint otherwise."

"Then it's a no."

Howard leaned forward. "It's this or you're fired, Miss Burke."

She belted out a laugh. "I'm already fired."

"I mean immediately. We can work around the missed *Oz* shots."

Her head began to pound. She couldn't lose her job immediately. She needed time to build a plan for what would come next.

"We have to create an antidote for the reel," Howard said, "and I'm heading off public relations problems with Francis here."

Billie studied Strong, wondering what he was thinking about all this, but she couldn't get a read. In her head, she pressed him: "Say something, damn it, and stick up for yourself." But she kept her mouth shut.

"He has a film coming out soon where he'll be introduced," Howard said. "The world has to see a normal man. And as for you, we can't have the headlines reading, '*Follies* Creator's Wife Interested in Women.'"

"I'm not interested in women. I've said that repeatedly. Dorothy and I are just friends."

Howard smirked. "That's a loud protest."

She banged her fists on the chair. "I won't do it."

Strong's feet tapped the floor; his cheeks turned ruddy. "I don't like this either," he finally said.

"You don't have a choice if you want to do your next two films," Howard said.

Francis grimaced.

"I don't have time to argue," said Howard. "Here's the central question: Do the two of you want your jobs tomorrow?"

Billie looked aside and tightened her jaw.

"Do you?" he asked again.

She didn't want to reply. She didn't want to lie.

"Yes," Strong said with a sigh.

"Miss Burke?" Howard said.

She bit her lip. "Do what you have to do," she said under her breath. "As long as it's just this once." Somehow, she would figure this out.

Howard patted his desk and gave a wry smile. "Terrific. You'll both appear at the Jewish Home benefit next

Glinda's Ruby Slippers

Wednesday. Francis, you're going to perform with the orchestra. Miss Burke, you'll be a table hostess. After Francis finishes, he'll join you at your table. You'll be a couple for the afternoon. You don't have to kiss or hold hands. You don't have to look lovingly into each other's eyes, but show mutual interest. You'll pose for pictures, walk the grounds, share a napkin, I don't know. But you get it, right?

She looked away as her jaw tightened even more. She was tired of being controlled by stupid men. She wanted to spit in Howard's face.

"Just this once, right?" Strong asked.

Howard rolled his eyes. "If I'm not satisfied, or if it doesn't work," he said, "there could be another, but I'm sure the two of you will figure it out and make me happy."

Billie turned to Howard and glared. "You said just a second ago it would just be once."

"As I said, it'll be once if it goes well . . . which I'm sure it will. You're an accomplished actress, Miss Burke. You've played everything from an auto mechanic to a fairy princess. You'll figure it out."

"What are we supposed to tell people?" she said, feeling resigned but still tense.

"That you met on the lot, and you have mutual interests. You can be coy about it. It'll up the curiosity."

Dread colored Strong's face.

"Mrs. Mayer asked you to attend," Howard continued. "She chairs the event, and she asked that you host a table. She seems to like you and asked for you, specifically. But before that, you and Francis should get to know each other. You don't want to appear like strangers. I want you to have tea tomorrow at the Formosa Café. Four o'clock. Work out the details between yourselves."

Billie sat up straight. She liked the idea of ingratiating herself with the boss's wife. If Mrs. Mayer liked her, maybe she'd defend her to L. B. when the time came to try to save Billie's job. Billie felt herself soften a little. Maybe this event wouldn't be so bad, if she could keep things with Francis Strong at a friendship level.

Billie turned to him, wanting to appear friendly while still presenting an honest question. "I want to learn more about classical music. Perhaps you can teach me?" Billie's "daughter of a circus clown" personality still ran through her, sometimes making her seem unsophisticated. She could always use a bit of tutoring on the finer things.

"Certainly," he said with a nod and a smile.

* * *

Billie drove the half-hour home with her thoughts in a blur. She felt tired, lonely, and regretful, but she couldn't pinpoint why. Her mind was spinning blank. It wasn't about what had happened with Howard. She knew she could make the event work for her, and this thing with Strong was just a one-time deal. No, there was something else she couldn't put her finger on, but she thought a chocolate-chip cookie might help. She ate one about twice a year. She didn't keep them around the house. That would be dangerous.

She parked in front of a small bakery and stepped inside as bells jingled above the door.

"May I help you?" a female clerk said.

The smell of butter and sugar in the room calmed Billie. She eyed the donuts, breads, and other pastries, trying to decide which would best take care of the craving.

"Chocolate-chip cookies. Do you have any? I only want one," Billie said, raising her index finger.

"Not right now. It's late in the day, so we're all sold out. We do have conchas, however." The clerk pointed to a tray on the counter.

When she first moved here, Billie had tried one of those, experimenting with Mexican foods that couldn't be found on the East Coast. The concha had been dry. Right now, she wanted comfort food. She scanned the other baked goods in the glass case. Her eyes landed on slices of Battenberg cake, a sponge cake covered in marzipan with a pink-and-yellow check pattern.

That kind of cake had been Stanley's favorite. Suddenly, she missed him. She put her hand to her mouth; a lump formed in her throat.

Stanley had been her fiancé in England in her younger, pre–New York days. Her career had just taken off, and he'd seen her in a performance.

A tear came to her eye. She wiped it away and bit her lip. Suddenly, she wanted two cookies. Tomorrow, she'd have to fast to make up for whatever she bought here.

"Miss Burke?"

Startled from her daydream, Billie shook Stanley out of her head.

"You are Billie Burke, aren't you?" the clerk asked as she lifted a tray of glazed donuts to the top of the case.

Billie adjusted her hair with her fingers. It was time to turn on her star persona.

"Yes," Billie said.

"What can I get you?"

"I'm still thinking."

She looked again at the cake. She wanted a piece. She pictured herself sharing it with Stanley.

"How about a dozen butter cookies?" the clerk asked. "I took them out of the oven just half an hour ago. I was going to take them home to my children, but I don't need twelve of them. They don't really need any of them, but I like seeing them happy."

Even as the clerk rattled on, Billie's thoughts drifted back to Stanley. Their breakup happened in 1907 in a London West End restaurant. She'd just finished an evening performance of *My Wife*. A half-eaten plate of chicken with Provençale sauce sat before her, and Stanley had the same.

Her mother had agreed to let them dine alone after Billie insisted, saying she had something personal to discuss with him.

"Most improper," Mother had puffed, but she'd relented.

Billie's agenda had been to decide what would happen next in their relationship. A week earlier, she'd signed a contract with American producer Charles Frohman to be one of his leading actresses in the States. She'd told Stanley about it a few days previously. She'd heard in his voice and seen in his face that he'd expected her to turn it down.

But she couldn't turn it down. This was what she'd always wanted, and she did want to return home to New York. She also wanted Stanley to go with her, and she assumed he would, in the end. He always spoke highly of the United States.

In the restaurant, gaslights hissed and forks clanged on plates like bent windchimes hanging from a tree. Guffaws, whispers, and conversations created a low hum in the dining room.

"I cannot live in America," Stanley said, facing the kitchen.

She stroked her engagement ring. "You could live in both places. You could come back here for a visit when I'm on tour."

He bit his lip. "My whole life is here. I have a responsibility to my father." Stanley managed his father's country estate. It would be his in a few years.

She tried to sound upbeat. "You've traveled the world."

"Indeed, and I've been to New York. It was a nice place to visit, and I liked the United States, but I can't leave England."

She straightened the cloth napkin in her lap. "We could live in Yonkers. A train would take me to the city. You could still have a country house with horses and all the other things you enjoy."

"And what would I do during the day?" he snapped, startling her. Stanley never snapped.

"You'd do the same thing you do here. You could buy a place and—"

"I am not going to buy anything in America. I do not understand why you cannot stay here," he said, his voice choking. "London's theater is better than America's, and you're widely known here." He gestured wide. "Why would you want to leave all this behind?"

"I only recently became known, and I don't know how long my fame will last."

"It'll last forever. I'll help you."

"I . . . I . . . I can't."

He exhaled.

"Mother and I want to go home," she continued. "America is home."

He looked around the room. "You've lived here most of your life."

"A little over half of it."

"You told me it was home for you. You said Mr. Courtneidge offered you a contract for West End plays." Robert Courtneidge was an English theatrical manager who had produced one of her recent plays.

"Yes, he did, but I turned it down."

Stanley's eyes darkened. He shook his head. "Why?"

"The money is better in the United States. I'll earn twice what I'm earning here. And I want to go home."

"You don't need money. I have money."

"I need my own money. I told you about my circumstances." Billie was determined never to be poor again. She'd been poor most of her life and had only been comfortable for the past eight months. Just a year ago, she'd buried her father in a pauper's grave, something she still regretted.

"I don't want to be taken care of," she said. "I want to take care of myself, and I owe this to Mother. My father is dead, and my mother's family lives in Washington, DC, and Ohio. She's been longing for home. We didn't want to come here in the first place. It was my father's idea, and now that he's gone, we can return. I have my two sisters in the States, and we haven't seen them for eleven years."

"They're adults now, with their own families. And they are half-sisters, twice your age."

"My mother misses them just like she'd miss me if distance separated us for so long. We're her children."

Stanley took a deep breath and closed his eyes. "Well, I can't go."

Billie swallowed hard. "What does this mean for us?" The word *us* rippled through her like an electric shock. She couldn't breathe. Tears filled her eyes. "Please, Stanley."

He opened his eyes and stared at her.

"Come with me," she begged. "We'll work it out. You can still own Sheldon Manor. Your father isn't going to take it away. You're the oldest. It's yours, and when I retire, we can come back and live here. The career of an actress is short. You can visit here whenever you want. You'd have two homes instead of one."

He ran his fingers through his hair. "I cannot. I cannot. I run the place. My father is getting older."

"You love me, don't you?"

He locked onto her eyes and held her hands across the table. "Of course I do," he said.

She sobbed. "Then come with me."

He let go of her hands. His glazed eyes looked down.

The strings inside her broke.

"Miss Burke?" the bakery clerk was saying now, forcing her back to the present moment. "Have you made up your mind?"

Billie could still feel the warm imprint of Stanley's solid hand on hers. She took a pink handkerchief from her purse and dotted the corners of her eyes. She had loved Stanley, loved him still. Maybe she should have stayed in England. She'd never stopped questioning the decision to leave, though if she'd stayed, she wouldn't have married Flo, and she wouldn't have had Patty. She also wouldn't have had her career. She loved Flo differently, in a way built on an appreciation for what he'd given her: a daughter, a career, a lot of humor, and plenty of fun.

"Miss Burke?" the baker said.

"I'm sorry, dear. Butter cookies are fine," Billie said. "Just one, though."

The clerk put a cookie in a brown paper bag and took Billie's money.

Billie smiled and accepted the bag while wondering was Stanley was doing these days. Did he ever marry? Was he still thinking of her as she was thinking of him? Should she send him a letter?

"Miss Burke," the clerk said. "Is everything all right?"

Billie shook Stanley out of her head. She had to move on. Thinking of him only saddened her. She needed to leave the past in the past and move forward.

* * *

Shortly after she got home, Billie threw the cookie into the trash. She'd resisted eating it all the way home, and now she knew she didn't need the treat. Instead, she sat in her home office dialing Patty in New York. It was 5:00 p.m. here and 8:00 p.m. on the East Coast. She was calling to hear Patty's voice and warn her about her possible press appearance with Francis Strong. Patty would know there was nothing between Billie and Strong, but she might still wonder what was happening if she found out about it without a warning first. Her mother had never been paired like this. Billie anticipated sarcasm about it.

"It's Monday night," Patty said when she answered the phone. "Why are you calling? You call on Thursdays."

"Can't a mother call her daughter anytime? I missed you. That's all."

"What happened?" Patty said, sounding suspicious.

"What do you mean?"

"You know exactly what I mean."

Billie twirled her hair. She wasn't going to tell Patty about her MGM contract. The girl didn't need to worry. It was going to be odd enough telling her about Francis Strong.

"Nothing happened," Billie said.

"Mother. Your life is predictable. You do things at the same time every day and for the same reasons. I've been in New York for weeks, and you've never called me on a Monday night."

Billie had rehearsed what she was going to say all the way home. Here it went. "You know about the annual benefit at Pickfair?"

"Mary Pickford's estate?"

"Yes. It's to raise money for the Jewish Home."

"I recall something about that, yeah."

"I'm going to be a table hostess."

"You called me on a Monday night just to tell me that?!"

"Yes, dear."

"Try again. You've done things like that before."

"Not at Pickfair."

"What's going on, Mother? I smell something rotten."

So much for easing into it. Patty's intuition was sharp, and it was only getting better with age, making it harder for Billie to hide things.

"Ouch," Billie said.

"What's wrong?"

"I pulled too hard on my hair."

"Let it alone, then."

Billie put her hand down and squeezed the phone's earpiece.

"Something's going to be in the papers, isn't it?" Patty said. "What is it? Does it involve me?"

Patty hated the press. When the girl was twelve, reporters had shown up at the front door of Burkeley Crest, hungry for gossip. Patty had unknowingly opened the front door to camera flashes, questions being shouted, and pencils scratching on pads. Flo had just had another affair with a floozie, and the press wanted to know about it. They'd expected a servant to answer the door, but Patty had been near it, so she answered. For the reporters, it was a jackpot: a young girl who let them in. They pushed right past her into the house, frightening her half to death.

Billie was in the next room and heard the commotion, but she was thirty seconds too late. Nowadays, the phone was on the wall or on a table nearby. You could easily call the police. But back then, the closest phone had been kept in a phone closet. Billie had done her best to get the reporters out, but only after she agreed to answer some questions.

Billie knew her current situation with Francis Strong wouldn't create that kind of fuss, but she still took a deep breath before answering Patty's question. "I'm going there with a beau of sorts. But before you say anything—"

"A what?! A beau?! You don't do beaus." Patty laughed aloud, something she rarely did.

Billie wasn't sure whether she should be upset about being mocked or relieved that Patty wasn't asking if the press would show up at her door. "He's not that, exactly. Um, I'm not sure what to call him, but that's the way MGM will present him in the press." Billie almost heard the girl sit down, cross her legs, and settle in to pick this story apart.

"It's a press stunt," Billie said.

"Oh, God. I haven't seen you try a press stunt since before Daddy died."

"Rumors are floating that your aunt Dorothy and I are, well, you know . . . like the last time."

"A novel way around it, for you, at least. A beau?"

"We're only doing it once. It's MGM's plan."

"So, you're calling to warn me?" Patty said.

"Yes."

"I appreciate it. Now, what's he like?"

"He's a classical piano player with a three-film contract."

Patty laughed again. "You don't know anything about classical music. The closest you've ever gotten to it is parlor songs."

"That isn't true. I sang in many plays in London and New York, let me remind you," she said. "And I'm singing in *The Wizard of Oz*."

"'Come Out, Come Out' isn't classical music, Mother. Opera is classical music, not movie tunes."

Billie bristled. "It's a lovely song. But back to our original discussion. The man's name is Francis Strong—the one accompanying me to the event. He's a very respectful gentleman, and it doesn't matter what he looks like or how old he is." She wanted to take that last phrase back as soon as it slipped out.

"How old is he? Older than Daddy?"

"No. Younger."

"How young?"

"I don't know his exact age, and it doesn't matter. It's a studio contrivance, dear. It isn't real."

"Ten years old?"

"Of course not!"

There was a moment of silence on the other end. Then Patty pressed on: "This sounds odd, Mother. Why did you agree to it? It doesn't sound like you."

"MGM wants it. I told you."

"That doesn't answer the question."

"He's a famous classical pianist. He tours the world, and MGM thinks it would be helpful for us to be seen together. It would smooth out my image as a scatterbrain comedienne and expose him as a new screen talent. That's all."

Patty was silent.

"Really, dear. That's all. Just a one-time experiment. This Mr. Strong is new. He needs it more than I do."

"Whatever you say, Mother."

Truthfully, this had as much to do with Billie's career as well as Strong's, but she didn't want to admit it to Patty.

It was embarrassing to be coupled with such a young man, and she needed to tell herself that it was for him and not her, and to follow through on that belief. Doing so made her feel less like MGM property and more like a career mentor, which is what she preferred to be.

Chapter Eight

Billie approached the Formosa Café, a red train car converted into a restaurant. Francis Strong was outside wearing black pleated trousers and a pullover sweater with a checkerboard design. When he looked up and saw her, his lips tipped into a smile, and he gently closed his book over a leather bookmark. He was tall, and his eyes seemed bluer, brighter than she remembered.

"Miss Burke," he said. His smile revealed dimples. "Thank you for coming. You're beautiful, as always."

"Thank you, Mr. Strong. Flattery will earn you extra points. Oh, and I love that sweater. Where did you get it?"

"From Adrian."

She smiled. "Of course."

Adrian Greenberg was an MGM costumer, the same one who had designed the costumes for *Oz*. He often gave or loaned clothes he wasn't using, and Billie had been a frequent beneficiary.

Strong opened the door for her, and they stepped inside to the smell of oyster sauce. The dining room seated fifteen or so, and the air buzzed with chatter.

"MGM reserved us a table," he said, pointing to the back corner.

The maître d' tucked two menus under his arm and led Billie and Strong to the back of the restaurant. Strong pulled out a chair for her and set down his book. It was a leather-bound edition of *The Summing Up* by W. Somerset Maugham, a friend of Billie's. She pointed to the book as she sat.

"Are you enjoying that?" she said.

"Not especially," he said. "I was expecting something like *Of Human Bondage*. It reads more like an autobiography, and it's rather philosophical."

"Willie sometimes writes like that," she said, smiling proudly.

"Who?"

"Mr. Maugham is a friend of mine, and that's what we call him. He's a playwright, too. He wrote some of my plays back in the teens."

Strong's ears turned red. "I hope I didn't offend you."

"Not at all. That book was made into a film five years ago by RKO."

"Interesting. I've read some of his earlier works," Strong said. "I would love to meet him someday."

"He lives in Paris now, although he's talking about moving to Los Angeles. Perhaps you'll get to work on a film together if he does."

"That would be splendid."

"But that's not why we're here, Mr. Strong." She folded her hands on the table.

"You can call me Francis."

"And you may call me Billie. We might as well get down to it." She straightened her back. "I've been in this business longer than you've been alive, I'm afraid to admit. I'm not excited about this arrangement between us, but here we are. It's nothing personal. You seem like a fine young man, and I'm looking forward to hearing your music."

His face tightened as he sipped his water. She noticed a wedding band on his finger, and she reflexively touched her own.

The waiter arrived and poured water into their glasses. Billie ordered a fruit salad and green tea; Strong ordered a bran muffin and black coffee. They sat in silence for a minute while Francis fidgeted with a spoon.

Billie took a deep breath. "Let's get on with the matter at hand. Is that all right with you?"

He nodded.

"You seem like a nice fellow," she continued, "but I don't want another relationship with a man, real or fake. Not even for one afternoon. My marriage didn't end when I became a widow. Flo is still my husband, and I don't want anyone to think I'm throwing him away."

Francis sat back and dotted his lips with the napkin. His fingers were long, and his movements were graceful. "I don't want to do this either," he said, "but Mr. Strickling is insisting upon it."

"I understand that. May I ask a professional question?"

"Yes."

"Are you planning a film career, or are these just cameos?" She couldn't help wondering why MGM cared so much about his reputation.

He looked at her. His eyes seemed dimmer, grayer now. "Cameos. I'm not an actor, and they aren't trying to make me into one."

"You're lucky."

"MGM approached me to do a film and then signed me for two more. To answer your question, I'm doing the films for two reasons. First, to earn extra money. With the economy in the hole, touring has declined. My European concerts are gone, and my American and Canadian concerts are fewer. I need the money because I'm caring for my father. He's ill."

"Oh, I am so sorry," she said. "Where does he live?"

"Here, actually. I recently moved him here so he'd be closer."

"Oh," she said. Francis was a good son. Billie could relate; she had cared for her mother in her later years. She'd even built a cottage for her at Burkeley Crest.

"The second reason for the films is to increase my profile. If people see me, I'll be better known and get more touring opportunities."

This didn't answer Billie's question about why MGM would be so concerned about a cameo actor. Francis was in the films because of his fame as a musician. Something was missing in his story. She had to press on.

"Tell me if I go too far," she said.

He nodded for her to continue, but his cheeks turned ruddy.

"How old are you, Francis?" she said.

"Thirty-five."

Older than she'd thought.

Before she could say anything, he sat back and folded his hands on the table. "I should be honest with you. There's something you should know."

Her stomach squirmed, but just then, the waiter arrived with their food and drinks, interrupting Francis. "Anything else I can get you?" the waiter asked.

"Billie?" Francis said.

"No. This is fine."

"No, thank you," Francis said to the waiter. The man left, and Billie motioned for Francis to continue.

"Like I was saying, there's something you should know." He ran his fingers through his hair. "I have a problem with this. I have to do it, but it could backfire." He leaned forward and whispered, "I'm going through a divorce."

She bit the inside of her lip. Divorce was a serious matter. "I'm so sorry."

"It's still in process," he said. He pulled a white handkerchief from his breast pocket and wiped his eyes. "It isn't going well. I got a call this morning. A threat. Oh, I'm very sorry. I shouldn't be telling you this."

"No, no, it's all right. Go ahead."

He loosened his tie and took another breath. "She wants more money. She heard about my film coming out. Her name is Louise." He stared at his food. "Miss Burke—I mean, Billie—I feel terrible about it. I didn't cheat on her. I didn't hit her. I was never even cross with her. We shouldn't have gotten married in the first place. We were miserable together. I married her because that was what men did. They marry women, and my parents pressured me. She was attractive, and her father was rich. She was kind to me, and she pursued me." He sighed, then continued. "I'm having trouble feeling anything for her right now. I don't want to hurt anyone, ever, including her. But all she cares about is the money."

"I imagine she cares about more than that."

"I don't think she ever loved me. She doesn't seem angry, at this point, just greedy."

"Well, it's hard to tell with these things."

"I met her at a concert reception, and she practically jumped into my lap. I was so surprised; I didn't know what to do. I had to marry somebody, so why not her? It was a stupid thing to do, but there was nobody else, and it took the pressure off. There was a lot of pressure on me."

Billie bristled. She understood women like that. Dozens had behaved similarly with Flo, even after he'd married Billie.

He paused and bit his lip. "Miss Burke?"

"Yes," she said softly.

He shook his head and put his palms on the table. "We can't do this together. We simply can't, but we don't have a choice. Can you imagine what will happen when we're in the papers, and the caption says I'm chasing you? Louise will have a fit, and she wants alimony. I don't begrudge her that, but she wants more than I earn."

"Do you have any children?"

"No, thank goodness, " he said. "Louise moved back in with her parents, and they're wealthy. Many people thought I married her for her money, but I didn't. I married her to get my parents to let it go, so I could live the life others expected. Her attorney is the real problem. He's demanding more than I earn on tour. That's why I need these films and more of them."

"I see."

Tension gripped his jaw. "We have to do this, I guess." His lips quivered, and he took a deep breath. "I've spent my whole life at the keyboard. I've been married to the piano, to music. My parents scraped to get me lessons, and they moved us from Colorado to Boston and put me in the best music school. I can't let my father down now."

Billie's parents had done similarly; she understood the urge not to disappoint your parents. When they sacrifice so much for you, it creates pressure to move, keep going, and be the best for their sake. You couldn't fail. The world would end.

"I don't want to do this any more than you do," Francis continued, "but if we don't agree, MGM will just pair us both with other people, and I think you're the best match for me." He pinched his lips. "Please do not be offended, Miss Burke, but when Mr. Strickling brought you up, more as a joke, I think, I leaped at it, and he said yes."

She threw her back against the chair and let out a snort.

"You look younger than you are, and you're beautiful, but I figured Louise would, well . . ." He hesitated, his cheeks turning red. He lowered his voice and said, "I thought she would see the age gap between you and me and be less concerned."

Billie chuckled. Oh, the irony of it. He'd chosen her because she was old. How about that? Well, at least he thought she was pretty. "I don't know what to say."

"I don't want Mr. Mayer to be angry with me, and you don't either," he said. "Nobody does. Your job is on the line, and my future is on the line. Please, Miss Burke. We have to do this. Can we figure out a way that we can both win? You're more experienced at this than I am. There must be a way."

She glanced out the window at a Model T chugging down the road, gray smoke puffing from its tailpipe. Her first car had been a Model T, though a new one. "Let me think about it for a minute."

"Then we are going to do this?" he asked, sounding half-relieved.

"Let's try this: We'll go, sit together, and be friends. If somebody asks, we'll tell them I'm mentoring you. Don't look at me when it's photo time, and I won't look at you. And we only give half-smiles. That might be enough. I doubt any photo of us will be published. Few people know you outside of the classical music world, especially here. Movie people and ticket buyers don't know a piano from a giraffe. And nobody would imagine you're my beau: no offense, but the age difference. But we also won't give it any petrol. If we take it step-by-step and simply be there, that will be enough. Neither of us has committed any crime, big or small. Sometimes the boys upstairs push people just to see what they will do."

"It sounds like it should work," he said.

Billie relaxed in her chair. Her intuition said she could trust him.

Chapter Nine

Pickfair was Mary Pickford's estate on eighteen acres in the San Ysidro Canyon above Beverly Hills. It reminded Billie of a Bavarian hotel where she'd stayed. Pickfair was in the same mold as Burkeley Crest, only grander: a four-story, twenty-five-room mansion complete with stables, servants' quarters, tennis courts, a large guest wing, and garages.

Billie drove her Buick slowly up the driveway, her tires crunching driveway stones. The place had views of the valley and mountains, a manicured lawn, and rivers of flower beds. Billie had been here a couple of times for parties—Mary liked to entertain—but Billie had never tired of the place. Pickfair seemed new every time.

"Miss Burke, welcome," said the valet as she stepped out of her car. She pressed two quarters into his hand, enough for lunch at Woolworths.

He tipped his hat and smiled. "Thank you."

The double-wide front door to the house was open. Ida Cummings was standing inside wearing a tailored beige suit draped over a dowager's build. Billie froze: Ida was L. B.'s sister and his second pair of eyes. Billie tamped down any hint of being at odds with L. B. Likely, Ida didn't know what had happened yet, so there was no need to give off a scent.

"Billie Burke," Ida said. "Thank you for coming. We're glad to have you here and helping, and what a lovely dress."

Billie switched on the actress inside of her. Ida could become trouble. Nobody ever knew what was going on behind her smile. Ida had her way of viewing things, and often those things got twisted around and relayed to L. B. That was true of everyone in this business. On screen or off, everyone was an actor. You could never tell what was real.

"I'm so excited about this," Billie said, smiling hard to make her cheeks lift. "Thank you for asking me."

Billie had chosen an outfit to make her look younger: a suit with a geometric design. The designer had said, "It's the newest thing. It looks superb on you." Billie hoped it worked. Ida seemed to like it, but she'd always been a challenging read.

Ida pointed down the hall. "Second door to the right and down the stairs. The orientation is in the Western Bar. We'll talk more later."

That had gone well, Billie thought as she made her way down the hallway. She relaxed a bit and stopped to admire the house's artistry. Flanking the hallway were rose-decorated porcelain vases big enough to hide kindergarten children. There were ceiling frescoes, mahogany-paneled walls, and gold-leaf-decorated niches. It was all so European.

At the bottom of the stairs, Billie stepped through the batwing doors of the Western Bar. It felt like she'd just left Paris and entered Tombstone, Arizona. Wood-beamed ceilings, cowboy gear, and noise made her want to grab a gun and shoot a can off a fence. Tables for four were scattered about, covered with red gingham tablecloths. The bartender wore a pinstriped vest over a white apron, a white shirt with a bow tie, and a pair of armbands.

Twenty or so ladies were chatting while they sipped chardonnay or iced tea; there wasn't a beer in sight. Most of the women were Billie's age or older. She walked to the bar and asked for iced tea. Taking a sip, she spotted Margaret Mayer, L. B.'s wife, talking to someone Billie didn't recognize. She hadn't seen Mrs. Mayer in a year. The woman's brown eyes seemed sad, and her gestures looked shaky and apprehensive. Makeup caked her face.

As Billie approached Mrs. Mayer, a slender woman pushed herself in front, slapping a paper into Mrs. Mayer's hand.

"My table is in the back," the woman said, her voice reminding Billie of the Wicked Witch in *Oz*. "But I want a table at the front." The woman pointed a scolding finger.

Mrs. Mayer crossed her arms over her chest. "I'm so sorry, Mrs. Horowitz, but the tables are all assigned."

"My husband is in the orchestra. I have to be near the stage."

"The table lists are finished, and the place cards are prepared. We will finish distributing them to everyone in a few minutes."

Mrs. Horowitz's face pinched. "I really need to move the table. My husband will be very angry."

Mrs. Horowitz's face made Billie wonder if the man was abusive. It didn't take much for many men to punch their wives—spill a glass of milk, serve dinner five minutes late, not look at him when he commands. Billie had been lucky with Flo; he wasn't physically aggressive and had never touched her in anger. Of course, maybe that was because he'd known she could handle a gun.

"I can't. Perhaps you can speak to him in advance," Mrs. Mayer said.

Mrs. Horowitz bit her lip.

"My sister-in-law has the list, and she prepared the seating. You can check with her. She'll be here shortly."

"Excuse me for interrupting," Billie said, "but if I'm up near the front, she can have my table."

A voice came from behind her: "Miss Burke."

Billie turned. It was Ida again, wearing her signature lopsided grin. Billie had always wondered was really behind it. The grin had always seemed like a mask for a quiet tornado brewing inside her.

"I don't know if you've ever organized an event like this, but it takes every inch of your being, and I'm running out of being."

"I can only imagine," Billie said. "My husband produced theater, and I know what that took."

Ida handed Billie a table list and place cards. "All you have to do is set the tags in front of the plates and greet people as they arrive." She handed Billie a map of the grounds. "The powder rooms and bars are marked. Your role is to make everyone feel welcome—not an easy task with some guests, but you have a lovely demeanor. You'll be fine. Now, I have to get rid of the rest of these." She held up the lists, then walked away.

Just talking to Ida raised Billie's blood pressure. It was as if L. B. himself were standing beside her, judging her, deciding Billie's future. They were a circle, these Mayers: L. B., Ida, Mrs. Mayer. Upset one, upset them all, and subsequently you could lose your job overnight.

Billie took a deep breath.

* * *

Billie stepped out onto the lawn. She pulled out the table map and spotted her table in the third row along the left. She walked to it, then stopped to leaf through the place cards Ida had given her. The last card in the Gothic-lettered stack contained the name Beatrice Century. Billie's jaw dropped. What was she going to do with that girl?

Everyone at the studio knew about her affair with L. B. An *Oz* carpenter told Billie he had seen the boss kissing the girl behind Studio 26. And the commissary cooks had spread the word after spotting Beatrice having lunch with L. B. in his private dining room.

Billie pulled out her chair and slumped onto it. She knew this table placement was no accident. Mrs. Mayer must have known about the affair and asked Ida to put the girl at Billie's table. She probably figured Billie would know how to handle the girl, given the way she'd chased away Flo's floozies, some of them publicly. It had earned her a reputation for being on top of her marriage, not to mention for her toughness.

The most widely known affair she'd handled was back in '27. She'd taken care of the floozie at their annual Halloween party, an event that brought Broadway to the suburbs. The floozie's name was Vera, and she'd come to network with the hundred or so others milling about.

At precisely 7:40 P.M., Vera walked in dressed as a magpie.

Billie bristled inside but smiled on the outside. By night's end, Vera's beak would be swinging like a palm branch in a hurricane.

Vera saw her, then stopped in the doorway and turned to leave.

Billie reached for her arm and grabbed her black sleeve. "Dear, please come in. You look like you've seen a ghost.

There are at least four of those at the party, but they won't hurt you. I'm so happy you're here."

Billie kept her eye on Vera. The young thing was drunk within an hour. Billie watched her plop into a chair. It was time to move.

"Do you have a part in *Simple Simon?*" Billie asked Vera. "I can't remember. My husband shows me the cast list, but there are so many names."

Vera simply smiled.

"Let me take you upstairs to freshen up," Billie said. "There are people waiting in line for the bathrooms on the first floor." Billie worked around the potted mum blocking the stairs and took the girl to Flo's bathroom.

"This is lovely," Vera said. "I live in a tenement. I wish I had a bathroom like this."

"Flo has a stall with showerheads above and along the walls. It showers you all over. Would you like to see it?"

"Yes. I don't have a shower, only a tub."

Billie tingled inside as she opened the glass door and helped Vera inside.

Vera touched the walls. "This so nice."

Billie turned on the water, which came out at angles. She shut the door and leaned against it with Vera inside.

Vera screamed.

Billie smiled.

And that was the end of the affair.

People sometimes asked her why she stayed with Flo despite his infidelity. It was a simple answer: She'd done it to protect Patty. The girl adored her father and would have been devastated if he left. Another reason was Billie's career. People always blamed the divorced woman: "She wasn't caring for her husband properly, so he found someone else." If she had divorced Flo, the press would have been all over it, and her career would have ended. She would never want a man to have that much control over her.

Billie shook Vera out of her head. She had handled that situation, but she couldn't deliver a blow to Beatrice on Mrs. Mayer's behalf. It just wasn't her place. She wanted peace and smiles today. No waves. No upsets.

The guests were due to arrive in about half an hour, which gave her a little time. She rummaged through the place cards: Miss Minnie Dupree, Mr. Francis Strong (Billie's fake beau), Mrs. Margaret Hamilton (Maggie), Mr. and Mrs. Alan Mowbray, and Miss Beatrice Century. Billie already knew everyone personally except Beatrice. She had worked with Maggie on *Oz*, Minnie on *Young in Heart*, and Alan on *Merrily We Live*. She'd met Alan's wife, Lorraine, at the studio.

Billie arranged the seating to maximize peace.

A woman stopped, but Billie didn't recognize her. In her mid-fifties, she wore a copper-colored, matronly rayon dress with buttons down the front. A mahogany mink stole draped her shoulders.

"You're Miss Burke," the woman said in a New England-y voice.

"Yes, I am."

The woman patted Billie's arm. "Well, I'm Mrs. Schneiderman." She leaned in closer. Her breath smelled like mint and breakfast sausage. "I wanted to tell you how much I loved your character in *Merrily We Live*."

Billie smiled. "Thank you. It is a confection of a film. I've received letters from many women who struggle to hire household staff."

"It's impossible to find reliable ones, isn't it, dear?"

"Sometimes." Billie sighed inside. The truth was, Billie hadn't hired staff in years except for a housecleaner, reminding her how badly she needed to hold onto her job. She didn't want to slip any further.

"Well, it was nice meeting you," Mrs. Schneiderman said, and then left.

Billie raised her chin and took a deep breath, returning her eyes to the registration tent and driveway. Still no Beatrice. Billie crossed her fingers and squeezed. Perhaps Beatrice had changed her mind and decided against attending. That would make for a peaceful afternoon.

Dorothy had arrived, wearing her usual tweed skirt, jacket, white shirt, and man's black tie. She waved in Billie's direction. Dorothy was like family, and having family nearby initially gave Billie a sense of relief. But the last thing Billie needed right now was more gossip in the press about their relationship. She felt her shoulders tense.

"I didn't expect to see you here," Billie said, squeezing Dorothy's hand while trying not to look around for cameras.

"I need to be here to hunt for a project. I am going to find every producer and present my ideas." She stepped back, eyed Billie's outfit, and smirked. "What are you wearing?!"

Billie made a proud, deliberate smile. "It's a Lentz."

Dorothy snorted. "It looks like a boomerang rack."

"I've had several compliments."

"It sure is interesting."

"*Modern* is the word, and it's quite comfortable. Perhaps you should buy one."

Dorothy scoffed. "Well, all right," she said as she eyed the bar. "I see Pan over there. I want to catch him before he gets surrounded."

One by one, Billie's table guests arrived, and everyone exchanged greetings, then moved the seating tags she had so carefully arranged to sit wherever they preferred. Billie rubbed her temples and closed her eyes to think, trying to convince herself that everything would be fine.

There were now empty chairs on either side of hers: Beatrice to her left and Francis to her right. Maggie sat to the left of Beatrice's place. Alan and Minnie must have negotiated the seating to avoid Beatrice, taking advantage of Maggie's ignorance.

Billie sat as the last chord of the song playing sounded, and a man she didn't recognize stepped up to the stage. He was in his mid-thirties, wore a dark suit, and grabbed the microphone stand.

"Ladies and gentlemen, I'm Bob Hope, master of ceremonies. We have a concert for you, but first, let me thank you for coming. If you have no charity in your heart, you have the worst kind of heart trouble. So, there shouldn't be any heart attacks today." He swept his arms wide.

Billie had heard of Mr. Hope, a new talent and a former vaudevillian. His first big film had recently been released. He lifted his lapels. "Don't I look good?" he said, pointing to his face. "I have a terrific makeup crew. They're the same people who restored the Statue of Liberty."

The crowd roared. The clarinet player played a run.

"But enough of that." He winced. "Ouch." He glanced over his shoulder. "The conductor poked me in the back with his baton. I think I'm leaking."

The conductor stepped forward, a short bony man with a horizontal mustache and an embarrassed look. He leaned into the microphone. "Ladies and gentlemen, we are the Little Symphony Orchestra. Thank you for inviting us to help raise money for your cause. Today, we will play selections from the movies. Mr. Bob Hope and Miss Shirley Ross will sing the theme song from their new film, *The Big Broadcast 1938*. The song is called 'Thanks for the Memory.'"

A whoosh of air brushed Billie as the music began. She looked up and froze.

"I'm Beatrice Century. You're Miss Burke, right?"

Billie's stomach churned. Why did the girl have to show up? She whispered, "Yes, dear."

Beatrice softened her voice. "I'm sorry I'm late."

Billie pointed to the empty seat to her left and smiled. "Please, sit."

The girl was older than Billie had expected, perhaps around Francis Strong's age. She had an enigmatic, voluptuous beauty: poppy-red lips, rose-pink dress, Gibson Girl figure. There was a pearl choker around her neck that glistened in the sun—a gift from L. B.? Billie wondered.

Beatrice's shoulder-length curls jiggled as she sat. "Whew. I need to catch my breath."

Minnie turned to the girl with a finger to her lips. "Shhh."

On stage, Mr. Hope continued singing.

Beatrice leaned toward Billie and whispered, "I've never been here before. I got a little lost in the hills. I'm terribly sorry."

Billie winked to let the girl know it wasn't a problem.

"I love your dress," Beatrice continued.

Billie silently mouthed, "Thank you," and smiled. Inside, she wanted to tell the girl to shut up. She hadn't wanted Beatrice at her table in the first place, and Billie wanted to listen to the music. Beatrice's eyes turned to the stage just as the song was ending.

Billie leaned over toward Beatrice. "Have you seen the movie?"

"What movie?"

"The movie the song is from."

"No, I haven't."

"You should. It's on my list to see it. I hear Mr. Hope and Miss Ross are magnificent in it."

"I'm too busy. I barely have enough time to see MGM's films."

"Well, there certainly are a lot of them. Five, six each week. That's all you'd be doing."

The applause died, and Francis Strong stepped onto the stage in a tuxedo. Billie held up a polite finger for Beatrice to hold her thoughts.

Mr. Hope turned to Francis and said, "Mr. Francis Strong, ladies and gentlemen."

The crowd applauded.

Francis sat at the piano and adjusted the bench. He was scrubbed and shiny in that crisp tuxedo. His yellow-blond hair was precise and in place. There was something boyish and vulnerable about him.

The conductor took the microphone. "Mr. Strong has been signed by Columbia Concerts Corporation and plays coast to coast with most prestigious orchestras, but he also appears in MGM films." He looked back and forth between Francis and the crowd. "Isn't that true?"

Francis nodded.

"We will now play 'Rhapsody in Blue,'" the conductor said. He turned around, paused, and pointed his baton at a clarinetist who began to play. The orchestra—and Francis Strong—followed.

Francis's head bounced as he played, and his fingers flew across the keys. The trumpet bells rose and swung, and the conductor's hair bobbed as he waved the baton. The ending measures built to a bold, crescendo finish, followed by a moment of silence. A couple of people applauded, building up a roar and a standing ovation. Billie leaped up, clapping. The song brought back memories of her Broadway days, and the music always had a magical way of heightening her mood.

Francis lowered his hand to his chin, took a deep breath, stood, and bowed.

Billie applauded so hard, her hands hurt, but someone lightly tapped her shoulder. She looked left. Beatrice was still clapping beside her seat. Then, Billie turned to the right.

It was Mrs. Mayer, leaning in with a mischievous smile.

Billie stopped clapping. She stopped breathing. She glanced at Beatrice, who was chatting with Minnie. Minnie pointed toward Billie, and Beatrice turned. Mrs. Mayer's lioness eyes locked onto the girl's.

Billie wanted to close her eyes and tune the whole scene out. Instead, she looked to the other guests for support, but they all glanced away. Billie felt her whole body vibrate.

"Excuse me, dear," Mrs. Mayer said to Beatrice in a sweet voice, her hands clasped in front.

Beatrice smiled. The girl likely had no idea who this woman was. Mrs. Mayer usually didn't come to the studio; indeed, L. B. kept framed photos of his two daughters in the office, but not one of his wife. Billie hoped Beatrice's ignorance would help prevent an incident.

"Are you enjoying yourself?" Mrs. Mayer asked, with the fake pleasantness of a Broadway villain.

"I'm afraid I was a little late, but so far, yes. The music is beautiful." Beatrice lifted her hand and extended her arm behind Billie's in greeting. "I'm Beatrice Century."

"Charmed," Mrs. Mayer said. Her hands stayed folded together.

Beatrice's smile dampened as she awkwardly pulled her hand back into her lap. "And what is your name?"

Mrs. Mayer ignored the question and called to Maggie: "Mrs. Hamilton!"

The corners of Maggie's mouth drooped.

"My husband says you make the most frightening witch."

"I try," Maggie said, rubbing her sweaty glass of iced tea.

"This seems to be a table of witches," Mrs. Mayer looked at Billie, then Maggie, then Beatrice. "I thought I'd stop by to say hello." She turned to Beatrice. "Thank you for coming, dear."

The girl's eyebrows squished together.

"Miss Burke," Mrs. Mayer said. "It's good to see you. And thank you for your help."

"Certainly."

Mrs. Mayer left, and Billie breathed.

"Who was that?" Beatrice asked Billie.

Billie's tongue went dry but managed to spit out, "That was Mrs. Louis B. Mayer."

Beatrice's face went pale. She grabbed her purse from the table, rose, and turned to leave.

Billie's mouth opened to stop her. She didn't want the girl to leave upset. She'd go back to L. B. and might even associate Billie with the incident. She might tell L. B., "I met your wife at the event while sitting at Billie Burke's table. Miss Burke introduced us."

The girl tripped on something and fell to the ground, hip first. The people near their table gasped.

Billie rose and hustled to Beatrice's side. Minnie followed.

"Oh, dear, are you all right?" Billie asked.

Beatrice's face was red; her eyes filled with tears. "I shouldn't have come."

Billie felt sorry for her, but the girl was right: She shouldn't have come, and she had gotten what she deserved. Then again, Beatrice looked like a vulnerable child, and Billie couldn't stop herself from wanting to help.

Beatrice brushed the grass off her skirt. "I need to go," she said, then took a step to leave.

Minnie grabbed the girl's wrist. "Certainly, you must have known his wife would be here."

Beatrice broke free. "I'm going."

She couldn't leave like this. Billie had to keep the girl here and smooth things over. "Please, wait," she said.

Beatrice stopped and turned around.

"Please, come back. Let's talk."

"No. I'm leaving." The girl's voice was shaky. She turned and hurried away.

Billie's heart raced as she followed her, but the girl had a ten-foot lead. Billie hustled, but the grass slowed her pace. Beyond Beatrice, up ahead, actress Rosalind Russell was coming toward them. Billie waved her arms for Rosalind to see, pointing toward Beatrice, and hoped she'd understand and stop the girl.

Rosalind saw Billie, smiled, and waved.

Billie tensed, pointed to Beatrice again, and mouthed, "Stop her."

Rosalind shrugged her shoulders.

Billie pointed at Beatrice harder this time. The girl was about five feet in front of Rosalind. Billie motioned with her arms, signaling a stop.

Rosalind nodded, stepped before Beatrice, and said something to the girl. Beatrice stopped, and Billie caught up. She took a deep breath and tapped Beatrice on the shoulder. The girl turned around and grimaced.

"Just give me a second," Billie said to the girl.

Beatrice puffed a curl off her face. "One second."

She led Beatrice to a quiet area. They faced each other, close enough for Billie to smell the girl's minty breath.

"What do you want?" Beatrice asked.

"I know why you ran."

"You do? How?"

"It doesn't matter, but I know you're embarrassed, and I'm sorry it happened. But leaving here right now, this way, with so many people looking, would be worse than staying.

I know you're worried about Mrs. Mayer, but don't be. She'll leave you alone from now on. She got what she wanted."

"That's not the point. I shouldn't have come here. It was stupid. Oh jeez, I have to go." She turned again to leave.

"Wait," Billie said.

Beatrice stopped but didn't turn around.

"I like your work," Billie said, "and I am sure others do, too. This event only occurs once a year, and who knows when you'll get another chance like this?"

"Why do you care?" Beatrice asked, turning back around and shoving her hands onto her hips. "We don't even know each other."

"I'm just trying to help out a fellow woman who's trying to make it. The producers are here. The directors are here. Even the investors are here."

"How many people know about . . . well, you know?"

The correct answer was everybody. But instead of telling the truth, Billie said, "Very few, and not enough to count. Those things stay quiet. Nobody wants to anger the boss."

"Miss Dupree knew. You seem to know. His wife knows."

"That's it, really. Very few, and those who might know don't care. Mrs. Mayer got her punch in. She's finished."

Beatrice's shoulders visibly relaxed.

"After the meal," Billie said, "I'll introduce you around. Come on. Let's get back to our table, dear."

They returned to the table to find salads at every plate and a woman singing a ragtime tune from the stage. Billie took a bite of lettuce as she listened to Beatrice's dreams about coming here to be in the movies and how she missed her family in New York.

Francis arrived and took the empty seat to Billie's right. Beatrice looked at him with a spark in her eye. Billie's heart stopped. Flirting with Francis would be dangerous. If L. B. found out, oh no!

Francis was wearing his wedding band, thank goodness. She took a breath.

"How did I do?" he asked Billie.

"You played magnificently. I have never heard a piano played so brilliantly. The music flowed out of you as if streamed from heaven. So smooth. So easily."

Billie glanced to her left and groaned inside. Beatrice was making goo-goo eyes at Francis. Didn't she understand the consequences? Billie had better warn Francis, Mr. Naïve. It was bad enough that the girl would earn L. B.'s wrath, but Francis? He didn't deserve it.

"The girl to my left is Beatrice Century, an MGM actress," Billie said quietly to Francis.

He glanced at Beatrice, and the girl smiled at him. He leaned toward Billie. "I don't recognize her. Is she famous?"

"Yes," Billie said, "but not for what you think." She bit her lip and whispered into his ear. "She's L. B.'s girl."

Francis's head lurched back. "He's married!"

"My goodness, you're young." She leaned in closer. "She's his mistress."

His jaw dropped.

"And she's interested in you."

Francis scoffed.

"Trust me; women know these things. If you show her any hint of interest, she'll be on you like a fly on a pie, and if L. B. finds out ... well, you can imagine the consequences."

Francis's cheeks turned ruddy. "I'll do my best to avoid her."

"I sure could use a cordial with this," Minnie said, gesturing to her plate.

"I'll get it for you," Francis said.

"You could use some help," Beatrice said, leaping up to follow him.

Billie patted the tablecloth near Beatrice. "Francis can handle it, dear."

"It's no bother," Beatrice said. "I have two hands." She got up and followed Francis.

A camera flashed from somewhere. Francis was a few feet away from the table, with Beatrice behind him. Another camera flashed. Billie pushed up and went after them, her heart pounding. After a few strides, she caught up with them and shoved her head between them.

"I need an iced tea," Billie said. She threaded her arms through theirs and scanned the grounds again for Hedda Hopper, the gossip columnist. Flash, flash went two cameras left and right. Billie smiled brightly as her heart banged against her ribs.

They walked arm-in-arm silently until they reached the line of bars beside the house, backdropped by Japanese boxwood shrubs. Bartenders opened beer bottles, shook mixers, and poured wine.

Billie dropped their arms and spoke to Francis. "Why don't you take care of the drinks? I need to talk to Beatrice."

As Francis approached the bar, Billie turned and addressed Beatrice. "We don't know each other very well, but I know this business, and I know L. B."

Beatrice pulled in her chin. "This isn't your affair."

Billie chuckled inside at the word *affair*. She couldn't help being shocked at the girl's abrupt change of tune after the earlier scare with Mrs. Mayer. "I'm stepping in for your own good," Billie said. "The cameras and gossips are everywhere. Do you want your picture in the rags with Mr. Strong when you're supposed to be L. B.'s girl?"

"That's never going to happen. The photographers don't care about me."

"Maybe not, but they would love to embarrass L. B. Embarrassing us is their game, and they're creative at it. They're also uncaring when it comes to miscellaneous victims. They could ruin you for good with a single photo."

Beatrice sighed but didn't look convinced.

"If L. B. sees you in a photo with Francis, you will be fired. At best. He doesn't take well to losing things."

"He *is* a bit possessive," Beatrice conceded.

"Possessive? Most men are possessive, and L. B.'s more so than most."

Beatrice's eyes softened, and her shoulders dropped. "I don't care anymore. I don't have any films scheduled, and I'd like to try something else."

"At MGM?"

"Anywhere."

"Don't be ridiculous. You'll never work again in this town if you cross L. B. Is that what you want?"

"Of course, I'll work again. Why wouldn't I?"

"I've been in the film business from the beginning, and L. B. owns this town. He founded the Academy Awards." Billie jabbed a finger toward her. "The moguls listen to him, and believe me when I tell you this: He will blackball you and make it stick. You'll be slinging hot dogs at Pleasure Pier until you're eighty. This may be Los Angeles, but it functions like Hannibal, Missouri. I can rattle off fifty blackballed actors if you'd like."

Beatrice's eyes went dark. "That won't be necessary," she mumbled. "But I feel stuck."

"I know the feeling."

"Miss Burke, I've heard terrific things about you, that you can be trusted and you're smart. If I tell you something, will you keep it a secret?"

"Normally, dear, if I were you, I wouldn't ask that question of anyone in this business. But yes, I'll keep your secret."

"I'm sick of the old man," Beatrice said, "and I want this to end. After two years, I'm no further along than when I started. I'm playing lousy parts in movies nobody wants to see."

"You're a talented young woman, but I'd hate to see you ruin yourself over Francis, especially since you can never have him."

"Why not?"

"He's taken."

"So is L. B. Besides, I want a man closer to my age."

"Find one outside of the business, then. I loved my husband, but being in the same business together, especially this business, meant hiding in the woods of Canada to get any rest."

"Oh, I'm not sure what to do."

"There's no easy path to stardom, dear; getting there is ninety percent luck. I sang in music halls when I was twelve and did every bit part my mother found for me. I put up with lecherous men, drafty theaters, and acting in silent films so bad, my own mother wouldn't even watch them. But the one thing I never did was have a relationship with a married man."

"But—"

Billie held up a hand to stop her. "That good reputation you claim I have? That's how I got it. Now, I'm not judging you. I understand the problem. All women face it. But if you anger L. B., he'll slam the door behind you on the way out and lock the other doors across the country. Don't throw everything away over Francis."

"But I can't keep going like this." Beatrice pulled a handkerchief from her purse and sniffed. "I don't know how to get away from L. B."

"Just do it. He'll be angry at first, but it'll pass, as long as you don't publicly humiliate him. You won't be able to work at MGM anymore, but you'll still be able to find work at another studio."

Beatrice's eyes brightened.

"I wish I had a better answer for you," Billie said.

"I should probably go home," Beatrice said.

Billie opened her mouth to stop her, but realized that Beatrice's staying here any longer could worsen matters. Bille felt like she was babysitting two children: Francis and Beatrice. With Beatrice gone, at least the girl wouldn't cause trouble or leave angry. If she got angry, the news would have found its way to L. B., upsetting him and making him blame Billie. Calm waters were Billie's priority.

"I would love to spend the afternoon with you, but for your own sake, you're right," Billie said. "You may want to head home."

They squeezed hands, and Billie left to help Francis at the bar. As they delivered the drinks to their table, someone tapped Billie's shoulder. She turned. It was Hedda Hopper. Billie wasn't sure whether to be scared or relieved.

"Follow me," Hedda said, nodding to Billie and Francis. "It's time for a photo." At Hedda's table were four twenty-something movie-star wannabes staring at the columnist with fake adoring looks. Hedda waved them off, and, like loyal subjects, they rose in unison and left.

"Hedda, dear. I love your hat," Billie said. Hedda was the queen of histrionic hats. This one was a brimmed thing the size of a bicycle tire with a fountain bouquet in the middle.

"Thank you," she said, touching the top. "It's a Lentz."

A notepad and sharpened pencil sat on the table in front of her. Billie wondered about the scribbles that were already on the paper.

Hedda motioned for Billie and Francis to sit on either side of her. "Let's get right to it, shall we?"

"Certainly," Billie said.

Francis rubbed the back of his neck.

"I understand the predicament the two of you face, and I don't agree with L. B. about this, but I'm playing along." She leaned toward Billie. "Not that you shouldn't have a younger man, Billie, but your reputation doesn't need one. And you, Mr. Strong, nobody knows you yet. Quite frankly, I don't know why L. B. is doing this, but my editor will decide what to print."

"Could you encourage the editor *not* to print it?" Francis asked.

Hedda gave him a curious look. "No. If anything, I should encourage him to print it, but I'm simply sitting it out. Mr. Strickling asked for something lovey-dovey. His words, not mine."

Francis bit his lip. "No."

Billie patted his wrist.

"Why not?" Hedda said.

"A photo is fine, but it can't appear like we're in love. That's all I meant."

"Again, why not?"

"He's doing it for me," Billie said. If Hedda learned about Francis's divorce, she'd run with it and cause trouble. "You said yourself this pairing was ridiculous. He doesn't want me looking foolish."

"Readers are going to love it," Hedda said. "And with your handsome face, Mr. Strong, you'll be a star overnight. Isn't that what you want?" She waved her arms. "Isn't that what just about everyone here wants?"

Hedda looked toward the bar and motioned to a photographer, a man in a gray suit. The man tossed down a drink, picked up his camera from the bar, and walked toward them.

Francis put his hands on the table, wrung them, and opened his mouth to speak. Billie patted his knee, and he snapped his mouth shut again.

"Mr. Strong," Hedda said. "You have a contract with MGM, and they decide what you do. To be in their films, you must do what Howard Strickling says. It's a business, not a charity, and there is no gray to it."

"Mrs. Hopper, I—"

"The photo won't harm you. You're a single, eligible bachelor. It'll build your reputation."

Francis shook his head. "Mrs. Hopper, I need to tell you something."

Billie kicked him under the table. Her lips pinched.

"You have two seconds, Mr. Strong," Hedda said.

He took a deep breath. "What I tell you has to be a secret."

"I promise not to tell," Hedda said. Billie knew Hedda was pretty good about keeping secrets if you asked her to, but still, Billie didn't trust her. When it came down to reality, Hedda's job was to divulge secrets.

"My wife—er, my ex-wife—will clean me out for thirty years if we take this photo. I can't let her think that I left her for another woman. It isn't true."

"I saw the wedding ring," Hedda said.

"But hopefully not for long."

"Then why in the world would they ask for this photo?" Billie shook her head. "Good question."

Hedda shrugged. "Oh well, it's a photo, Mr. Strong, that's all, and your wife will probably never see it. If she does, you can explain this to her."

"More like to her attorney," he muttered.

The photographer tapped his watch between puffs on a Marlboro.

"We have to get this done," Hedda said.

"May I have a minute with Francis?" Billie asked.

Hedda's eyes narrowed. "Half a minute."

Billie leaned toward Francis, cupped her hand over her mouth, and whispered in his ear: "Everything is theater in this business, so I'm going to script this for you. First, think old-world stoic, and then raise the corners of your mouth ever so slightly. Look at the camera. Don't touch me."

He nodded.

Billie turned to Hedda. "We're ready."

The photographer adjusted his lens. Francis pulled out Billie's chair, and they rose and got into place. Billie adjusted herself to leave a few inches between them, then whispered to him, "Keep your eyes on the house's side door. Lock them there. Only a slight smile."

"Can the two of you look like friends, at least?" Hedda said. "Smile or something?"

"I spent a lot of time on these eyes this morning," Billie said, pointing to them. "I want the fans to see them."

"It's the best I can do," Francis said. "I don't often smile. I'm a classical musician."

"Can you hold her hand or put your arm around her back?"

Billie folded her hands behind her back and smiled a tiny bit more. Francis froze.

Hedda threw her hands in the air. "Take it," she said, sounding disgusted. "We don't have all day."

Click-flash went the camera.

Hedda shook her head at Billie. "You know, you need some fun in your life."

"What makes you say that?" Billie said.

"I can see it on your face and I know how hard you work. Once in a while, everybody has to go out and go dancing, get rousing drunk, go surfing, something."

Billie scoffed. "I don't have time for that."

"You should make time."

Francis smiled at Billie. His eyes told her he had an idea.

As they returned to their table, Francis said, "I know a place to go where you could relax and enjoy yourself. It's a club. Club Café on Sunset Boulevard."

"I've heard of that place. It's for twilights, correct?"

"Yes, but the press doesn't dare enter. It's a safe space."

"I'm being fired for my friendship with another woman. Club Café would make that worse. If one word of it got out, my career would be even more over than it is now."

"You have nothing to worry about. There's a code of privacy. Besides, the club is on Sunset in the county, not the city, so there are no raids or worries."

"It's on the Sunset Strip?" Billie said.

"Yes. People respect each other there."

"The Strip is also full of casinos and gangsters."

"They won't be at the club. It's a sacred, careful space."

A night out brought memories to Billie's mind of similar outings with Flo, making her smile inside. She had enjoyed those edgy evenings. But she was a lot older now. Would she enjoy it as much?

"I'll think about it," Billie said.

Chapter Ten

Two days later, Billie was in her home office answering fan mail when the phone rang, startling her. It was Patty.

"I saw it in a movie magazine," Patty teased.

"What, dear?"

"The photo of you and your beau."

Billie stiffened. "I told you. He's not my beau."

"It's pretty tame. It looks more like a family photo than anything else. Like a mother-son or brother-sister kind of thing. It shows you and Mr. Strong walking arm-in-arm."

"Were there any other photos?"

"No. Do you want to know what the caption says?"

"Not really, but I guess I should know."

"It says, 'Miss Billie Burke enjoys the afternoon with Mr. Francis Strong, a classical pianist.'"

Billie realized she might be forced to appear in public with Francis Strong again because the photo may have been tamer than what Howard Strickling wanted. She dropped into the chair and shut her eyes.

"There's a woman to your right in the photo, or at least a piece of woman. You look more like a threesome than anything. What was that all about?"

"Now, how about that job of yours?" Billie asked, ignoring Patty's question.

A beat of silence followed. Billie heard the quip-dust settle. Patty needed to get a career.

"The job is the job," Patty said with a measured voice. "All I do is get coffee and run errands. At least at the paper I was writing." Patty had been working for the *Beverly Hills Citizen* before she left for New York.

"That paper was a career dead-end. It's always like this at the beginning, dear, but you'll show them what you can do, and they'll respect you and give you better things."

"I suppose," Patty said, but her voice was dragging.

"Only three months to go."

"An eternity."

"I love you, dear," Billie said.

"Me, too."

"Oh, and one more thing," Billie said, scratching her head. "Do you know anything about the Club Café?"

* * *

Two days later, Billie stood outside the Club Café wearing dark sunglasses and a hat with a brim that would have made Hedda proud. Billie's watch read 8:28 P.M. Francis was to arrive by 8:30 and then escort her inside.

She'd decided to meet him, if only to learn. She prided herself on appearing and thinking younger. She researched her characters, so she would use this opportunity to research today's youth. Club Café was a stretch, but she needed a stretch. She'd commit to staying for an hour. That's it.

Francis's head peeked out from behind the entrance door. He motioned for her to join him.

"I was wondering if you'd show up," he said. He smelled like Acqua di Parma—a light floral blend, sweet and refreshing.

"I committed," she said.

"I got here early to hold a table for us. This place can get crowded."

She took a deep breath and stepped inside to a gush of warm air mixed with cigar smoke and men's cologne. A woman sang "Moonlight Serenade" from the stage. Standing there was a man in his mid-forties with the face of King George and a green carnation pinned to his lapel. He was laying down the rules to a smiling male couple holding hands. They looked to be in their early twenties.

"No touching of any kind," King George said, frowning down at their hands. He sounded like an English butler: pithy, precise, impeccable.

"But this is the county. The laws don't apply here," one of the men said.

"We do not take chances. That's why we stay open."

The two men dropped their hands.

Billie froze. She'd thought she would be safe here. Was it possible that sheriff's deputies might show up? If so, would she have to call MGM to bail her out of jail? MGM had a quick response system for its contracted stars to get them out of trouble quickly.

"Maybe this is a bad idea," Billie said to Francis.

"Don't worry," Francis said. "They're just being careful. We're safe here." He offered his arm to her, but she hesitated.

"Really," Francis said. "It's safe."

She reluctantly took his arm.

One hour, she reminded herself, and then she was going home. Bar mishaps usually happened later in the evening, after people drank too much. She would be out of here by then.

"I would take off your sunglasses for now," Francis told her. "He has to see who you are. You can put them on later if you want to."

Billie removed the glasses.

"Miss Burke. It's good to have you here," said King George, bowing. "Welcome to the Club Café. I'm Mr. Walsh. Mr. Strong told me you were coming. You wouldn't mind if we asked you to perform, would you?"

She chuckled and shook her head. "It took every ounce of courage just to walk inside. Besides, I'll only be here for an hour."

"We always ask stars to perform. Some say yes, some say no. If you decide to perform, let me know. I am a fan, and I know the boys will enjoy it."

"Thank you." A part of her wanted to do it, and another part didn't. She was flattered by the request, which would allow her to engage a younger crowd. But she wasn't an improvisational actress. She liked to prepare thoroughly before a performance. She was known for perfection.

Francis escorted her to their table in front of the stage.

"There's Miss Billie Burke," a woman said from the right.

"I heard she was a lesbian," another woman said from the left.

Billie cringed as she balled her hands into fists. She wanted to correct the woman, but she also wanted peace.

"Don't worry," Francis said. "What happens here stays here."

Billie told herself to let the women think what they wanted and then muttered, "Rabbits, rabbits, rabbits."

At the table, Francis said, "May I get you a drink?"

"Just tomato juice," Billie said.

Francis left for the bar, which gave her time to look around. The decor was Venetian and made her think of King Umberto's parlor.

The next singer, a man dressed as a woman, crooned, "I bring you and sing you a moonlight serenade. Let us stray 'til break of day in love's valley of dreams."

Billie crossed her legs and listened. It reminded her of when she was fifteen years old and her mother had booked her to sing in a music hall in a small port on England's east coast. She was one of a series of acts, and the song was some silly confection. The place was an old, small music hall doubling as a pub. The sailors sat on benches on the main floor, drinking cask beers and eating shelled peanuts and whole tomatoes. She had looked down at the floor the whole time and kept forgetting the words. The booing started, followed by people throwing tomatoes at her. She finished the song in tears with a heavily stained dress.

Francis returned and set a glass of tomato juice in front of her. It had a celery stick propped in it.

"Don't worry," he said. "It doesn't have any vodka. It's straight tomato juice, but I thought you should at least look like you were having a good time."

She laughed. "I'm getting there."

The singer finished, and the room applauded. After the noise quieted, someone tapped Billie on the shoulder. It was a woman around Billie's age with dyed red hair and white roots, a hefty gal with sagging cheeks. She wore a well-crafted flower-print silk dress.

"Are you having a good time, dear?" the woman asked, bending closer. She smelled of roses and whiskey. "I don't believe I've ever seen you here before."

Billie managed a smile, but the back of her neck prickled. Was this woman interested in her? She hoped not.

The woman touched Billie's shoulder and squeezed. "I'm Baroness Catherine d'Erlanger," she said in a French accent. "I own this place."

Francis leaned over to Billie. "She greets every new person."

The baroness smiled, and her wide blue eyes grew wider. "You're Miss Billie Burke, aren't you?"

"Yes."

"You should bring that lovely daughter with you the next time. I see her with you in the papers. She looks so sweet."

Billie shook her head. "Yes, she's sweet and smart. But tonight, I'm just visiting with my friend Mr. Strong."

The baroness squeezed Billie's shoulder. Billie cringed.

"We don't usually get women of your refinement in this place. You add a touch of class to the place."

"Thank you," Billie said. "But quite frankly, I was raised in a series of cold-water flats, and I sang in places I don't care to describe."

"Someday, you will have to tell me about it." The baroness winked at Francis. "Where is Ben?"

Billie smiled. "Who is Ben?"

Francis's cheeks turned ruddy. "I told him tonight was just for us," he told the baroness, pointing back and forth between Billie and himself.

Someone called for the baroness from the bar. "Well, my dears," she said, "enjoy yourselves. And Miss Burke, please sing for us. You have a lovely voice."

"Perhaps."

Francis turned to Billie. "I would love to hear you sing."

The baroness squeezed Billie's shoulder, and her hand lingered. Billie held her breath until the hand moved away.

Billie leaned toward Francis. "Is she a . . . ?" Her voice trailed off before she could utter the word *lesbian*.

"Yes," he said. "It's why she opened the place. She wanted to give people of that inclination a nice place to go that was just as good as other clubs. The show and decor drew the men, but when word got out, it attracted a broader crowd. It's still mostly twilights, and nobody cares."

Billie scanned the room. There were same-sex couples, opposite-sex couples, groups, Orientals. Nobody seemed "on" or self-conscious. She sat back, sipped her tomato juice, and crossed her legs. She felt comfortable here.

"Who is Ben?" Billie asked again, smiling from the corner of her mouth.

"He's a music professor at the University of Southern California. He teaches piano, among other things. We are not . . . as you think. We're friends, that's all, but we enjoy this place, and neither of us wants to come here alone. The baroness thinks we're a couple. We told her it's not true, but she doesn't believe us."

Billie didn't believe him, either.

* * *

A little while later, Mr. Walsh stepped onto the stage: "Ladies and gentlemen, welcome to Club Café. We have several more performers this evening, and one I hope we can add." He winked at Billie.

She was tempted. She felt safe here, so performing would probably be all right, but she wasn't prepared and didn't want to look bad. What would she perform? Maybe she could sing the theme song from *Mind the Paint Girl* or something from *The Belle of Mayfair*, though she wasn't sure she'd remember the words of songs she'd performed over twenty-five years ago. She'd love to sing "Come Out, Come Out" from *The Wizard of Oz*, but the piano player probably wouldn't know it, given that the movie wasn't out yet.

Francis grinned. "Are you ready to sing?"

Billie wrung her hands, still frantically trying to choose the right song. She closed her eyes and sat back. There had to be something she could do, even if it wasn't singing. Tell jokes? The studios promoted her as a comedienne, but she wasn't funny on her own. She didn't know any jokes.

"Miss Burke?" Mr. Walsh motioned for her to join him on stage.

Glasses clinked. Hands clapped. "C'mon, Miss Burke," someone called out.

She took a deep breath, stood, straightened her dress, lifted her skirt, and walked to the stage.

Mr. Walsh greeted her, then turned to the crowd: "Miss Billie Burke, ladies and gentlemen ... although she needs no introduction." He stepped back, applauding, and left the stage.

A rush of adrenaline shot through her. She'd sing the song that had launched her career when she was nineteen.

She leaned toward the keyboardist, a peroxide blond with sharp features. "Do you know 'My Little Canoe' from the musical *The School Girl?*"

"Sing a little," he said.

She hummed a few bars.

"Yes, I do."

She took a deep breath, turned on her smile, grabbed the microphone stand, and tossed her curls back. "I'm going to sing a little song that none of you will be old enough to know."

Laughter rumbled. All eyes were on her.

"I'll tell you a little story about it first," she said. "It's a song that has special meaning because it launched my career in London's West End. It was my job to sit in a canoe and sing a song. Nothing more. The audience loved it; before you know it, I had my own leading-lady roles. After that . . . well, here I am. " She looked over at the keyboardist.

He played the introduction.

She took a deep breath and sang: "Mamie, if you've nothing else to do, my Mamie girl. I'm going to invite you to come along with me." She motioned to the audience, inviting them to come along.

The room fell silent. Billie smiled all over. She felt lighter.

"Mamie, you'd have something to do," she sang, pointing to the audience earnestly. "And when I've told my worries to you, then Mamie, we might canoodle, we two."

She sang one more verse. The keyboardist played the last couple of bars, and then Billie bowed.

The audience jumped to its feet and applauded. "More, more," they called out.

She felt the vibration of appreciation, and it fed her. A tear ran down her cheek. She was tingling all over.

People jumped to their feet, applauding above their heads. "Sing us another!" a man called out.

She shook her head. It was better to leave them cheering. "You can hear me in the upcoming MGM film *The Wizard of Oz*."

"Encore, encore," people yelled.

Billie curtsied. Her body was filled with energy.

"Tell us a joke," a man called out from the bar.

She stood and wiped a tear from her eye. She didn't want to leave the stage, but her years of experience told her it was always best to step down when you were on top. She didn't want to ruin things with a bad joke. She curtsied again as Mr. Walsh stepped up, waving his handkerchief.

"That was wonderful, Miss Burke," he said. "You're going to be tough to top."

Billie waved at the audience, left the stage, and sat. She loved performing for a live audience and swore she'd start doing more stage work. It had been too long.

She shoved her tomato juice aside and turned to Francis. "May I have a tiny glass of chardonnay, dear?"

Chapter Eleven

Billie sat on the pink chaise-longue in her studio bungalow, munching on a bite-sized piece of Swiss cheese with bread and a sliced apple. It was lunchtime between *Oz* recording sessions, and her song was coming up. The phone rang; she swallowed before answering.

"I have another one for you," Howard Strickling said. He sounded preoccupied, as if juggling multiple tasks at once.

"Another what?" she said.

"I want you to attend the *Stagecoach* premiere with Francis Strong."

She'd been afraid of this. "No."

"It's a Walter Wanger film. A United Artists premiere," he said, talking right over her.

"No." She slammed her plate on the table. Apple slices fell to the floor. "You promised it would only be one time."

"No, I said there could be another if the first one didn't go as planned."

"But it went well, I thought."

"Not in my opinion. Miss Burke. We wanted a photo of the two of you that would make people think there was some romantic interest between you. Instead, we got a stoic-looking family shot from 1865."

She bristled. "I agreed to one event." She eyed a picture of Flo on her dressing table. She wished he were here. He'd have found a way to make all this go away. "I'm not doing it." She leaned down to pick up the apple slices from the floor.

"You have no choice. It's in your contract."

"No."

"You don't have any choice."

She knew she had no choice, yet she felt the need to push back. She wasn't going to be ordered around by someone younger than herself. "Have you spoken to Francis?" she asked through clenched teeth. She was pretty sure Francis would do what he was told, yet she hoped he had put up some resistance.

"He's in. He didn't have a choice, either."

Billie hated being forced into things. And what made Howard think the next photo would be any better?

She paused, sat back, and closed her eyes. "One more, and that's it. When is it?"

"The details and tickets will be in your dressing-room mailbox tomorrow." He hung up before she could say another word.

She slammed down the receiver and eyed the plate, wanting to smash it to the floor. Since leaving New York, she hadn't smashed a plate, vase, or glass. There was little point to it now. She'd usually done it to get Flo's attention, and he was gone.

She took a breath and looked at the clock, trying to slow her racing pulse. It was time to return to the recording studio; she was a professional.

* * *

She stormed out the door and took an alley route to Studio Two to burn off her anger. Ten minutes later, she arrived, still tense. She needed to calm her nerves if she hoped to sing well. She took several deep breaths.

"Relax," she told herself. "Relax, relax." She took a few more deep breaths, then opened her eyes. She sang the first line of her song, "Come out, come out, wherever you are." It sounded okay.

She opened the door and stepped into the studio, where a soprano was singing a run, the violins were being tuned, and wooden music stands scraped the floor. She found a quiet corner to warm up, faced the acoustically paneled wall, and straightened her spine. Quietly, she hummed the scale, "Do, Re, Mi, Fa, So, La, Ti, Do," up and down four times and made "brbrbrbr" vibrations to loosen her lips.

"Places, please," Mr. Stothart, the music director, called out. He was about Billie's age, a stoic with a boxer's face and slicked-back hair. She'd met him several times in New York through the Gershwins. He'd been younger then and had occasionally smiled. But the older a stoic like him got, the less often his lips curved up at the corners.

Billie moved into place in front of the microphone, a seventy-piece orchestra and chorus behind her. To her right, inside the sound booth, Victor Fleming was talking to someone behind the plate-glass window.

Judy Garland stood to Billie's right, wearing a granny-apple-colored dress with puffed sleeves and shoulder pads. She looked mature, but there was a naive child inside. Someday, Billie hoped, things would smooth out for the girl.

Judy smiled, exposing her white teeth and brightening her brandy-colored eyes.

Billie touched Judy's back. "I'm happy to see you, dear. Are you ready for our song?"

"I suppose I'm as ready as I can be."

Stothart tapped the music stand, and the room quieted. "Come Out" wasn't a hard song, and it was short. This shouldn't take long. Stothart folded his arms across his chest and waited. Billie rotated her neck and shoulders and shook her hands loose.

"One minute," Stothart called out, holding up a stubby index finger.

While waiting, Billie reviewed the lyrics and melody in her head. She wanted to sing the song like a lullaby. The thought of lullabies made her mind drift back to memories of singing to Patty when she was little. Billie reached over and stroked Judy's brown hair. It was soft and shiny like Patty's had been.

Stothart motioned to the projection room behind him. A light beam shot across the space to a screen hanging high on the wall above the chorus behind everyone to ensure the music synced to the film.

Billie rehearsed her first line in her head: "The small folks . . ."

The room was silent. Stothart lifted his stick and looked at the screen. He flicked it at Judy. Billie's eyes locked on the baton. She had to be ready to begin the instant it pointed at her.

"Oh. But, if you please—what are Munchkins?" Judy said, her hands gesturing, her curls bouncing.

"The little people who live in this land—it's Munchkinland," Billie said in her fairy godmother voice. "And you are their national heroine, my dear. It's all right—everyone come out and thank her." She swung her arms as if motioning to the Munchkins as she'd done during filming. It helped keep the rhythm.

Stothart gave the downbeat, and the orchestra began to play. After several music bars, his eyes went to the screen, and he flicked the baton at Billie.

She sang the first line of "Come Out," but there was a warble in her voice. She sounded like an eighty-five-year-old church lady and didn't know why. This had never happened before.

Stothart gave a cutoff sign.

"I'm sorry," Billie said. She knew he had stopped because of the warble. She had a trained, sweet soprano voice, somewhere between opera and jazz, which was one of the reasons why they'd chosen her for the role. Her voice was usually as clear as a nightingale's.

Stothart perched his hands on his stomach. "Miss Burke," he said in a patient, measured voice. "Take a deep breath and sing from here." He pointed to his stomach.

Billie coughed to clear the saliva from her throat. Maybe that had been the problem.

"It won't happen again," she said, fingering her necklace. She closed her eyes, took a deep breath, filled her diaphragm with air, and puffed in and out. Sing naturally, she told herself. She opened her eyes and motioned for him to continue. That's all she needed. One more second to relax.

Stothart cued the projection room. "Roll it back." He turned to Judy. "You don't need to speak this time. We've got that part."

Judy nodded. Violins tuned.

"Same with you, Miss Burke," he said. "We'll begin with the song. I'll give you the cue."

Judy squeezed Billie's hand. Billie smiled. It was something Patty would have done, too.

Stothart motioned to the projection room, and the light stream shot across the space. He gave the downbeat. The orchestra played, and then he cued Billie.

"No need to hide. Come join us," she sang.

The warble was still there, but she continued, hoping it would clear. It didn't. Her stomach churned. What was happening?

Stothart gave the cutoff, and Billie froze. She didn't feel any different today than she did yesterday. She looked at Victor but couldn't get a read. He seemed calm, for now.

Judy coughed and stepped to the side.

Stops and starts were common during recording, but they were usually because of the difficulty of synchronizing music to film, not because a singer's voice failed. Thankfully, Victor's face looked understanding.

"Let's work on it," Stothart said, sounding gentle. "The sound, I mean. You're near the pitch but not on it."

"Oh, my stars," she said. "I'm so sorry." She covered her mouth. She sounded like an old church choir soloist, the kind she'd heard at funerals. She wasn't that old. She was fifty-four, not seventy-four. Her voice couldn't have changed that much overnight.

She bit her lip in determination.

"Don't worry," Stothart said. "We're going to restore your voice. I need a cleaner sound. More like what we had in rehearsal. Do you remember what that felt like?"

"Yes," she said, but she felt the same way now, and the sound of her voice was nowhere near the same.

"You're too tense," he said. "I can hear it in your voice. Take a minute and relax."

She checked her body. He was right. She was tense; thank goodness it had nothing to do with her age. Her body was still in knots, and that was a problem she could fix. She was a professional, after all.

"Relax your neck and shoulders," he said. "I know you did that earlier, but do it some more."

She rolled her neck and shoulders, took several deep breaths, and closed her eyes. She felt better.

He gestured toward her. "May I give you some suggestions?"

Billie froze. She didn't want to hold up the recording session, but she also didn't want her voice to ruin the scene. "Yes, please," she said.

"Let's start with your stance."

She straightened her back, assuming that's what he meant. Her London music teacher had taught her that a straight back helped with airflow.

"Spread your feet apart six inches," he said, demonstrating. "They're too close together. You look like a nutcracker."

Judy giggled. The choir tittered.

Billie studied her feet and then moved her right foot out six inches.

"Now, roll your neck slowly again. Up, down, left and right." He demonstrated. "Loosen the muscles. Not too hard. Easy, so you don't strain anything. That would make it worse."

Billie did it all and felt better, even happier.

"Before you sing, bend a little at the knees. Pretend you're a baseball player." He demonstrated. "Pretend you're getting ready to sit down on a chair. It will loosen your stance."

His squat was too low for her, so she bent at the knees about half the distance, afraid of falling over if she went further. She felt relaxed. Problem solved. "It won't happen again," she said, smiling. "I'm ready."

He nodded.

She saw Victor staring at her from the corner of her eye. He still seemed fine. Hopefully, he would stay that way.

"Is everybody ready?" Stothart said. The orchestra and choir quieted. Judy returned from the food table. He motioned to the projection room. The light beam streamed.

Billie took a deep breath into her diaphragm and focused on sending it back up through her lungs, across her throat, and into the music.

The orchestra played. Stothart cued her.

"Come out, come out, wherever you are," she sang, "and meet the young lady who fell from a star." The warble was still there. Billie's jaw tightened.

Stothart dropped the baton on the stand and rubbed his temples.

Victor stepped out of the sound booth with a slight smile on his face. Was this the calm before the storm? Would he slap Billie across the face like he'd done to Judy? She kept her eyes on him, ready to flood him with apologies, though she had no idea how to correct this problem. All she knew was that if she didn't correct it, they'd have to call everyone back, driving up the production costs.

Victor stopped and motioned for Stothart to join him. As the two men talked, sweat formed on Billie's brow, and her heart beat quicker. They were going to pull her and dub in somebody else's voice. She was sure of it. That was what they did in cases like this. Billie's voice had never been dubbed. She could sing, dagnabbit. Maybe not as loftily as Judy—there was a whole orchestra in that girl's voice—but Billie was good, and she wanted to prove it.

She watched the men's lips as they talked. She wanted to step in and defend herself, but she stayed put. Stothart was fifteen feet away, yet she saw his pinched face and could hear his voice. She couldn't make out the words, but his tone was sharp. Victor folded his arms across his chest and tapped a finger to his chin. He seemed to be listening. Stothart shook his head. Victor's eyes tightened; he dropped his arms and pointed at Stothart. He seemed to be insisting on something. Stothart threw his hands up, turned, and walked toward Billie with cold eyes.

She lowered her head and closed her eyes. It was over. They were going to replace her with another voice. If this got out, she'd be stuck playing granny roles for the rest of her career—if she even had one.

Stothart stopped five feet before her and took a deep breath.

"Miss Burke," he said. "It turns out the director likes the sound. He says it's fairy-like and unique." He looked her in the eye. "Now, you'll have to replicate it." He turned and stepped to the podium.

Her shoulders relaxed out of relief. Yet her mind spun over the unwanted change in her voice. Billie had always worked at staying young, a necessity for maintaining her marriage and career. Exercise, a healthy diet, sleep, skincare routines, you name it. She did it, and it worked. Her ability to keep herself young was a part of her professional identity. It had never occurred to her that her voice would change like this, and she felt blindsided by it. What else would come out of nowhere and turn the dial left on her career?

Chapter Twelve

Still in her Glinda costume, Billie hustled down the alley, breezing past the people calling out: "Hey, Miss Burke!" and "Slow down! You're gonna get hurt!" She ignored them and kept moving. She had just received word that she'd been nominated for an Academy Award, and she needed to find out more.

Which film was it she'd been nominated for? She'd been in seven movies last year, and they'd all done well. Her best had been *The Young in Heart*, but the nomination couldn't be for that one. She had been on loan to another studio for that film, and that studio would have told her, not MGM. It must be an MGM film. She hoped it wasn't *Everybody Sing*. That was a horrible film, and she didn't want to be known for it.

She reached the Thalberg administration building, lifted her skirt, and walked through the glass doors and to the elevator bank. Luckily, the elevator bell went "ding," the doors opened, and she walked forward to enter, but her hoop skirt didn't fit, bumping the sides of the door. She didn't want to break the hoop underneath, so she tried squeezing in sideways. That didn't work, either.

"C'mon, lady," a man said from behind her.

She felt her blood pressure rise. She grabbed the hoop on both sides and forced the skirt through the door, hearing a "snap" and feeling a dent on the left side of the dress. Her heart sank. Adrian, the costume designer, was going to be angry. The dress was complicated, and the hoop was expensive. Thankfully, there was a replacement dress. She could only hope he would forgive her.

She rode up the elevator with her eyes closed and leaned against the wall to steady herself, her blood racing. The doors opened after a seemingly endless ride, and she strode out to L. B.'s office suite across the hall and entered. Inside, The Mount rose from her desk and smiled. The Mount rarely smiled.

"Which film?" Billie asked her.

"Not the one you think." The Mount smiled like a kid trying to hold in a secret. "*Merrily We Live*," The Mount said. "They loved your Emily Kilbourne."

Billie rolled her eyes. Emily had been a society matron who cut melons with a wooden spoon and called her pet fish "fishy wishies." Billie was capable of far more depth.

"It was nominated in five categories."

Billie's jaw dropped. "You're kidding!" The movie had been okay, but it was not Academy-worthy in Billie's opinion. Still, a nomination was a nomination. She smiled as she squeezed her skirt. This suddenly felt real. A win—maybe even just the nomination—should be enough to renew her contract. Why would L. B. throw away an Academy Award nominee?

"Sound, song, art direction, cinematography, and best supporting actress were the categories," The Mount continued. "Those are a lot of nominations for a single film, so it's sure to win one or two. Mr. Mayer is lobbying the Academy for all of our nominees."

The Academy Awards had been L. B.'s idea, back in 1920, when he called a group of studio moguls together and proposed the ceremony to promote their films. His politicking and opinions still held weight.

"Let's keep this short," The Mount said. She handed Billie a sheet of paper.

Billie scanned it.

"Those are the directions for the night of the awards. We'll call you around six at home to let you know if you've won."

Billie took the paper and nodded, feeling a little numb.

"Mr. Mayer wants you at the ceremony if you win, but it's optional if you lose. Will you be there regardless? Mr. Mayer wants a big showing from MGM. It'll promote the films and the studio."

"Yes. Absolutely. I will be there, no matter what happens." Billie knew she might never get another opportunity like this, and just being at the ceremony would give her exposure. Every magazine, newspaper, and newsreel crew would be there. She wasn't going to miss this chance. She wanted Patty there, too. She'd fly her daughter home and send her back to New York when it was over. Patty being there wouldn't just make Billie feel better; it would be good for Patty's career. The room would contain some of the country's top scenario and press writers—a perfect networking opportunity.

Chapter Thirteen

The next evening, Billie walked downstairs, adjusting a dangling diamond earring. Francis would be here to pick her up in fifteen minutes. The *Stagecoach* premiere was tonight, and she'd decided to make the best of it. She'd chosen a pink chiffon gown that covered her from chin to ankles. It felt light and free-falling.

She'd put behind her the angst of not wanting another MGM-engineered date. She and Francis had agreed to appear platonic, and he was excited about the film. He'd never been to a premiere, and she always enjoyed the glamour of one. This was going to be fun.

The doorbell chimed as she reached the tiled foyer. She opened the door to a tuxedoed Francis, his blond hair combed back, his face flushed, the corners of his mouth drooping. He wasn't wearing his wedding ring.

She was afraid to ask what was upsetting him. "You're early," she said in a cheerful voice, hoping to avoid the issue.

He stepped in, closed the door behind him, leaned against it, and looked at the floor. "Something happened," he said.

"What's wrong?" she asked, motioning to the couch for him to sit as she sat in a white-cushioned chair across from him.

He leaned over and handed her an envelope, "Read it," he said. "I got that today from Louise's attorney. Did you get one?"

"No. Why would I get one?"

He shook his head. "This is what I feared. But I thought that common sense would prevail. Obviously, there's an age difference between us. You are a beautiful woman, but, well . . ."

She pulled out the one-page letter, read it, and laughed halfway through. "Imagine. Me, a floozie!" Oh, the irony of it after all of those years with Flo, and at her age. She was flattered. Maybe she could use this as ammunition with L. B., given that he was thinking she was too old. She snorted a laugh.

He pointed to the letter. "My wife's going to double my alimony, saying that I cheated on her with you and lied during the divorce proceedings."

"But the photo was bland."

"Her attorney thinks otherwise."

"He's fishing for pike in a frog pond. There's nothing there."

"It doesn't matter." Francis stood, paced, and combed his fingers through his hair.

"What are you going to do?" she said.

His eyes narrowed. "What are *we* going to do is the question."

She held up her palms and shook her head. "This doesn't concern me."

"She mentions you and blames you for taking me away from her. She wants an apology letter."

"For what?! I did no such—"

"I know. I know, but . . ."

Billie lifted her chin in defiance. "If I write an apology letter, she'll use it as proof. That's what her barrister is looking for: written evidence. Well, of course, I'm not doing it. It would be a lie, and it would hurt both of us."

"If you do it, this will go away. She told me so on the phone."

Youth. Francis was so naïve. "No. It will make it worse. Can't you see that?"

"Maybe, but then again, maybe it would be enough. She said that if you did it, she would back off."

"No."

"Please."

"Let your barrister handle it. That's why you pay him."

Francis looked aside, stopped pacing, and bit his lip. "We can't go tonight. It will only make this worse. It will be in the news, providing even more fictitious proof."

"And so will a letter." She sighed. "We have to go to the premiere. Howard's requiring it, of both of us. I can't go on my own."

"Can't you call him and ask for a replacement?"

"Do you mean another man from the MGM warehouse of men?"

"I don't know what I mean, really."

She gave him a gentle smile. "Francis, believe me. Your barrister will take care of this problem. Things like this are part of the business. Didn't you warn your wife about our arrangement? You were supposed to warn her."

"Of course I did. I'm not an idiot." He resumed pacing.

"Well, that was the right thing to do, even if she's reacting the same as if you hadn't." She pointed to the couch. "Sit down, and let's figure this out. Can I get you a cup of tea?"

"No, thank you." He dropped back onto the couch like a teenager expecting a lecture.

"Let's figure this out rationally," Billie said. "Does Howard know about the letter?"

"Not yet."

"You're going to need to tell him eventually, and sooner is better than later."

Francis dropped his chin. "I know."

"We can't upset Howard and L. B. We have to think of something. Give me a minute."

Francis put his hands to his face. "I'm going to lose everything I have. I just know it."

"You should turn this letter over to the studio's legal department and let them sort it out. They have the best barristers in the country. They might even be able to make the alimony go away. Let MGM legal work it out. If they can make a murder disappear, they can make this disappear."

"A murder?"

She waved it off. "Clark Gable. According to good sources, he didn't intentionally murder the person but may have accidentally killed someone while driving drunk. It may have been real. It may have been a rumor. Who knows for sure? But Howard was brilliant at covering it up. Howard is amazing. Sometimes scarily so."

Francis shoved himself up and turned to the door. "If you won't write the letter, I guess we have nothing more to discuss."

"I'm sorry, Francis."

"Not as sorry as I am," he said, and headed for the door.

"Hold on a minute."

He stopped.

She dialed Howard and handed Francis the phone. "You had better tell him now and let him get to work. We also need some advice on how to handle tonight. It's too late for him to replace you, but I'm sure he'll tell us to stay home until he figures this out."

The operator put her through.

Francis reluctantly accepted the phone and asked for Howard.

"I'll put you through," the MGM operator said.

"I hope he's there," Francis said.

"He works twenty-four/seven. I assure you. He'll answer."

"Howard Strickling, here."

Francis shared the earphone with Billie. She pushed an earring away to hear.

"I am here at Miss Burke's, and there is a problem."

"Unless somebody died, the two of you are going," Howard said.

Francis's body stiffened as he explained the letter and situation.

"Crap," Howard said. "This stuff never ends. You're right. The two of you stay home. Come by tomorrow with the letter. We'll think of something."

Billie backed away from the phone.

Francis shoulders relaxed as he exhaled and hung up. A small smile grew on his face.

"Too bad," Billie said. "I was actually looking forward to it. Can I get you some tea?"

Francis reached for the doorknob. "I just want to go home and curl up with a book."

"I understand that completely," she said. "We'll talk later, and good luck. Don't worry. It will all work out."

Chapter Fourteen

"Flight fifty-nine is approaching from New Jersey via Chicago," squeaked the announcement from a ceiling speaker. Billie was in the marble waiting room at Grand Central Airport, anticipating Patty's commercial flight. It had been expensive, but sometimes you had to spend money to make things happen. She looked to the left at the windows along the far wall, but didn't see an airplane.

A redcap opened the door to the tarmac, letting in a rush of cool air. People filed out the entrance to the waiting area on the tarmac.

"Flight fifty-nine has arrived," the announcer called out. "Please meet your parties at Door Two."

As Billie moved toward the door, a group of women suddenly surrounded her, asking for her autograph. These days, she rarely attracted a crowd, but news of her Academy Award nomination had been in the paper recently, which was likely why people were even more eager than usual to meet her. She could sign a few autographs while she waited for Patty to get off her plane. Billie exhaled and conjured a smile. She reached for the notepad closest to her.

"Mrs. McNaughty," the woman said.

"Mrs. Johnson," said the next woman.

And so it went. Billie signed six pads and envelope-backs with "It was nice to meet you, Billie Burke."

Passengers began walking through the door from the tarmac.

"I really must go," Billie said, pointing to the door. "My daughter is here."

A couple of the women thanked her, but one stepped before her, stopping her abruptly. Billie's heart thumped.

"Excuse me," the woman said. She was a pretty young thing who reminded Billie of Claudette Colbert. She had the same tight waves of hair hugging her scalp.

"Oh, please, Miss Burke. My name is Mary. One more?" She held out a pad and pencil.

"Me too," said another, running up, waving a pad. "I'm Paula."

Billie scrawled two more signatures, then locked her eyes on the tarmac door, looking for Patty. Another woman stepped in front of her, a thread-thin woman with tight lips.

"Please," the woman begged. She seemed frail, almost sickly. "Please, Miss Burke. It's for my daughter. She's in the hospital."

Billie's shoulders dropped, and she took the woman's pencil.

"Ethel is her name," the woman said, her grin showing crooked teeth.

Billie scribbled on the back of the airmail envelope: "Dear Ethel. Get well soon. All my love, Billie Burke." She returned the envelope and pencil and said, "Now, if you'll excuse me, I need to get to my daughter."

"Mother!" It was Patty's voice.

Billie pushed through the clinging crowd of fans and opened her arms to her daughter for a hug. Billie could feel Patty's tears on her cheeks. Nothing else mattered. Nothing else existed.

Outside the airport, Billie squeezed Patty's hand and looked her up and down. She seemed taller, and her body shapelier. She wore a navy-blue beret—very New York—and a polka-dotted blouse.

Billie's body chilled. In only a month, her daughter seemed to have grown up like corn in the night. Every day for over twenty years, Billie had listened to her breathing, counted her toes, and counseled her through first bras, first boyfriends. Today, a woman stood before her. When did that happen? She straightened Patty's collar and felt Patty melt at the touch.

"I'm glad to be home," Patty said.

Billie's lips quivered. "I'm glad you're home, too."

A porter opened the driver's side door of Billie's car.

"May I drive?" Patty said.

"Certainly, dear."

It wasn't ladylike for women to drive, but Billie loved the freedom and power driving gave her, and she wanted Patty to have that, too. Patty pulled out of the parking spot quickly.

"Take it slow," Billie said. "You haven't driven in over a month."

"Believe me; I know what to do."

"And where are your gloves?" A woman in public without gloves was the equivalent of walking barefoot into a formal ball.

"Gloves are on their way out, Mother. It's a modern world."

Billie pressed her lips together. She considered herself "modern," but there were still basic standards to uphold.

Patty's eyes narrowed. "You're staring at the beret, aren't you?"

Billie gave a fake smile. "It's lovely, dear."

"You don't like it."

"It makes you look . . . well, artistic. Very New York."

"I bought two." Patty winked.

Billie winked back. "Wonderful," she said. "You might lose one." After a few miles had passed, Billie asked, "How's the job?" She tried to make the question sound casual.

Patty tapped the wheel. "I have two feet of unsolicited radio plays to read. Two feet. You should try lifting my luggage when we get home."

"Your job sounds important. You might find the next Mr. Shakespeare in that pile."

"He didn't do radio."

"You know what I mean."

"Mr. Ellison gave me strict orders: 'No more *War of the Worlds*.' I think he wants light, fluffy things. Comedies, mostly." Her eyebrows lifted. "In fact, you could help me. You could read them all. You know what to look for better than I do."

Billie leaned toward Patty and patted the bench seat between them. "Everyone starts this way, dear, but if you work hard, they'll notice, and they'll give you a chance."

"You've told me that before."

"Your father had it rough at first. Your grandfather made him file a lot of music. When your daddy complained, his father would say, 'Do that vell, then move on. *Das Leben ist kein Ponyhof.*'"

Patty squinted. "English, please."

"Life isn't always easy."

"I know that."

"Your grandfather also said, 'The first time I gave him a real responsibility, vut did he do?'" She shook her head. "'*Es war eine Zerstörung.*'"

"What does that mean?"

"Such a mess." Billie laughed.

Patty teared up, probably at the thought of her father. She had always been a daddy's girl. A muscle moved in her jaw. "Can we change the subject, please?"

Billie didn't want to upset her daughter. They could talk more about this later. After a pause, Billie said, "There's a gift for you on the kitchen counter."

Patty's face brightened. "What kind of gift?"

"Something you'll like." Billie smiled to herself at the thought of the gift. It was that Amazonite pendant she'd purchased from the RKO cashier. It was Patty's favorite color.

"Thanks, Mother." Patty relaxed into her seat, and she even smiled a little.

Billie didn't want to ruin the moment, but she couldn't stop pressing on: "I'll read one-fourth of the scripts. How about that?"

One of Billie's worst fears stood before her: her daughter's disinterest in building a career. Patty didn't seem to understand that you had to tough out boring activities until your opportunity to go big arrived. The girl was smart, a good student, and kind, but trying to help her build a career was like pushing an elephant uphill.

Billie's whole body suddenly felt exhausted. She sat back and closed her eyes, looking for something to talk about instead of listening to honking horns.

"We should go dress shopping and get something new for the Tailwaggers Ball," Billie said, assuming her daughter would like this topic better than the last. Patty loved shopping.

Patty sniffed. "What ball?"

"Tailwaggers. It's an event to raise money for a dog hospital." Billie was a member of the organization. "There'll be dancing. You like to dance."

Patty stopped at a light and looked at Billie. Her eyes were pink. "I get to choose the dress?"

"Absolutely."

"At any price?"

Billie stiffened. "Well, no. I don't have unlimited funds, remember." Billie wouldn't let her daughter go wearing something cheap and unfashionable, yet she had limits. They'd find something.

Chapter Fifteen

Billie stepped into the Crystal Ballroom at the Beverly Hills Hotel for the Tailwaggers Ball wearing an amaranth-colored gown with a layered lace collar. Patty wore an ivory-colored satin dress with a plunging neckline and Empire waist. The dress was so low-cut, Billie had wanted to throw a shawl over Patty's shoulders. Now, at the ball, she wished she had.

As they entered the room, Louella Parsons, the film columnist for the *Los Angeles Examiner*, called out. Though Louella was a kinder, less judgmental columnist than most, Billie still felt her guard go up. She tapped Patty's arm. "You go ahead. I'll meet you at the table." Patty was here for fun. Billie was here for work.

"Congratulations on the nomination, Billie," Louella said. "We should talk later."

"Thank you, and certainly," Billie said.

"You've long deserved this," Louella said. "I want the paper to print something. Don't forget. Come find me later."

"Oh, I won't forget."

Patty was waving in the distance. With her at the table were actor Eddie Cantor and his daughter Marjorie, both family friends. Eddie had worked for Flo back in the *Follies* days. Billie joined them.

"Madame Burke," Eddie said as he stood. He was a short man with exaggerated brown eyes and a Greek nose. He kissed the top of Billie's gloved hand. "You look scrumptious."

She batted her eyelashes and fanned herself with a free hand. "Why, Mr. Cantor, you are married."

He motioned to the table. "Do you see my wife here?"

"Where is she?" Billie said.

"Home sick with the flu."

"The poor dear."

"The girls are caring for her," he said, meaning his four other daughters.

Marjorie rose. "I'm Mother's stand-in," she said.

"Give her my regards," Billie said.

Eddie pulled out a chair beside his for Billie, and they sat. He sipped his water, paused, and said quietly so only Billie could hear, "So, New York's a problem?"

Billie pulled off her gloves. "How do you know that?"

"Patty writes to Marjorie."

Billie sighed. "I don't understand that girl sometimes."

The microphone squealed as actress Bette Davis took it from the stand at the head table.

"Later," Eddie said, nodding toward the girls, who were close enough to overhear if he said too much. His eyes told Billie he had information for her. "We'll dance, and then we can talk."

"Everyone find your seats," Bette said from the stage. "It's time to eat."

Billie unfolded her napkin and tried changing the subject. "Are you working on a film right now?"

"Just cameos," Eddie said. "I've been focusing on the radio show."

"You're not slowing down, are you?"

He scoffed. "I'm not getting old, Billie, if you're suggesting that." He pointed back and forth between them. "When we dance later, I'll prove I haven't lost my pep."

"Count me in."

* * *

During dessert, Bette Davis returned to the microphone and raised her arms.

"Attention, please," she said. "I know the studios want you in bed early, but we need to raise thirty-four hundred dollars before we leave here tonight, and you'll stay until we get it done, even if you have to sleep here to do it." She pointed to a few people in the back of the room. Her fingernails were long and painted scarlet. "That amount will be a down payment on the eighty thousand we need to keep this wonderful organization going. Checks, cash, who cares? Just do it." Her nymph-like blue eyes scanned the room from left to right. "Now, who will give us the first check?"

Bette pointed to a man in the second row. He was in his mid-forties and had wavy dull-brown hair and a mustache.

Billie began to wring her hands. She hadn't realized they'd be confronting people like this to encourage donations. She hadn't brought her checkbook with her, and there were only eight dollars in her purse. She hoped this little confrontation had been staged to get things rolling.

A man from the Tailwaggers Association whom Billie knew as Jim approached the man in the second row, who handed over a check.

Jim raised the check in the air. "I have a check for a hundred dollars."

That was enough to buy a mink shawl.

"Vonderful," said a man from the fourth row in an Austrian accent.

Jim hurried over to the man. "Can you give us a hundred dollars, too?"

The man shook his head.

"Do you have a dog?"

"No."

"Children?"

"No."

"But you direct movies."

"Yes."

Who was that man? Billie wondered.

"Movies are like puppies," Jim said.

The man scoffed.

"You once said that directors were like doctors," Jim said.

"I did."

"If something goes wrong, you diagnose it and fix it; sometimes that fix takes money. Puppies are the same. Like movies, they bring joy to people, but they won't if they're sick and need a doctor." The man folded his arms across his chest.

"How about fifty dollars?" Jim asked.

The man shook his head.

"How about ten dollars, then?"

A waiter came in, carrying a cocker spaniel puppy inside a cage. Gasps and "awws" spread across the room, creating a soft vibration that made Billie smile.

"Bring that over here," Jim said, motioning to the waiter. The waiter gave him the cage, and Jim held it up for the man to see. The puppy paced with a wagging tail.

Spoons clinked glasses, and the man pulled a leather wallet from an inside jacket pocket. He removed a bill and gave it to Jim with a resigned look.

Jim waved the bill like a flag. "Ten dollars it is. Thank you, Mr. Sternberg." He handed the puppy back to the waiter. The man must be film director Josef von Sternberg, and it was no surprise he was here. Actress Marlene Dietrich, who starred in many of his films, was at his table, laughing. The two were friends, and she'd probably insisted on his coming.

A man's arm went up in the last row, and he waved a check. She couldn't see his face, just his jacket sleeve. A silver cufflink shimmered in the light.

"Mr. Bing Crosby," Jim announced. Bing was a singer who sold more records than the church sold Bibles.

Jim jogged over to the table, plucked the check from Bing's hand, and read it. "Seventy-five dollars," he bellowed. "It sure ain't pennies from heaven, is it?"

People groaned and applauded.

"Thank you, Mr. Crosby. Now, who's next?"

Dozens of hands waved checks in the air as Jim jogged and plucked them from their fingers. Billie recognized Henry Fonda, Constance Collier, Hedda Hopper, Louella Parsons, and Mary Pickford. Jim took checks from them all.

Eddie slapped his checkbook on the table as if he planned to write a big one. He opened to a blank check, filled in the spaces, signed it with a flurry, and raised it in the air.

Jim headed toward their table with a bounce in his step. The guests' eyes followed him, and Billie held her breath as he got close. Everyone would expect her to wave a check or bill. Eddie had a lot of money, but she didn't. She could give what she had in her purse, but she needed more than eight dollars.

It was a common misconception that she was still rich, which seemed odd because the press had announced she'd lost everything. She'd been wealthy once—half a million dollars in the bank, an estate in Yonkers, five furs in storage, annual trips to Europe. When the stock market crashed, though, her assets crashed with it. She'd put up a good front all these years, which was probably why people thought she still had money. Today, her home in Beverly Hills was rented, and she often wore borrowed clothes by well-known designers. She pulled it off as a trained actress, but it was all an act. Too bad there weren't Academy Awards for real-life acting. She'd have earned several by now.

Jim reached their table and Eddie gave him the check. "From the eternal funny man," Jim said, waving the check. "Eddie Cantor, one hundred dollars."

Jim lingered behind her as her heart raced. She tried to get her daughter's attention with her eyes, but Patty was staring at her water glass and wiping the sweat from its sides, likely bored. She had a good attention span for most things, but there was still a teenager inside of her from time to time.

Eddie motioned for Jim to wait, scribbled a note on a piece of paper on his lap, and tapped her hand with it under the table. She looked down, took it, and opened it on her lap. It was another check. He motioned for her to take it.

She felt her face turn scarlet. It was for thirty dollars, and the memo read, "From Miss Billie Burke, who forgot her checkbook."

"Oh, I couldn't," she whispered to Eddie.

She could feel Jim breathing behind her.

Eddie whispered, "For God's sake, Billie. Just do it."

She felt the heat of all eyes on her. She smiled and lifted the check in the air.

Jim took it and said, "From the amazing and ever-beautiful Miss Billie Burke, thirty dollars. Thank you. Now, who's next?"

Billie breathed as Jim turned and left to collect the other checks. Her shoulders relaxed. "I'm going to pay you back."

"Don't be ridiculous," Eddie said, waving off the idea. "After what your husband did for me, it was the least I could do."

Bette Davis looked at the pile of checks and smiled. "Thank you," she said. "And now let me introduce your dance teacher for the evening, Mr. William Stephenson."

A young man rose and waved. He was a tall, slender boy with shiny black hair and was dressed in a navy-blue suit at least one size too big. His face had an aw-shucks look brushed with a New England demeanor.

Bette rubbed her hands together. "Okay, everyone. Thank you for coming, and get moving." She motioned to the crowd. "C'mon, c'mon."

Mr. Stephenson stepped onto the parquet floor in the center of the room with the ease of a courtier. Two dozen young people joined him, including Marjorie and Patty. He lined them up facing him and said, "To do a swing dance, we first learn the parts."

The orchestra struck up "Have You Got Any Castles, Baby?" featuring a male soloist. The beat was playful, steady, and straightforward.

"Mrs. Ziegfeld," Eddie said as he stood and offered his hand.

Billie nodded and smiled, putting her hand in his. His fingers were thick and strong.

"It'll give us a chance to talk," he said. "No children around."

As they reached the dance floor, Eddie asked, "Foxtrot?"

She nodded, then put her hand on his left shoulder. As they moved through the steps, light and airy, she realized it felt good to be back in a man's arms for a dance.

"I spoke with John Ellison the other day," Eddie said.

John was the head of the radio station where Patty apprenticed, her immediate supervisor. He'd also been a family friend for years.

Billie stopped, worried that she'd hear bad news. She wanted to believe things were going well for Patty in New York, but her intuition told her otherwise.

Eddie stopped. Their hands stayed in place.

"Why?" Billie asked.

"It was about an appearance. We were talking about Flo, and John mentioned Patty."

A chill ran through Billie, but she realized they must look ridiculous standing still in the middle of the dance floor. She gave Eddie a nod and they resumed dancing, but lightly. She forced herself to look him in the eye.

"Now, Billie," Eddie said, "I've known you and that girl a long time. I've watched her grow up, and I think of her as part of my family."

"I feel the same way about your girls." She bit her lip. "So, what did John say about Patty?"

Eddie took a breath, glanced to the side, and looked back at Billie. "Her heart isn't in the job."

"He complained?"

"Not exactly. I could tell when he described what she was doing."

Billie missed a step. "Sorry." She paused, then got back into the rhythm.

"You know how he is," Eddie said. "Now, Billie, you and I go way back."

"We certainly do. Twenty-two years. Our children practically grew up together."

"I'm going to be frank with you."

"You usually are."

"I know you've been trying to help Patty develop a career, but—"

"But what?"

He looked down. "Marjorie tells me that that apprenticeship isn't going too well. They've been writing each other."

"I knew that, but eventually, things will kick into place."

"Are you sure?"

"She's had some ups and downs with the job, but it's an apprenticeship. It isn't supposed to be fun, and I've told her that. She has to start somewhere. She can't expect to start at the top. She needs this. You know what I've been through since the crash. If I didn't have my acting career, I'd be selling apples in front of the Biltmore. Building a career is like planting a garden. You plant the seeds now, and they bloom later."

"Well, perhaps you know best."

"She agreed to go to New York, you know." She raised her hand in dismissal. "I didn't force her." Billie looked over at Patty, who had found a dance partner. She looked back at Eddie. His eyes were sincere.

"She isn't you, Billie," he said. "Keep that in mind."

"I know that. She never wanted to be an actress. We tried. I even put her on stage in Philadelphia to substitute for an ill actress. It didn't go well."

"I remember Flo mentioning it."

"I paid for two years of college, so she should use it and become a writer. That's what she said she wanted. She's wanted it since grade school." Billie tensed. "She needs a craft to fall back on if something happens."

"Don't be mad at me when I say this, but she wants to please you. She always has, even more so since Flo died. A part of her is excited about New York, for sure. It's home for her, but she's also seen you struggle. She saw both of you struggle, and she wants something different for herself."

Billie stopped dancing, stepped back, and put her hands on her hips. "Why are you telling me this?"

"I'm trying to help, that's all. I'm sorry. I didn't mean to offend you."

Billie's shoulders dropped. "I'm sorry," she said. "I hope I wasn't rude. I appreciate what you're trying to do. Frankly, I don't think Patty knows what she wants. She's been lost since her daddy died, and I want to keep her safe. If the apprenticeship doesn't work, so be it, but I still think it will."

Eddie took her arm and led her back to the table, but she kept her eyes on Patty.

"I've got a busy day tomorrow," Eddie said as he pulled out her chair. "Perhaps I should collect my daughter."

"Me too. Thank you for the dance. I really appreciated it."

He bowed. Billie got up and walked over to Patty, tapping her shoulder.

"Are you ready to go?" Billie said in the girl's ear. "I'm exhausted."

Patty looked over her shoulder. "In a minute," she said, then returned her gaze to the man she was dancing with. Billie frowned. Patty had never been boy crazy. This seemed out of character.

Billie tapped her foot.

"Tomorrow?" the man asked Patty.

"Yes," Patty said in a soft tone.

"Splendid," he said. He turned to Billie. "I'd be happy to take her home."

Patty gave Billie a begging eye, but Billie whispered, "A young lady shouldn't go home in a man's car the first night they meet."

Patty gave her mother a mutinous glare. "We're having fun, and it's only ten o'clock."

Billie gave her a warning look, the kind she used when Patty was little and had already been told to stop a particular behavior for the hundredth time. "Ten minutes, then meet me in the lobby," she said, jabbing a finger in Patty's direction.

Billie stormed off to the lobby to wait, bristling and forming fists. This wasn't a good time for Patty to find a local man to latch onto. Boys were nothing more than distractions. She needed to return to New York to finish that apprenticeship. Billie would see to it.

Chapter Sixteen

Filming with *Oz* was finished for now, although Billie knew there might be requests to return and refilm a few scenes. No film was ever finished until the last reels were made. Until then, Billie was getting ready for her next film. She stood in Adrian's studio for a costume measurement for *Bridal Suite*. Along one wall were manufacturing plant–sized windows with work tables lined in front of them, each big enough to play ping-pong. Mannequins stood by, cloaked in Munchkin costumes, ball gowns, and dinner jackets.

The ever-lithe Adrian tapped a two-tone Oxford on the linoleum floor, his flint-colored pleated trousers jiggling with every tap. He was a twilight, but Billie still cringed at being measured by a man.

He thrust his hands to his hips. The dimple on his chin deepened. "Oh, come now. Be a sport." Adrian stepped forward, tilted his head, and laid a finger on his chin. "You look thinner. Have you lost weight?"

"Don't patronize me." She grabbed the table behind her and squeezed. "Can we make a deal before I let you touch me?"

"Deal?" he said, folding his arms across his chest and nodding curtly.

"May I borrow a dress for the weekend?"

He stepped back. "You know the answer to that question is always yes.'"

"I know, but I need something special."

"What's it for?"

She explained the beauty endorsement project arranged by Tom and Lydia. The first meeting hadn't been scheduled yet, and she had vowed to remind Tom to set it up over lunch, but she wanted to plan ahead. What if the meeting were suddenly tomorrow? She might as well pick something out now while she was here.

"Something businesslike?" he said.

"Something that makes me look pretty but focused," Billie said. "Nothing too frilly."

"Not frilly? You? You are Miss Frilly."

"I know, but I'm trying to look more modern. But nothing too unusual!"

"More like a Joan Crawford than a Kate Hepburn?"

"Yes, but not sexy. You know . . . business-y."

"When do you need it?"

"Tomorrow morning?"

He frowned. "What's the real reason for this dress? You seem tense about it. Something doesn't feel right."

She paused, looked out the window, then said, "Can you keep a secret?"

"Of course."

Billie locked her eyes on Adrian's, and felt her stomach sink. "L. B. may be letting me go."

"What do you mean?"

"He's threatened to refuse to renew my contract."

Adrian stepped back with "If that's true, then he's nuts."

"I might be doing an endorsement that could help change his mind, and you know I need my job."

Adrian put a finger to his chin. "I have just the thing for you." He held up the tape. "But first, this."

* * *

After the fitting, Billie returned home and called Tom.

"I'm sorry, Miss Burke, I should have called Lydia by now. I've been so very busy," Tom said. "I'll call her as soon as I hang up."

"I don't want to upset a beauty columnist, that's for sure. She arranged this thing, and I want her to arrange more."

After hanging up the phone, she sat back and closed her eyes, her mind drifting back to 1910. She had been labeled nationally as the "Most Beautiful Woman in America." People copied her hair, her voice, her clothes. A "billyburke" was a cute way of speaking. People named racehorses and first-born children after her, and curly hair extensions modeled after her own style sold like horseshoes. By the mid-1920s, though, interest in her appearance waned. By then, she was in her forties, and plenty of younger women were coming up. In the entertainment business, youth reigned supreme.

Today, she was still considered beautiful, and she looked younger than her age. But these days, she had to work harder to look younger. She wasn't sure how long it would last, and it had to last if she hoped to keep her career going.

The phone rang, and she jumped. It was Tom. He'd scheduled an appointment for her on Sunday at 1:00 P.M. in the Chandelier Room at Santa Anita Park.

A gambling facility? Billie's shoulders tightened. Flo had lost thousands at New York's Belmont Park, and she'd long refused to step foot inside another racetrack. She'd almost divorced him twice over his gambling. Now, it looked like she was going to have to break her own rule.

* * *

On Sunday, she stood in front of the wide-open entrance to the Chandelier Room at the track. She straightened her hat, held up her chin, and walked in. It was 12:57 P.M. She was on time, but how was she going to find Lydia among the diners? She'd never met the woman and wasn't sure what she looked like except for the photo published in her column. The maître d' wasn't at his post to direct her, so she scanned the room for a waving hand or a smile aimed in her direction.

She turned, expecting the maître d', but it was a woman. "Miss Burke?" the woman said. "At last, we meet in person. I'm Lydia Lane. Thank you for coming."

They squeezed each other's hands. Lydia had a firm touch.

"It's a pleasure to meet you," Billie said.

"Shall we get going?" Lydia motioned for Billie to follow her as bangles jingled on her arm.

Halfway into the dining room on the right was a flat-chested woman in her mid-thirties standing at a table with a broad smile. She reminded Billie of a flapper. "Miss Burke," the woman said in a chirpy voice as they approached. "I'm Rachel Johnson. I've wanted to meet you for a long time. You're the epitome of a beautiful, charming woman, And what a lovely dress."

"Adrian," Billie replied. "You know, he has his own shop now."

"Oh. I didn't know that. How nice!" Lydia stepped back to admire the dress. It was a bubblegum-colored, calf-length dress banded at the waist, with two-inch-wide buttons down the front. "I'll have to stop by his shop," Lydia said.

"I'm sure he'd appreciate it." Billie touched Lydia's wrist. "And I'm sure he'd love a mention in your column."

"Yes, I think I will mention him."

A waiter pulled out their chairs and seated them. Once they had ordered, Rachel leaned across the table, peering at Billie's face. "Your skin is marvelous, especially for a woman your age. So smooth. So pure."

"She used to take milk baths you know," Lydia told Rachel. "Or maybe she still does?"

Billie shook her head. "I never really did that. It was all Flo's—"

Interrupting, Rachel stood, reached across the table, and grabbed Billie's chin. Billie fought not to flinch.

"I don't see one wrinkle or sag," Rachel said as she caressed Billie's left cheek.

"Miss Burke takes care of herself," Lydia said, nodding. "She always has."

"And the hair," Rachel said. "What a complicated shade of ginger, yet natural."

"Miss Burke is a Max Factor client," Lydia said, promoting Billie like a product. "She's extraordinarily beautiful, isn't she?" Lydia folded her hands on the table. "Let's get down to business, shall we? Rachel studied with a Paris doctor to learn to do facials for older women."

"Older?" Billie said out of the corner of her mouth with a hint of joking. To her, older meant over sixty with a sagging chin, drooping breasts, and U-shaped smile.

"Over forty-five, I mean," Lydia clarified.

Billie turned to Rachel. "What's this new treatment of yours?"

"It's a chemical process," Lydia broke in before Rachel could answer. "It doesn't hurt the skin like the others. She uses croton oil. It's an extract of the seed croton tiglium." She turned to Rachel. "Am I getting it right?"

"Perfectly," Rachel replied.

Billie had always been a natural-process skincare person. Her extensive research had told her there were only four ways to keep your skin young and fresh: regular exercise, a healthy diet, a daily facial scrub, and nightly creams. She'd never heard of croton oil, and wondered if it included harmful ingredients. She would only put something on her skin if she was sure it was natural and safe.

"Who else have you treated?" Billie asked Rachel.

Rachel shifted in her chair. "Nobody you would know."

"Are there other women I can talk to?" Billie said. "It isn't that I don't trust you, dear; I just need to learn more."

"I'm going to pay you handsomely," Rachel said.

"She's completely reliable," Lydia said, patting the white tablecloth beside Billie's plate.

Billie's chest sagged. The last thing she wanted was a fight with a beauty columnist, but she couldn't be in the press representing a treatment if it caused scars or other damage. Yes, she'd endorsed Lucky Strike cigarettes last year, and the ad showed her holding a pack and asking everyone to try one. But women had known for years that cigarette smoking damaged their skin. If they chose to smoke, they understood the risk. However, chemical treatments of the skin were new, and once they damaged your skin, you were scarred for life.

"Don't overthink this," Lydia said. "It's perfectly safe."

Lydia must be getting a cut from sales, Billie thought.

"I know you're worried, Miss Burke," said Rachel, "and I was worried too, at first, but they removed all the dangers."

You know how it is. When something is new, it has kinks, but they eliminate the kinks until they get it right. It's like those automatic bread slicers. My father is a baker, and he purchased one in twenty-nine. The thing cut somebody's finger off."

Billie winced.

"He has a new one now, and it has safety latches and whatnot," Rachel said. "It's the same kind of situation with skin treatments. They're risky at first but safe later, and we have the French doctors to thank. It's so exciting, and you could be the face of it."

"Do you have a list of clients I could talk to?"

"Certainly," Rachel said. "They're all in New York and Chicago, though. I've only been on the West Coast for a week."

"I'm sure they'll tell me how pleased they are," Billie said. She hoped they would, but then again, what if they lied?

The breadbasket arrived, but Billie couldn't look at the bread for fear of eating it.

Rachel took a slice and then lifted the basket. "Anybody?" she said.

Lydia and Billie shook their heads.

As Rachel buttered her slice, she said, "Come in for a treatment, Miss Burke. That way, you can see for yourself."

Billie touched her cheek.

"Then, when you endorse it," Rachel continued, "you can show people how it worked."

Lydia sat back and smiled. "Splendid idea."

Billie squeezed her skirt in angst. She didn't want to go through a dangerous process, and she also didn't want to say no and lose the endorsement. Why did so many good things come with such awful attachments?

"I can make an appointment for you for next week," Rachel said as the waiter set their meals in front of them.

"No, thank you, dear," Billie said once he'd left the table. "My skin is good as it is."

"What are you worried about?" Lydia asked, stabbing a chunk of lettuce with her fork.

"I just don't need it."

"But you'll be endorsing it," Lydia said, "so you should try it."

"I can endorse things without trying them. I endorsed Blue Bonnet margarine, but I didn't eat it, and I endorsed cigarettes but didn't smoke them." She took a deep breath, hoping she hadn't sounded too snippy. "If I agree to do this, all you will need is my name." Billie sprinkled vinegar on her salad. "Have you tried the treatment?" she asked Lydia.

"No, but I will, at some point. If it's the chemicals you're worried about, keep in mind that everything has chemicals in it these days, from that lovely dress you're wearing to your lipstick and lotions. It's the age of chemicals."

"I know, but—"

"From face powders to lipsticks to lotions," Lydia said again, seeming agitated. "Powder has talc in it, and talc is a silicate mineral. Lipstick has emollients."

"Yes, I'm aware of that," Billie said, carefully and politely. "But those are in the form of makeup and wash off. Chemical treatments change the skin; they are forever."

Billie pressed her knees together. She was faced with either irritating a columnist or promoting a product that might hurt someone. There was no third, better option. "I research new products before I put them on my face, that's all. I haven't researched this one yet."

"Speak to Mr. Factor about it," Lydia said. "He understands these things. He knows all about it."

"And he thinks it's safe?"

"He's considering using it."

Had Lydia told Max that Billie was considering endorsing it? She stabbed a piece of cucumber and put it into her mouth.

"Don't worry, Miss Burke," Rachel said, leaning forward with her elbows on the table, pressing her hands together. "I spent six months in Paris learning to do this. It's perfectly harmless. I'm an expert, and I know what I'm doing."

"Really, Billie. Try it," Lydia said.

Billie swallowed. "Have you tried it?" she asked Rachel.

"No," Rachel said. "It's for women over forty, and I have a good five years before I get there. I'll give Lydia the references; she can call your agent."

"You mean Mr. O'Donough? He's my press representative."

"Yes, him," Rachel said. "We want to sign you up, and there is no better face to put on this than yours."

"And the fact that you are Flo Ziegfeld's widow, well, it's perfect," Lydia said. "Can we get back together at Rachel's office in two weeks?"

"Yes," she said. She hoped (with fingers crossed) that the process was safe and that she wouldn't be pushed further to experience it. She'd research the process in the meantime to ensure she wasn't telling women to do something that might harm them.

Chapter Seventeen

Tonight was Oscar night. Billie sat at the kitchen table in a pink terrycloth bathrobe over a white satin slip, her ball gown patiently waiting on a hanger upstairs. Her face and hair had been completely Max Factored.

Her stomach was in knots.

She'd banished Patty to the upstairs and the dogs to the outside as she sat at the kitchen table with the phone in front of her, her hand inches from the earpiece. A stack of heavy books was in front of the doggie door to keep the dogs from climbing back in.

She was ready and supported by a curated collection of good-luck souvenirs. Billie admitted it: She was superstitious.

Something old: In her lap was a pair of her mother's white satin gloves, yellowed with age.

Something new: a fist-sized silver elephant figure from Flo's collection. Elephants were symbols of good luck. She stroked the figurine.

Something borrowed: a color-printed postcard of Pelagia the Penitent, the Catholic patron saint of actresses, suggested by actress Rosalind Russell. Billie wasn't Catholic, but why not try it? She picked it up and kissed it.

Something blue: a ceramic blue jay. Blue jays represented creativity, mental clarity, intelligence, and self-expression. She smiled at it.

Billie folded her hands on her lap and squeezed them. It was 5:56 P.M.; four more minutes to go. She closed her eyes and repeated, "Rabbits, rabbits, rabbits."

When the dogs barked and began scratching at the door, she jumped and gritted her teeth. The two ham bones she'd tossed into the backyard apparently hadn't been enough. The stack of books before the doggie door rocked as if jarred by an earthquake. The books on the top tumbled to the floor. Then, more fell. Two pink noses thrust through the leather flaps.

She pushed herself up and pointed at the noses. "Stay," she commanded.

Ziggy's white head poked through.

She jabbed her finger at him. "Outside."

Ziggy backed out, and then Pippin poked his head through and jumped inside, knocking down the rest of the books.

Billie's shoulders slumped. Was this disruption, this break into her curated space and time, a sign that she hadn't won the award? She shook her head. Stupid dogs. She loved them, but they were impossible to control. Both dogs ran inside and danced around her, tails wagging.

Then the phone rang, vibrating the tabletop. It was 6:04.

She raced to the phone amid barking dogs. Her heart pounding inside her chest, she slipped on the waxed linoleum and caught herself with the table's edge. She reached for the receiver, picked it up, and took a deep breath.

"Hello," she said, trying to sound relaxed.

"Did you win?" Dorothy said.

"Good grief," she said as she dropped into her chair.

The dogs ran up to her and put their front paws on her thighs. She pushed them away, but they sprung right back. She closed her eyes.

"I have to hang up," Billie said, sputtering. "They're going to call any minute."

"You have half an hour."

"MGM said six o'clock."

"Should I call back?"

"No. I have to hang up."

"You have plenty of time."

Billie squeezed the earpiece. "No, I'm sorry, but I have to hang up."

"But—"

Billie hung up. She'd apologize later.

She rose quickly, jogged to the counter, pulled a handful of doggie biscuits from the box, opened the door, and threw them outside. The dogs raced out toward the biscuits. She closed the door and crossed her fingers.

It was 6:09. MGM was calling the winners first. Hopefully, there were a lot of them. They probably started with Best Actress, Best Actor, and worked their way down to Best Scenario. She'd be midway. It was still early. "Relax," she told herself.

A "clack, clack, clack" sound came down the stairs.

Billie hung her head. Nobody was paying attention to her requests for privacy. What was next? Would Patty's new beau William appear at the front door? He was coming to be Patty's escort.

Patty reached the bottom of the stairs, fully dressed, diamond earrings dangling. She opened her arms wide and walked over for a hug. "Congratulations," she said.

Billie held out her hand in a "stop where you are" gesture. She'd spent too much money on her hair and face to risk destroying it all with an embrace. "It was only your aunt Dorothy."

Patty dropped her arms. "Oh."

"I asked you to stay upstairs," Billie snapped.

Patty's eyes narrowed. "The phone rang," she said in a "stupid mother" tone. "Can I stay?"

Billie sighed. "Why not?" She wasn't going to rid of Patty now, and frankly, a part of Billie wanted her here. Her lavender smell made Billie smile.

Patty pointed to the table and smirked. "What's all this?" She picked up the Pelagia card.

"Don't touch that."

Patty turned the card over. Billie plucked it from her hand and put it back.

Patty waved her arm over the display, her bracelets jangling on her wrist. "Mother. You know this hocus-pocus stuff doesn't work."

"We obviously disagree."

The phone rang. It was 6:16. Billie gripped the table.

"Do you want me to answer it?" Patty said.

Billie shook her head, bit her lip, and reached for the receiver. "Miss Billie Burke," she said.

"How are you, Miss Burke?" the caller said in a chirpy voice.

"I'm well, thank you," she replied in an even chirpier voice.

"It's Betty from Mr. Mayer's office. I have a lot of calls to make, so I apologize for keeping this short. I know everyone's sitting by their phones, waiting."

Billie stopped breathing.

"I'm sorry," Betty continued, "but the award went to Fay Bainter for *Jezebel*."

The air leaked out of Billie as she sat back down in her chair and closed her eyes. She felt a tear form.

"It should have been yours," Betty said. "You were marvelous in the film, and Mr. Mayer wanted you to know that."

Billie opened her mouth to thank Betty, but nothing came out.

"Miss Burke?" Betty said.

Billie opened her eyes. "Thank you, dear."

Patty walked over and touched her mother's shoulder.

"I hate to ask this," Betty continued. "I know you must feel sad. I sure would. But are you still going to the ceremony?"

Billie hung her head but didn't say anything.

"I'd understand if you didn't," Betty said, "but Mr. Mayer would like you to go if you could."

Billie's mind went blank. She'd told The Mount she would go no matter what, but hearing "No, you didn't win" had sucked the energy out of her.

"Miss Burke?" Betty said.

"Do you want me to take the phone?" Patty whispered.

Billie shook her head and took a deep breath.

The front doorbell rang. "Damn it," Billie said, but only in her mind. It was probably William, Patty's date, early as usual.

Billie sat up straight, squared her shoulders, and breathed deeply. "Yes," she said. "Of course. We'll be there." She wanted L. B. to see her full of smiles and energy.

"I'll send a car," Betty said.

* * *

Later, Billie, Patty, and William were inside the Biltmore Hotel, waiting in line behind the Cagneys in the hall to enter the ballroom. The hall was decorated with a Renaissance theme: hanging tapestries, marble fountains in niches, electric candle chandeliers.

Billie had worked through her pain and disappointment on the way here and was in a happier, more anticipatory place fed by the party atmosphere. Jewels glistened around women's necks, and black bow ties ribboned men's collars. The scent of Joy by Patou perfume and Nat Sherman cigars thickened the air.

Billie had never met the Cagneys, a next-generation couple. She tapped Mrs. Cagney on her shoulder and said, "Excuse me."

The woman turned to look, and raised her eyebrows. "Why, if it isn't Miss Billie Burke," she said. Mrs. Cagney had high cheekbones above a wide, natural smile. "It's such a pleasure to meet you. I love your work."

They squeezed each other's hands.

"My name is Billie, too," Mrs. Cagney said.

Billie wondered if Mrs. Cagney had been named after her. Many parents had named their female children "Billie" a few years back when "Billie Burke" became a household name.

"More like billy club," James Cagney said with a smirk.

Mrs. Cagney ignored her husband. "What a lovely dress," she said to Billie, touching its puffy sleeves. "I love the embroidered flowers." Green and yellow poppies, cornflowers, and marguerites were woven into the fabric.

"It's an Adrian design," Billie said, pulling her shoulders back.

Mrs. Cagney pointed to Patty. "Is that your daughter?"

"Yes," Billie said with a smile.

"I recognize her from photos in the paper."

"She's almost as tall as her father," James said.

"Which wasn't very tall," Billie said.

Mrs. Cagney slapped him on the shoulder. "Don't be rude."

He shrugged it off.

"And who is that striking young man behind her?" Mrs. Cagney said with a wink, nodding to William. William straightened his lapel.

"Patty's friend, Mr. William Stephenson," Billie said. "He's an architect, or soon to be."

"Are the two of you . . . ?" Mrs. Cagney asked Patty.

"We're friends," Patty said, responding as she'd been told. Billie didn't want the tabloids to run with fake, unflattering stories.

The line moved forward, and James took his wife's arm. They were next to enter.

"Congratulations on your nomination, Miss Burke," Mrs. Cagney said over her shoulder. "I'm afraid to ask. You won, didn't you?"

Billie shook her head.

Mrs. Cagney's shoulders dropped. "I'm so sorry," she said. "You were splendid in the film and have had such an incredible career. I laughed and laughed." She nodded at James. "He even tried cutting a melon with a wooden spoon."

James scoffed.

Billie shook her head. It had been such a stupid scene. As the Cagneys stepped away, into the ballroom, she moved to the door. An Academy secretary stood there with a clipboard. She was a petite young thing with bright red lipstick and curly brown hair. Billie straightened her skirt, fluffed her hair, turned to Patty, and whispered, "Get ready as we discussed."

She'd told William he could escort Patty, yet they should appear as friends. The two had been dating for a few weeks, and Billie was getting worried they were becoming serious before they'd thought through the possible result. The press would pick up on their coupling and pressure the two to discuss the relationship and its future, something they might not be ready to do. A loving appearance by the two would also lead to more media prying. To protect Patty and William's privacy, Billie told them not to hold hands, not to make loving glances, and when asked, to simply say, "We like and appreciate each other, but that is it for now." Every industry gossiper was in the room wanting to write the scoop headline "Flo Ziegfeld's Daughter Getting Married." All of them were more than willing to stretch the truth.

Inside the packed ballroom, Billie could see hundreds of people at round dinner tables with rose centerpieces, pewter starter plates, and crystal glassware. Billie smelled Old Spice.

"Ten seconds," the secretary whispered to Billie.

"My daughter and her friend, too," Billie said, pointing to them.

The secretary asked, "Table number?"

"Thirty-two," Patty said.

"It's in the back corner of the room," the secretary said, pointing into the distance to the right. "The two of you can go in through those doors at the end by your table. Miss Burke enters here."

Billie's heart sank. "They can't enter with me?"

"Sorry, no. Only the talent and their escorts."

"See you inside," Patty said as they moved away.

Maybe it was for the best, Billie thought. The cameras and eyes would have been on them if they entered here. This way, they'd go in unnoticed. Billie straightened her skirt. There was a camera at the far end of the entrance aisle, so she lifted her head high and turned on the biggest smile she could muster. The room's buzz lifted her heart.

"You'll turn right at the end," the secretary said.

Billie stepped off.

"Ladies and gentlemen," the announcer said. "Miss Billie Burke, MGM comedienne extraordinaire."

The applause roared as people stood in two waves from the aisle. Billie's skin tingled. What a relief to know she was still valued. As she approached the director Frank Capra, the emcee, she nodded.

"It's so good to see you, Miss Burke," Capra said.

She turned right and saw L. B.'s table up ahead. Seated with him were teen actors Mickey Rooney and Judy Garland, L. B.'s wife, and actor Spencer Tracy and his wife. Judy smiled big and waved, but L. B. didn't look at Billie, which made her freeze inside. She wanted a contract extension, so she told herself to stay calm.

"L. B.?" Billie said as she approached his table, smiling as naturally as possible, although she was trembling inside with a mix of anger and fear. "It's good to see you."

The microphone squealed. "Can somebody help me with this thing?" Frank Capra said.

L. B. gave Billie a big smile. "Miss Burke, I'm glad you're here. We need our talent in the room."

"Thank you," she said.

"Attention, please," Capra announced. "We need to get started."

Billie's shoulders tensed. She wanted to get a sense of whether or not the nomination would win her a seven-year renewal, the standard for most contracts.

"I need to talk to you," Billie said, trying not to be insistent.

"I'm sorry you didn't get the award," L. B. said. "We had two of our own up for it, and neither of you got it. It should have been a tie between you and Beulah Bondi. Damn shame." He shook his head.

"Everyone, please take your seats," Capra said. "We're going to begin."

"I need to talk to you," she said a little louder.

"Can it wait?" L. B. asked, gesturing to Capra. "We're about to begin."

She spoke louder over the noise. "It will only take a second."

L. B. turned away.

Resigned, she gently patted his arm and said, "We'll talk later."

* * *

"Welcome to the Eleventh Annual Academy Awards," Capra said from the podium.

Silver spoons clinked crystal glasses. Patty sat up straight, eyes on the microphone, her face in a polite, ladylike pose. William reached over and took her hand. Rule number one, already broken. "Ahem," Billie said.

William let go of Patty's hand. He and Patty turned to look at the rabbi now standing at the microphone.

"Before we eat, let's have a prayer," he said. "You are lucky that a rabbi is doing this because the Jewish prayer is shorter than the Christian version."

Everyone laughed.

"The majority of you in this room are Jewish, given that this is a very Jewish business."

Again, everyone laughed.

"I will do the Hebrew, then the English versions, to be sure you are all covered." He paused. "*Baruch ata Adonai Eloheinu melekh ha'olam shehakol niyah bidvaro.* Blessed are You, Lord our God, King of the universe, Who brings forth bread from the Earth."

"Amen," everyone said.

Frank Capra took the microphone and smiled. "Let's eat."

Conversation buzzed as white-jacketed servers balanced silver trays topped with individual dinner salads.

Billie leaned toward Patty. "Remember what we said, dear?"

"Yes, ma'am."

"I don't want people suspecting that you have a relationship with this young man."

Patty's eyes turned to slits. "But we *do* have a relationship."

Billie whispered, "You've seen each other twice before. That is not a relationship. It takes months, even years, to develop a relationship. And you know how the press is. Do you want them all over you? This time when you answer the door and they burst in, I won't rescue you."

Patty looked down. "We'll be more careful."

"Thank you."

"He follows my lead," Patty said, nodding toward William. "You don't have to worry about him. He's a bit nervous about being here with all of these stars. I explained to him that all the people in here are simply flawed human beings, but he's having trouble grasping it."

Billie scanned the room for people her daughter should meet—reporters, columnists, scenario writers—people who could give her a job and get her career moving once her apprenticeship ended.

"Patty," Billie said as she pointed across the room.

"Yes, Mother?" Patty poked a piece of romaine lettuce with her fork.

"The film critic for the *New York Telegraph* is two tables away." She motioned with her nose. "You should talk to him." Bob Harvey was in his mid-forties with slick-backed brown hair and a dark mustache.

"Why? He works in New York."

"You live in New York."

"I'm not going to stay there."

"I know, dear, but these people have connections everywhere. He might be able to open a door for you here. I am sure he'd appreciate the distraction. And because you're my daughter, he'll want to speak to you."

Patty looked in the man's direction.

A piano began to play "Begin the Beguine," but Billie could barely hear it over the noise of the crowd talking and eating.

"Maybe you could tell Mr. Harvey your plans for the future about wanting to write," Billie said. "Maybe he can help. He might even write an article about you and tell the world about your career dreams. If he does that, you'll get all kinds of offers."

"I think I'd like to enjoy the evening, and besides, I don't want to leave William alone with you."

"Why not?"

"You'll interrogate him."

Billie rolled her eyes. "That's not true."

"Oh, yes, it is."

Patty was right. Getting William by himself and talking to him had been Billie's plan. "I promise to leave him alone. We'll only talk about movie stars. How about that?"

"Remember, Mother. We agreed. I'm here to support you and to have fun. You have your rules, and I have mine."

"You could do a better job following mine," Billie said.

Patty snorted. "Maybe I'll talk to the man later." But Billie sensed she wouldn't.

Billie unfolded her dove-shaped napkin and spread it out on her lap. Dorothy appeared beside the table wearing a tan wool pantsuit with chocolate-colored buttons down the front. Billie looked toward L. B., but he was too busy eating to notice Dorothy's arrival, thankfully.

"I completely missed you on the way in," Billie told Dorothy.

"Aunt Dorothy," Patty said with a surprised look. The girl stood, and the two hugged.

"It was like an obstacle course to get to this table," Dorothy said as she pointed to the empty chair to Billie's right. "May I?"

Billie bit her lip and looked back at L. B.'s table. He wasn't looking. She nodded to Dorothy, who sat. She would make good use of Dorothy while she had the chance. Dorothy was entrepreneurial about her career, and Billie hoped Patty would listen to her, given that she wasn't listening to Billie.

"Dorothy, you're here for a reason. Tell Patty why you're here."

"John Ahlberg's film didn't win, so he gave me his ticket."

"Who is John Ahlberg?" Billie asked.

"Sound director for *Vivacious Lady*. The film was nominated for sound," Dorothy said.

"Oh. All right. But why did you accept the ticket? Why are you *really* here?"

"I'm onto you, Miss Billie Burke Ziegfeld," Dorothy said as she turned to Patty and folded her hands on the table. "I'm here to work the room for director jobs, plain and simple."

"But you have a job," Patty argued.

"Not after this film. Unlike your mother, who gets long-term contracts, my career has long been a film-by-film thing."

Billie sat back and let Dorothy and Patty talk, tuning it out and trying to relax. Patty idolized Dorothy, and this was a perfect chance for Patty to connect the dots. Billie glanced over at L. B., who was still working on his salad. L. B. lifted his head and looked in Billie's direction. She looked down quickly to avoid meeting his gaze.

Apparently, Dorothy had seen L. B. looking, too. "Yes, I know we can't be seen together," Dorothy said, rising.

"I just wanted to stop by and say hello." She scanned the table with a surprised look. "You have the emptiest table in the room."

Billie put her napkin to her lips and swallowed. "*Merrily* didn't win a thing," she said, her voice dropping. "Not a darn thing."

"I'm sorry. It was such a cute film." Dorothy touched Billie's shoulder, then stopped beside Patty. "I'm four rows over along the wall." She pointed. "Come by and see me." She nodded toward William. "Is this him?"

"Yes," Patty said, grinning. Billie could see that she was blushing beneath her face powder.

The boy stood and bowed. "I'm William Stephenson, ma'am."

Dorothy extended her hand to him so he could kiss it. He complied.

"This is my aunt Dorothy," Patty said to William. "I told you about her."

"The famous female film director?'

"That's the one," Patty said.

"Handsome," Dorothy said to Patty.

"He's from Virginia and studying to be an architect," Patty said. "He teaches dance to support himself right now."

"He looks like Clark Gable," Dorothy said. "Bring him along to my table when you come. Your mother will have plenty to do here tonight. She always does. Being here is work for her, too."

As Dorothy left, Billie felt a pinch of sadness. She'd love to have Dorothy sit with them. She felt lonely, with Patty focusing most of her attention on William. Billie couldn't remember the last time she had felt so lonely. She found herself wondering: Is this what life would be like once her daughter got married? And if she had no work, what then? At least Billie didn't feel lonely on the set or a stage. She squeezed her eyes shut as tears formed. She felt like crawling into a hole.

* * *

With dessert in front of her, the ceremony progressed. Billie's hands were under her thighs for self-control and to remind herself to leave the dessert alone. She'd chosen fresh fruit, but it arrived heaped with whipped cream. She knew she'd eat the entire thing if she took even one bite, so she shoved it far away.

She looked to L. B.'s table as studio mogul Harry Warner accepted an award. L. B.'s eyes faithfully faced the speaker and never glanced in her direction. After Harry, this whole thing would be over. She would need to get to L. B. quickly to check whether his mood had changed. Everyone would be after him, and she needed to be first.

The room applauded. Billie pushed up. L. B. stood. Billie lifted her skirt and hustled toward him through the crowded aisles, bumping into others also getting up. She accidentally knocked someone's mink to the floor, hesitated, picked it up, and apologized.

L. B. turned to leave the table.

Billie blurted out, "L. B., wait."

He gave her a smile that held a touch of a grimace.

She reached him, her chest pounding. "Can we talk now? I know you're busy, but it will only take a second."

His shoulders dropped. "Just for a minute."

The others at his table had already left. Billie had him all to herself. She folded her hands in front and squeezed them.

He pushed his glasses up his nose. "What do you want to talk about?"

"My contract. I assume that, well, considering the nomination, you must have reconsidered."

"Nothing's changed, Billie. What made you think so?"

She curled her toes in frustration. How thick could he be? "I was nominated in a major category. That should mean something."

"I knew about the nomination before I made the decision to let you go."

She threw her head back, shocked. "You knew, and you still did it?"

"That's what I said."

"That makes no sense."

"Keep your voice down," he said, patting her hands as if to soothe her. She yanked her hands away.

"I've explained all of this to you," he said. "There's nothing more to say. The newsreel didn't help your case."

"I did everything you asked. I stopped publicly socializing with Dorothy Arzner. I made a public appearance with Francis Strong. And on top of it, I was nominated for an Academy Award. Isn't all of that enough?"

"I warned you a long time ago, Billie," he said. "And even after all my warnings, the two of you were together here, tonight, before dinner."

He had seen? Billie stiffened. "She's my friend."

"You can have dinner with her at home or go for a country drive. I don't care. But you can't be seen in public together, not while you work for me. That woman is in trouble, and she'll pay for it."

Billie's jaw dropped. "What do you mean?"

"Nothing. I had to make cuts. I have too many of . . . your type. Now, if you'll excuse me."

She moved to block his exit. Security guards couldn't protect him here. "I have a right to live my life."

"You do, but not as an MGM employee."

"What if I'd won tonight?"

He scratched his chin. "I don't know what to do with you performers. Last year, it was scandal after scandal—affairs, public drunkenness, immoral behavior."

"I didn't do any of those things!" She wanted to yell, "Beatrice," to throw his hypocrisy back in his face, but she bit her lip to stop herself. Sure, he was a man, but why should that make it right? The urge to throw something at him, anything, washed over her. She eyed Mickey Rooney's fruit salad, the whipped cream long gone. He hadn't touched the fruit, and it would decorate L. B.'s face nicely.

"You name it, actors did it," L. B. said. "Audiences love reading about it, but they don't buy tickets afterward. The censors are sick of it, too. I can't even put a man and a woman on the screen in the same bedroom. And this economy is killing us. No, I'm not taking any chances. Nobody is."

She reached for the plate with her left hand, but her right hand stopped it. If she threw the plate at him, she'd spend the rest of her working years cleaning grammar school toilets. She put her arms behind her back and laced her fingers together.

Hedda Hopper walked up. Talk about something that checked actor behavior. Billie's mind felt fuzzy.

"It's good to see you again, Billie," Hedda said. "I'm sorry you didn't win. You were marvelous in that film."

Billie had trouble unfuzzing enough to offer a charming reply, so she just smiled and said, "Thank you."

Hedda turned to L. B. "L. B., thank you so much for all you did for tonight. I want to interview Spencer Tracy. May I?"

"Certainly. He's here, somewhere. I think he's on the dance floor with his wife. You can use this table. It's empty now."

L. B. and Hedda walked away. That was it. It was over that quickly and irrationally. Billie didn't matter to either of them. Her thoughts raced as three male singers crooned, "Whoopi-ty-aye-oh, rockin' to and fro, back in the saddle again." They were silly lyrics, and they made the entire room seem empty-headed and uncaring.

Patty and William were on the dance floor, but Billie was more than ready to go home. She struggled to get to them, squeezing past couples who didn't know how to dance, rocking back and forth like drunks, not even bothering to do a real dance step.

"I'm back in the saddle again," the singers in the band sang. It was some cowboy song, but they weren't even real cowboys. Cowboys don't wear suits, for God's sake. Everything was fake in this business. Nobody was trying anymore, except for Billie. She'd worked hard all these years, and here they were, happy-looking young people bouncing around like Kewpie dolls. Someday, what had happened to her would happen to them, too. They'd better wake up.

She reached her daughter and said, "I'm going home. You can stay. I'll get a taxi."

Patty stopped. "Why?"

Billie thought maybe she needed to be alone. Instead of trying to explain, she simply said, "If anyone asks where I am, just tell them ... well, I don't know." She looked down. "Just tell them I had somewhere else to go."

"No, Mother, we're coming with you."

Billie's eyes watered at her daughter's willingness to give up her own fun for her mother. It felt good to have that kind of support, especially in a room in which everyone seemed to care only about themselves.

* * *

When they arrived home, Billie was drained. Even opening the front door felt like a labor. She headed upstairs to get ready for bed and heard Patty follow her. As much as she wanted to be alone, she knew spending what energy she had left offering motherly wisdom was important.

"Dear," Billie said, "do you have a minute? Let's step into your room for a chat." She wanted to tell her daughter what had happened with L. B. If she had any hope of salvaging a career tonight, it would have to be her daughter's instead of her own.

They entered Patty's room and sat across from each other in padded armchairs. Billie crossed her legs. "I'm sorry about this evening," she said. "I know you and William were having fun, and I spoiled it for you."

"No, Mother, it was fine. We understood."

The word *we* sent chills up Billie's spine. "It wasn't losing the award that upset me. It was something else." She looked to the side, paused, then looked back at her daughter. "When I approached you, I'd just finished speaking with Mr. Mayer."

Patty nodded.

"He's decided not to renew my contract when it ends in a couple of months. He said there were too many of my type in the MGM talent pool. The studio is letting go of people because it has to cut expenses. Actually, all the studios are doing it."

Patty's eyes widened. "That's ridiculous."

Billie held up a finger. "With the economy the way it is and all the turmoil going on in Europe, fewer movie tickets are being sold. I thought Mr. Mayer would reconsider after I was nominated for the award, but I was wrong." She sat back and sighed. "I got upset and didn't want to appear upset in front of all those people."

"That is so unfair, especially after your career and all you've done for the studio."

"Well, I agree with you. But it is what it is. I didn't want you to worry. That's why I didn't tell you. But now, well, you should know."

"What are you going to do?"

"I'm fortunate that I built a long career, and I'm grateful to your grandmother for pushing me into it."

Patty sat back. "I think I know where this is going."

"Not entirely, you don't," Billie said. Damn, this girl was smart. "Anyway, because of all of that, I'll keep going. Things will be different. That's all. I have a few films to finish at MGM, and I hired a public relations consultant to help me. Other studios will hire me as an independent artist. Aunt Dorothy is helping me come up with some ideas. I'm sure everything will be fine," Billie said, still trying to convince herself.

Patty pinched her lips. "This may be bad timing, but I have to tell you: I'm not going back to New York."

Billie sat back and clenched her jaw. "You're right. It *is* bad timing. Why not?"

"Because you need me here."

That wasn't the correct answer. The correct answer was wanting to stay here to be with William, an answer Patty knew her mother wouldn't like.

"I love you, dear," Billie said, "but you need to finish your apprenticeship. You made a promise. They're counting on you."

"But it costs you money."

The girl had a point, yet Billie couldn't admit it. "Keeping you there costs no money, really, just food and transportation. And phone calls. But it's not like I'm making no money at all. We are not going to go broke. Things may be different now, but I'll still be working and earning money. Just in a different way."

"But—"

"I already paid for your return ticket to New York, and it isn't refundable. You only have a little more time left, and I'm still under contract with the studio through those months and beyond, so there is no reason to worry. I also have savings in the bank."

Patty opened her mouth to speak.

Billie held up a finger to stop her, then stood. "Not another word about it. You're going back."

Patty's face seemed resigned to her mother's command, which relieved Billie. After a few more days, the girl would return to New York; she would be all right and would finish this thing. Billie just had to get her on the plane.

Chapter Eighteen

Billie was back in the Emerald City on the *Oz* set the next day, standing on a silver gazebo refilming a scene. The Kansas girl, Cowardly Lion, Tin Man, and jumpy Scarecrow were with her. She touched the railing to keep herself from teetering over.

"Oh, good grief, cut!" Victor Fleming yelled, sounding about ready to punch a wall. He'd stopped the scene because Judy had missed a line. It was take twenty-two.

Judy dropped her head.

This was what it was like working with children. Billie bent over to relieve the strain on her back as she waited. It felt good to bend over. Besides, she had a tennis match with Dorothy after work and didn't want her muscles to kink up.

"Two minutes," called the second assistant director as workers scurried around, picking up stray feathers and fallen tree leaves.

Hopefully, the girl would get her lines right this time. She'd been taking acting lessons, but there was only so much a sixteen-year-old could do.

"Places," Victor said. "Take twenty-three. Action."

The cameras purred.

"Good-bye, Mr. Lion," the Kansas girl said, holding Toto in her arms.

The Lion dried his teary eyes.

"I know it isn't right," the girl continued, "but I will miss you. You have more courage inside you than you know."

"Aw shucks. I wouldn't have been able to muster any courage without you. That's for sure," the Lion said.

Billie's back tightened with a quick spasm. She hid a grimace and tried to breathe deeply into the pain. It didn't help.

The Scarecrow wiped a tear from his face with a straw-stuffed sleeve, the signal for Billie's next line.

"Are you ready now?" Glinda asked the girl with a smile and a tilt of her head. She kept her voice bright. Having had a child prepared her to work through any pain, unpleasant as it was.

"Yes, I'm ready," the girl said, nodding.

Glinda waved her wand, lifting her arm as best she could, hoping this wouldn't trigger a spasm. "Then close your eyes, click your heels together, and imagine home, your home," Billie said.

"Cut," Victor said as he bent over and put his hands on his knees. "We're finished, finally, I hope."

Sadness rippled through Billie. She was usually happy when she finished a film, but this was going to be her last major motion picture under this contract; it felt like an official ending.

She wanted some ruby slippers of her own.

* * *

Later that afternoon, Billie was on the court in a frilly white tennis outfit, the sun blinding her eyes like car headlights. Dorothy was winning, but Billie was working to turn it around. She shouldn't have scheduled a tennis match after work. She felt drained.

The score was five–five, and the game score was thirty–forty. It was Billie's turn to serve. She squeezed the racket, stretched on her toes, and begged her adrenaline to deliver an ace. Tennis was her game; golf was Dorothy's. Billie usually won their matches.

Dorothy stood across the clay court, crouched inside her baseline, twirling the racket in her hand.

Billie tossed the ball into the air, bent at the knees, dipped her racket behind her back, and stroked the ball. Bang, whoosh. It felt like a solid shot, but the ball clipped the net and landed in the service box.

She bristled. Dorothy tipped the brim of her straw hat like a gunslinger.

Billie shook her head and mumbled, "I'm not too old for this. I did it last week. I can do it again."

Dorothy tapped the ball back.

Billie returned to the baseline to serve again and adjusted her pleated skirt around her waist. She was determined to clear the net this time. She took a deep breath, hit the ball as hard as possible, and watched it whiz over the net and land on the "T" within the baseline. She smiled.

Dorothy lunged at the ball, her white skirt swinging. Her backhand missed.

Yes! I'm back, Billie thought. Everything would be okay from here. She could feel it.

"Deuce," she called out with a pep in her voice. She bounced the ball on the clay court once, twice, three times.

Dorothy moved farther back, bent over, and hit two practice swings. A chill ran through Billie. She'd never seen Dorothy so determined to win a match.

Billie bounced the ball a few more times, threw it in the air, jumped to hit it, and swung. Though the swing was smooth, Billie landed on her left ankle. It buckled. She winced, bent over, and took several short breaths.

Dorothy ran to the net and called, "Are you okay?"

"Yes," Billie forced out. Her chest pounded. Her ankle stung. "I'll walk it off."

She pushed herself up and gingerly took a test step. The ankle wasn't too bad—just a little stiff. She took another step and felt a dull pain. "No, no," she said to herself. This wasn't about age. Even children got sprains. She wasn't giving up. She limped to the net to retrieve the ball, assuring herself she'd be okay in a minute or two. Each step sent a spark of pain up her leg.

Dorothy put her racket over the net, scooped up the ball, and handed it to Billie. "Should we stop?"

"I'm fine. It's nothing. I birthed a child. I can handle this." She limped to her corner to serve. "Rabbits, rabbits, rabbits," she said aloud as she bounced the ball three times. But the ankle hurt too much and she couldn't focus. She couldn't do any more. It was time to stop.

* * *

They finally reached the café, chose a table by a bay window, and ordered iced teas.

Billie laid a napkin on a nearby chair and set her bad foot on it. The ankle was throbbing, but she was sure it would be fine by the time they left. It already felt better up on the seat.

Dorothy pointed to the ankle. "How is it?"

"It isn't a sprain," she said, trying to reassure herself. "It'll be fine. I just need to rest it."

Dorothy dropped two teaspoons of sugar into her iced tea and stirred. "Well, okay. Let me know if I need to take you to a hospital."

Billie brushed off the comment.

"You told me on the phone you had something to tell me," Dorothy said.

"Your news first," Billie said.

"You're the injured one. You get to go first."

She looked to the side. "L. B. told me something." She paused. "He said you were in some kind of trouble."

Dorothy threw her head back. "What did he mean by that?"

"That's all he said. He walked away, and I was too self-absorbed to ask."

Dorothy looked away and puffed. "I know what this is about. I didn't want to bother you with it. I was waiting until after the Academy Awards to tell you."

"So, there *is* something."

"Yes."

Billie folded her hands in her lap.

Dorothy took a deep breath. "RKO doesn't have a film for me after this one."

Billie closed her eyes and shook her head. "I'm sorry to hear that. It must be frustrating."

"It is."

"Well, it's probably just a lull before the next one. There's usually a gap at MGM between projects." Dorothy always landed on her feet. If work was light, she dug up more. She was also a lot younger than Billie.

"I sense something going on, some kind of setup," Dorothy said.

"What?" Billie gulped her tea.

"*Dance, Girl, Dance.*"

"What about it?"

"L. B. was right, and I had already smelled it. I was set up with an unrevivable film to sink me."

"Nonsense. RKO fired the last director and put you in to fix it because you were good. They wouldn't have done that if they didn't believe in you."

Dorothy scoffed. "There's nothing I can do to make the film better. Lucille Ball is saving it for us, but some others are struggling. It's a cute story, but the dialogue is sophomoric."

"Like some of my films."

"Worse," Dorothy said.

"That's hard to believe."

"Well, it's true."

"You could bring the talent out of a rhino," Billie said. "You did it with me."

"You're packed with talent. I didn't have to do a thing except to give you a chance to shed that silly air-headed stereotype you're forced to play. You have decades of training and experience that give you tremendous depth. All I had to do was unlock the door on it."

"Tell that to L. B.," Billie said.

"The cast is lovely, but some of them are struggling to grasp their roles. Louis Hayward, mostly, and Maureen O'Hara, too."

"I've heard of them…"

"They're relatively new actors," Dorothy said. "Louis comes from Broadway. Noël Coward trained him, so I expected more. He's handsome enough, but he pauses between lines and seems aloof. Maybe it's because Lucille is bold, but she's also talented. I'm not going to tone her down. Maureen has talent, and I've seen her work. There's a punch to her, but the character she's playing is meek. I think she's having trouble being meek."

Billie shoved her tea aside and adjusted her raised foot. The ankle was stiff, but it didn't hurt anymore. "I don't think it's a setup, dear."

"I'm not so sure."

"All right," Billie said. "Let's say it *is* true. You're an expert at coming back from the dead."

"As are you."

"It gets harder the older you get."

Dorothy smirked. A pause followed.

"What?" Billie said. "There's something else."

"It's not what you think. I hired an agent," Dorothy said.

Billie rolled her eyes. "I know where this is going." Dorothy had encouraged her to hire one a year ago, but she hated the idea. Film agents were a new thing, and most were drunks.

"Well, I'm glad for you, dear," Billie said, "but I'm not going to do it. I hired a public relations consultant, and that should be enough."

"Terrific. But he cannot get you jobs, and you need jobs."

"Hiring someone may work for you. You're tougher than I am, and it's different for directors. You don't have to be young or pretty. You just have to create a sellable film to generate a profit."

"Being a woman matters. Something I'm sure you know." Dorothy sat back and smiled. "The agent I hired was Minna Wallace."

Billie dropped her jaw. "A woman? You found a woman agent?"

"You think I would hire a man?"

"You would if he respected you. I didn't think women agents existed."

"She's like a glimmer of light and takes no prisoners." Dorothy shoved Minna's card across the table. "In case you change your mind."

Billie shoved it back. "I won't do it, even if she is a woman."

"You know Maggie Hamilton's story, don't you?"

"I know she's a single mother and recently divorced. I know she's from Cleveland, Ohio. I know she's a nice person and a gifted actress."

Dorothy sipped her tea. "She quit RKO in September, and now she's on her own."

"I knew she was independent."

"It's how she landed the *Oz* part. Her agent set it up." Dorothy paused and tapped the table. "Now, brace yourself."

Billie leaned forward. Her ankle complained. "For what?"

"She's making twice what you're earning for the same film."

"She's being paid by the film, and I am on salary. Of course she would earn more."

"That's not the point. She strings those bigger checks together and earns more than you earn. You could do the same."

"How do you know what she earns?"

"Pan Berman told me," Dorothy said. "He's having problems at RKO and thinks he's being pushed out, too. We were talking about career solutions."

Billie shook her head. "When will they learn? He's one of the most talented directors around."

"He and Maggie are friends."

"Maggie's young," Billie said.

"Is thirty-nine young?"

"To me, it is," Billie said.

Dorothy was forty-two.

"And she has a two-year-old son." Dorothy shook her head. "Talk about brave."

"We all like her on the set. She's as sweet and talented as they come, but I don't want to spend my time and energy searching for work at the end of an agent's chain. I need a steady income. I have Flo's creditors to pay. I can't take the risk."

"You have to do something. What's it going to be?"

Billie looked at her feet. Her ankle was stinging. "I don't know, really."

Dorothy shoved the card toward her.

"No," Billie said.

"Hear me out."

"Do I have a choice? It's not like I can run out of here on this ankle."

"I know this whole agent thing is new, but it's like a small rock tossed into a pond. It ripples out."

"I am not turning my career over to a flesh peddler," Billie said.

Dorothy leaned forward. "You heard about Miriam Hopkins?"

Billie had worked with Miriam on *Becky Sharp*. "Heard what?"

Dorothy leaned forward and pointed at Billie. "You know the deal she got?"

"All I know is she got hired."

"She got sixty thousand dollars for eight weeks and ten percent of the gross over eight hundred thousand."

Billie dropped her bad foot to the ground as if to stand. "Ouch," she said and then grabbed the table's edge. She moved her throbbing foot back up onto the chair. "Where did you learn that?"

Dorothy shrugged her shoulders and smirked. "I went to one of her parties."

Billie lifted an eyebrow. "Those parties are wild. You are not wild."

"True, but sometimes I have to do things I don't want to do to network."

At Miriam's parties, people danced naked on the tables and threw wine bottles at each other. "How did you get an invitation?"

"You're jealous."

"Hardly." Billie's idea of a fun night was reading the newspaper dressed in her robe.

Dorothy sat back with a proud face. "I met her on a loan-out. I wanted her for a film, and she asked me to a party at her house. Miriam said she found me exotic, like a rainforest plant." Dorothy batted her eyelashes.

"Next, you'll tell me she has an agent."

"Of course."

Billie earned less than forty thousand dollars a year, and she'd like to earn a lot more, but she wasn't convinced that an agent could help.

"It's the new way, Billie. The old way is dying. It's time for you to try the new route. It won't cost you anything to at least talk to a couple of agents. It will give you an idea of how they work. You can always say no."

Billie sighed. Dorothy had a point. Billie had nothing to lose except a little time. *Oz* was finished, and rehearsals for her next film weren't scheduled yet.

"Who represents Miriam?" Billie asked.

"Selznick-Jones. If you go that route, Myron Selznick is the one to talk to."

"I've heard of the agency. It's a big one."

Dorothy pushed Minna's card across the table. "This gives you two to can talk to. I don't have a phone number for Selznick, but you should be able to get it easily enough."

Billie picked up the card.

"I would try the Orsatti Agency, too. I've heard good things about them. I can get a number for them if you want. I know somebody who uses them."

Billie studied the card. It wouldn't cost anything to do this, and she supposed she could find the time to at least talk to an agent.

"All you have to do is go and listen," Dorothy said. "You don't have to sign anything."

Billie tapped the card in her hand, trying to convince herself to take a first step. Trying new things was easy when she was younger. For some reason, it felt harder these days.

Chapter Nineteen

Billie sat in reception at Rachel Johnson's office for her appointment regarding the endorsement. The office was cluttered with French neoclassical furniture and potted palms. The air smelled pungent, a mix of rotting apples and grease paint.

Mumbled voices came through the closed door across the room. One voice sounded a complaint, and Billie wasn't surprised. She'd learned a few things about this treatment since their first meeting that had confirmed her worst fears. Billie crossed her legs and felt stiffness in her bad ankle, which reminded her how the pain had almost controlled her these past few weeks.

A copy of *Movie Fan* sat on a nearby table. Her name was on the cover, along with an article announcing the film *Gone with the Wind*. Were they going to offer her a role, and she didn't know about it? She grabbed the magazine, turned to the article, and smiled. Fans had selected her as the second choice for the role of Aunt Pittypat Hamilton, a "plantation scatterbrain." Billie sat back, closed her eyes, and let out a relaxing breath. She still mattered.

The door across the room opened, and the awful smell got thicker. Billie put her hand over her nose and mouth and tried not to breathe. She wanted to vomit.

Rachel stepped out in a white doctor's coat and pulled down a mask. "Miss Burke," she said with a smile. Her teeth were perfectly shaped and straight. "Thanks for coming." Rachel closed the door behind her.

"You have a client in there?" Billie asked

"My assistant is taking care of her. You're probably wondering about the smell."

Billie nodded.

"You'll get used to it."

Billie shook her head. "I'm not sure about that."

"Please. Come into my office." Rachel pointed to a door to the right. Billie followed, sat, and straightened her skirt.

"I'm sure Lydia will be here in a minute." She folded her hands on the desk and lightly pumped them. "She stopped by the attorney's office to pick up the contract. Are you with us, Miss Burke?"

"Meaning?" Billie asked, though she already knew what Rachel meant. Billie stiffened her chin. She only wanted to give her answer once, so she'd wait for Lydia to arrive. "Perhaps you can answer some questions before she gets here?"

Rachel motioned for her to go ahead.

"After the chemical treatment, how long does it take for the skin to heal?" Billie asked.

"A shorter length of time than traditional treatments. You smelled the cider?"

"My parents are from Ohio. That didn't smell like cider."

"Well, it has apple in it, so I call it that."

Billie bit her lip. "How long does the application take?"

"Depends. An hour, sometimes longer."

Billie touched her cheek. "It must hurt when you go outside, the air brushing against raw skin."

"The skin does become more sensitive, but we ask people to bring a broad-brimmed hat and stay out of the sun for a while. It's seventy-two degrees today, and there's no breeze; the client won't feel the air at all. Most clients come in on Fridays, which gives them the weekend to recover."

Billie squeezed her purse.

"It's a light tingling. No burns," Rachel said. "Nothing like the old way."

One of Max Factor's assistants told her about an article published in *Petticoat Journal* a few months ago. She read it in the library. Some women had undergone the treatment and experienced skin damage.

"How long have you been in Los Angeles?" Billie asked, tapping her knees.

"A month. It's cold in the East, so I love it here, although I miss the greenery."

"And your assistant? Is she from the East, too?"

"Yes, I brought her with me. She's the best."

Billie wondered if the assistant was the one who had done the damage to the woman in New York. The treatment had discolored the clients' faces, leaving red splotches from burns and irritations. The splotches didn't go away.

Rachel leaned forward. "You have such clear and smooth skin, and this would take it up a step. You would simply glow. I have a slot available tomorrow morning." She opened her appointment book and picked up a pencil.

Before Billie could answer, the door to the office flew open, and Lydia rushed in. Billie's shoulders relaxed.

The pungent smell followed Lydia inside. Billie wondered how Rachel could stand being around that stench all the time.

Lydia closed the door and placed a folder on Rachel's desk. "I'm sorry I'm late. Street parking in Beverly Hills. Forget it!" She turned to Billie and took a deep breath. "Miss Burke, thanks for coming. I know how busy you are."

"We were about to talk business," Rachel said.

"I'm ready," Lydia said, sounding rushed, as she sat. "Now, where were you?"

"Mostly small talk so far," Rachel said.

"Do your assistants apply all of the treatments?" Billie asked Rachel.

"Yes. They are all trained professionals." Rachel sat back with a satisfied look. "The one finishing up is Greta. I sent her to Paris to learn the technique. She will be doing the treatments here."

"And you have other assistants in Chicago and New York?"

Rachel's smile dropped. "I have three in New York and two in Chicago. I hope to have three here, eventually. How did you know about my other assistants?"

"I read an article in *Petticoat Journal*, and called the reference in New York you suggested. She gave me the name of another woman to call."

"I was unaware of any article," Rachel said. "I'll have to read it."

"You had to fire an assistant in New York, correct?"

Rachel's hands on her desk were white-knuckled. "I did. Who gave you that information?"

"I can't say."

Lydia's eyebrows drew together. "You have to fire incompetent people. It shows commitment and professionalism."

Billie closed her eyes and reopened them, shaking her head. "I can't do the endorsement. I'm sorry."

"Why not?" Lydia said, sounding surprised.

"It turns out that the chemical mix caused facial burns for two New York City women," Billie said.

Rachel's nostrils flared, and she banged her fist on the desk. The leather pencil canister rattled. "I compensated those women with cash settlements."

Lydia raised her eyebrows and tilted her head.

"You can't compensate for lost husbands or incinerated careers with a cash payment," Billie said.

"I solved the problem with the treatment," Rachel said. "I fired the assistants who were responsible and I compensated the women. I assure you; the chemicals are safe if they're applied correctly."

Lydia's eyes turned flinty. "I've booked seven customers for you. How many received treatments?"

"Four, so far," Rachel said, sounding defensive.

Lydia closed her eyes and shook her head. "How many did you do?"

"One."

"Nobody complained?"

"That's correct," Rachel said. She turned to look at Billie, glaring.

Billie stiffened.

"I demand to know who told you all of this," Rachel said to Billie.

"I told you, I can't say." Billie's voice shook, but she held firm.

"If you knew about this, why did you even come today?" Lydia asked Billie. "You could have canceled and told me over the phone."

Billie turned to Lydia. "We don't know each other well," she said gently, carefully. "I thought you should hear this in person. I also wanted to give Rachel a chance to explain. You meant well, Lydia, but your career could be in danger if you continue to promote this. I wanted to protect myself, but I wanted to protect you, too."

Lydia put a finger to her lips. "I need to speak with Rachel. Will you excuse us?"

"Certainly." Billie rose, put her hand over her nose and mouth, and left the room. As she closed the door behind her, a shouting match erupted inside. Billie was angry, too, because she'd really wanted to do the endorsement. It would have been a huge boost for her reputation as a youthful-looking beauty, an image she'd worked hard to maintain. Perhaps Lydia would think of her again for another opportunity, but for now, Billie was back where she started.

* * *

Once home, Billie called Tom and explained what had happened, her tone stiff.

"That sounds horrible," he said. "I am so sorry."

"Before you connect a client to something like this," she said, "you should thoroughly research the situation."

"I am sorry, Miss Burke. I must admit that I don't know much about ladies' skincare."

Tom was too new, too male, and too inexperienced. Maybe he could do this job someday, but she couldn't take any more risks with him. He had almost damaged her reputation with Lydia, a woman who was as much a gossip columnist as a beauty expert. Working with him was too dangerous.

"At this point, we won't be working together anymore, Mr. O'Donough. You're dismissed."

"But—"

"Good day," she said as she hung up and closed her eyes. Firing Tom made her miss Flo. If her husband were around, he'd find a way to get her into the press favorably and keep her there. But alas, that wasn't an option. Perhaps she should listen to Dorothy and contact a couple of agents. At this point, she didn't know what else to do.

Chapter Twenty

Billie stood on the set of the B film *Bridal Suite*, next to her costar, Gene Lockhart. Gene played Cornelius, a dismissive fifty-something. Billie played his wife, Lillian—simple-minded, of course. All over the floor lay white cornflakes, to double as snow.

"In five," said the director, Wilhelm Thiele, in his Austrian accent.

Billie sighed in relief. She wanted a break and was glad she wasn't the cause of the delay. The ankle was stiff and sore, but it was holding up.

"A light is out," an assistant called.

Gene plopped onto a nearby wooden bench to wait out the break. "Aah," he said as he looked at Billie and patted the seat beside him.

She approached him, gingerly stepping over the crushed flakes, trying not to slip. She pulled off the fur coat she was wearing and sat next to him.

"This is a horrible film, isn't it?" Gene said, shaking his head. "I can't believe I agreed to do it."

"You have refusal rights, don't you?"

"Yes, but I had no idea. I should have been more careful. But here you are, a big star and widow of the famed Ziegfeld. You have refusal rights, too, don't you?"

She laughed and shook her head. "Unfortunately, not."

"Too bad. You should."

"Well, that isn't going to happen anytime soon."

"These contracts are something else, aren't they?"

"They sure are. May I ask you something?"

"Of course," Gene said.

She folded her hands on her lap. "Do you have an agent?"

He put his hands behind his head, making his potbelly stick out. "Why in the world would I want one of those?"

"I'm thinking of getting one," she said.

"I heard about your contract. I'm sorry."

Her heart sank. "Who told you?"

"You know how this place gossips."

She rolled her eyes. "I do. All too well."

He lowered his arms and crossed his legs at the knee. "All kidding aside, if I were in your shoes, I *would* consider getting an agent. You're an accomplished actress, but it's harder for ladies than for male actors. Even I can see that. I got a reasonable deal from MGM. They let me do many things outside the studio, and they don't even take a cut."

She bristled. MGM had always taken a cut from her loan-outs.

"I told them," he said, "'if you want me, that's the deal,' and after a lot of posturing, they said yes."

Gene did theater, movies, and playwriting. Work flowed to him. Work used to flow to her; maybe an agent would be able to remove the dam. "Do you know how much agents charge?"

He opened his mouth just as Wilhelm shouted, "Places!"

Gene pushed himself up. "Later."

She rose, put back on her coat, walked to her mark, and eyed the microphone, an intermediary between her and the audience. There were no microphones on the live stage. Live theater was so much more natural. She could play a whole other person for three hours and do it in her own way without all the stops, starts, and detailed direction required by film. And you didn't need microphones. You projected your voice in such a way that you were truly heard.

Robert Young, who played their son, Neil, joined them. He was a tall, dark-haired man who reminded Billie of a younger Flo. Next, the porter appeared, a woman dressed in a man's uniform. Billie pressed her lips together. At the young woman's age, Billie had once repaired a Model T while wearing overalls in a silent film. She had been paid more for that role than she'd earn now for an entire year. Much more.

The light atop the camera switched from red to green. The machine purred. Billie reviewed her lines inside her head.

"Action," Wilhelm said.

In a lilting voice, Billie, as Lillian, said, "Neil, darling, whomever are you talking to, dear?"

"The porter," Neil said, stepping off the train.

"The porter?" Lillian said. "That sounds like a girl's name." Billie cringed inside at the Dumb Dora line.

Neil walked over to his mother, and Lillian ripped into her son for arriving unmarried. He was supposed to have married a week ago, but he'd left the girl crying at the altar. She'd been one of a string of girls he'd dumped.

"Leave him alone," Cornelius snapped.

"I'll do nothing of the kind until he's married," she said.

"Cut," Wilhelm said. "Break for lunch."

Billie groaned in relief. How could she do a good job with such horrid dialogue? Wilhelm was doing his best, but he was probably wondering the same thing. That did it, Billie decided. She'd call Minna and see about hiring her as an agent. She limped a bit, but she kept pace.

As everyone hustled to the exit, Billie looked for Robert. Like many of the younger actors, he had an agent, and she wanted to know who it was, to expand her pool of people to talk to. Spotting him, she hurried to catch up, her breath quickening. She limped a bit, but she kept pace.

"Robert, wait!" she called. He didn't hear, so she cupped her hands around her mouth and tried again. "Robert!"

He stopped, turned, and smiled. "Miss Burke, I'm sorry. My mind was on my sandwich."

She tried to catch her breath. "I know you're in a hurry, but before you go, may I ask you something?"

"Certainly, but walk with me. I'm starving."

He opened the door, and the sun's rays pinched her eyes. Then it happened: Her left shoe hit the step's edge and slid off, forcing her left leg to the ground with full force. Her ankle folded, and she fell to the asphalt.

She screamed as a flash of pain seared through the nerves and muscles of her ankle. It was the same ankle she'd injured playing tennis.

Robert crouched at her side. "Miss Burke!"

She pushed up to a sitting position, her ankle throbbing.

"Are you okay?" Robert asked as he offered her a hand.

Her hands were scraped and a little sore. They weren't bleeding, just skinned a bit at the palms. She accepted Robert's hand and tried to hop up on her right leg, but she couldn't get her balance and dropped back down. She cringed. She must look like a goof, like a dizzy old woman.

"Are you all right?" Robert asked again.

"Yes," she said breathily, trying to control the pain.

"Can you stand? Can I help you?"

She shook her head.

"I can lift you and set you on the stoop, if you'd like."

She nodded. He put his hands under her armpits and lifted her. She was amazed at his strength and felt safe in his grasp. He helped her hobble to the wooden stoop as a knot formed in her stomach. She swallowed hard once, twice, three times, and leaned to the left to throw up, but nothing came out. She took deep breaths.

A small crowd had gathered, and she heard someone from behind and turned to see him. It was Andrew, one of Wilhelm's assistants, a short boy with rust-colored hair.

"I called a studio ambulance," Andrew said. "It should be here soon."

"Thank you," Robert said as he sat beside Billie and folded his hands in his lap.

All around them, the crowd shouted questions and advice, the words falling on top of one another, making everything a blur.

"Leave your shoe on."

"Can I get you anything, Miss Burke?"

"Are you okay?"

A studio ambulance backed into the space, its red lights flashing and rear doors opening. Two male attendants in white jackets jumped out and pulled out a stretcher. The device banged the ground as it wheels landed with a clang.

Billie feared she'd cause a delay on the set, making L. B. even angrier. She could do this. She tried to stand up and walk, but she felt a sharp pain when she put weight on the ankle. Tears filled her eyes. Injuries like this kept an actor off the set, slowing filming and driving up the cost of production. If costs rose because of her, it would reinforce L. B.'s belief that he'd made the right decision to get rid of her.

* * *

That evening, Billie was home in her favorite beige chair, her ankle wrapped and resting on the ottoman, the dogs resting nearby. The doctor had determined she was suffering a bad sprain. Dorothy sat in the far corner of the couch reading John Marquand's *Wickford Point* and guarding Billie like a pit bull.

Billie rustled the pages of the *Los Angeles Examiner* in her hands. The clock read 6:55 P.M. Where was Patty? She was out with William and was supposed to have been home by six.

"She'll be home soon," Dorothy said without looking up. "Quit fidgeting."

"I'm not fidgeting," Billie said. "How does a one-legged person fidget?"

Dorothy snorted, licked her finger, and turned the page. "And stop staring at the clock."

How did Dorothy know? She hadn't looked up from the book for half an hour. "It's dark out, and the picnic was hours ago."

"I am sure she's fine. She's a big girl now. Can I get you another cup of tea?"

"I'll get it," Billie said. She was tired of sitting. She needed to get back to work, so she might as well push herself now. She placed her hands on the chair's arms and maneuvered in her seat to find the correct position to push herself up.

Dorothy closed the book and stood. "Don't be stupid. I'll get it."

"No, I will. This is my house." Billie reached for her crutches, gritted her teeth, and held her breath. "I can do this."

"We've been through this, and it's getting old." Dorothy pointed at Billie. "Stay put, or I will tie you to the chair."

Billie tried to push up, but she felt weak. She sat back in defeat and closed her eyes. "Fine."

The grandfather clock in the foyer chimed seven o'clock as a pair of headlights beamed through the picture window. Billie recognized the engine's roar; it was her Buick, which Patty had borrowed. A wave of relief swept through her.

The door from the kitchen squeaked open, and Patty walked into the living room, unbuttoning her pink jacket, the dogs pawing at her legs. "Hello, Aunt Dorothy," she said.

"It's good to see you," Dorothy said, then pointed at Billie's feet.

Patty's eyes widened. "Good grief. What happened to you?"

Billie managed a smile. "Just a little spill, dear. It isn't a big deal."

"Just a little spill?" Dorothy said. "Hardly. She'll be on crutches for the next two weeks."

"What happened?" Patty said as she walked over to her mother. "Are you all right?"

"It will mend, dear. It's just a sprain."

"She came out of Studio Sixteen and tripped on a step," Dorothy told Patty. "The studio took her to Cedars Lebanon."

Patty put her hands on her hips. "To a hospital? My mother went to a hospital? Mother hates hospitals. She hates them so much, she sterilized a hotel room and gave birth to me there with Grandma's help."

Billie shook her head. "It was either that or the MGM infirmary," she said.

Dorothy continued: "It's a low-level sprain. She'll be back to her old self in a few weeks, or at least enough to function." Dorothy pointed to the crutches on the floor. "Warning: She's awkward on those. She lacks coordination."

"I am *in* the room," Billie said.

"The doctor said she needs to use a wheelchair if she leaves the house," Dorothy said.

"I've only used the crutches twice," Billie said, "and your aunt Dorothy wouldn't let me practice. I'll get better as I use them more."

"You need one full day of rest," Dorothy said.

Patty kissed her mother on the cheek, leaving a warm, lingering sensation on Billie's cheek. "Can I get you anything?" Patty asked.

"No. Just come and sit with us." Billie pushed herself up an inch with a groan. "Dorothy has been waiting on me like an Irish maid. It's driving me nuts."

"German maid. My family is German."

Patty sat on the couch. "I'm sorry I'm late. I suppose you want an explanation."

Billie nodded.

"We went out to dinner and lost track of time," Patty said.

"What happened to the picnic?" Billie said.

"They needed me at the *Courier*, and by the time I was done, it was too cold and dark to picnic in the park. I was helping to write a movie review." Before leaving for her internship in New York City, Patty had written for the *Courier*.

"You should have called," Billie said.

"I did, but nobody answered."

Billie sighed as she pointed to her ankle. "There's why. Sorry."

"Mother, I know I'm supposed to fly back to New York tomorrow, but given your condition, I think I should stay home a little longer."

Billie shook her head. "Absolutely not. I hired a nurse to help. It'll be fine. You need to get back to your job. They're expecting you."

"But—"

"No," Billie said, shaking her head again, more firmly this time. "No."

"But you can't even drive me to the airport with that ankle," Patty said.

"Aunt Dorothy volunteered to take us."

Patty's shoulders dropped.

"I'll drive you tomorrow," Dorothy said. "We have about an hour's drive to Glendale, depending on the traffic, so I'll be here by five in the morning."

"We'll be ready," Billie said.

"*You* are not going anywhere," Dorothy told Billie.

"I most certainly am." She pointed to the crutches. "I'll figure it out."

"Mother, I—"

"You're going back to New York, and that's that. I already paid for the ticket, and you know I don't like wasting money."

"The work is about as interesting as a rainy day on Long Island," Patty said, "and I miss working here, at the paper."

"You wrote a weekly movie column," Billie said. "What could you be missing?"

"I liked working there. I liked the people. I liked writing about film. All I do in New York is read scripts and fetch coffee."

"I understand that the kind of work you are doing now isn't very creative, but it will have a long-term benefit because the station is respected and it's in New York, which carries more weight automatically than Los Angeles. You will finish this assignment in New York, and the world will open up to you. Remember: Success comes to those who see things through to the end."

"What's that supposed to mean?"

"What do you think it means?" Billie asked.

"I see things through to the end," Patty said.

Billie lifted her right hand and counted off on her fingers. "Two years of college. Two months at MGM. Now only one month in New York?"

"Five weeks in New York."

"Fine. Five weeks."

"Two years was the end of university for me. I didn't need any more education. Was I supposed to go four, six, eight? Maybe return for a doctorate?" Patty snipped. "I didn't need any more than two to become a writer. As for MGM, I couldn't stand it any longer. Those lecherous men. And you agreed, remember?"

The girl was right about MGM, but for now, Billie wasn't giving in. A jolt of pain zipped through her ankle. She gasped and tensed.

Patty stood. "Mother, are you okay?"

"Yes, dear," Billie said. She took a deep breath. "I'm fine. And you're going to be on that plane tomorrow as promised, and you're going to finish that apprenticeship. You're lucky to have it. Most girls your age have nothing."

Patty looked away.

Dorothy motioned to Patty. "Come outside and see me to the car."

Patty put on her jacket.

Being a parent is a daily challenge full of surprises, and it doesn't end when the child becomes an adult. Patty needed to finish this apprenticeship, but Billie was also worried about pushing her too hard. She didn't want to alienate her daughter, and she wasn't sure where the boundary was between not enough and too much. It was like navigating a choppy sea without the stars in the sky. One false move and you hit a glacier.

* * *

The next morning, Billie was in the front seat of Dorothy's '37 Packard with Patty in the back. The wiper blades squealed on the windshield.

"Are you excited to go back to New York, just a little?" Dorothy asked Patty.

"Not really," Patty said.

Billie stared out the window. She was glad Patty was going back, but she didn't want the girl to return angry. "This rain is terrible, isn't it?" Billie said as she squeezed the armrest.

Silence.

"What are you going to do when you get there?" Dorothy asked.

"What do you mean?" Patty said, her tone strained.

"Get to New York, I mean. Go to a play, eat dinner with friends? Things like that."

"I'm not sure."

Dorothy pulled up to the airport's entrance. An attendant came to Dorothy's window, and she rolled it down. He was a tall, lithe young man with dark bushy eyebrows and a toothy smile. "Unload here?" he asked.

"Yes," Dorothy said. "By any chance, do you have a wheelchair available?" She pointed at Billie. "This is Miss Burke, and she recently sprained her ankle and can't walk the distance."

Billie smiled at him. She didn't want to appear as an invalid.

"Yes, ma'am. I'll get one," he said.

"The suitcases are in the trunk," Dorothy continued. "Be careful, though. They're heavy."

"I'm used to it," he said.

"Patty, dear, can you bring me those crutches?" Billie said.

"You're not supposed to be using them in the airport," Patty said.

"I'm just going to use them to steady myself as I get in and out of the car."

"I guess that's all right," Patty said. The wheelchair arrived, as Patty stepped out.

"Miss Burke," the redcoat said. "How do you want to handle this?"

"Hand me one of the crutches and guide me out with your hands. I don't know exactly how to do this. I'm learning as I go."

"Yes, ma'am." He held out his arms as she swung her legs around, put her right hand on the door frame, and used the crutch in her left as he helped her into the wheelchair. She put on her sunglasses and pulled the brim of her hat down over her face.

"I'll drive around and be back for you in twenty minutes, Billie," Dorothy said. "But first, I need to hug Patty good-bye."

Dorothy and Patty stepped out of the car, shared a long hug, and Dorothy said, "I'll miss you."

The attendant's hands reached for the wheelchair handles, but Patty said, "I'll drive her in. Thank you."

He tipped his hat. Patty gave him a tip, wheeled Billie inside, and claimed her ticket from the window. She looked at Billie's ankle.

"Mr. Mayer is a bad man," Patty said, seemingly out of nowhere.

"He's not, really," Billie said. "He saved us by giving me that seven-year contract. We could have been out on the street."

Patty sat in the chair next to Billie and crossed her arms over her chest. "Maybe, but I don't understand why he's doing this."

"The economy is bad, so he says he has to drop expenses."

"That's ridiculous. Jonah did an article on that for the paper."

"Who is Jonah?"

"Staff reporter," Patty said. "MGM is only losing money overseas, not here."

Billie shifted in the chair. "Who knows what's true? But what's done is done, and on we go."

Patty said nothing.

"Are you still angry with me because I'm sending you back to New York?"

"I'm sorry about being silent in the car. I was missing William."

"Oh."

"No, I'm not angry. Not anymore. Aunt Dorothy explained everything to me last night. I'm still not thrilled about going back, but I understand why you're pushing it, and you're right. I need to follow through and finish this. After that, I can decide what's next."

Billie felt her heavy energy lighten, and she smiled. She removed her sunglasses, pulled Patty toward her, and held her tight. "You'll miss William, and I will miss you. I understand what missing someone feels like."

"TWA Flight Twelve to New York, now boarding at Door Three," came an announcement over the loudspeakers.

Billie let go and kissed Patty on the cheek. Patty returned the kiss. "I'll call when I get there." Patty rose, waved, and walked to the door, turning twice to wave good-bye.

Billie watched her daughter go, then put her sunglasses on, sat back, and cried quietly.

Chapter Twenty-one

The next morning, Billie sat up in bed feeling stiff, sore, and pessimistic. Last night, she'd leaned the crutches against the lamp table, and thankfully, they were still there. The doctor had been right. She needed time to recover, and she was resigned to it. The doctor had said that if she pushed herself too hard, the injury might not fully heal, and that could pose long-term mobility problems. The possible impact of long-term problems trumped the inconvenience of waiting it out.

She pushed herself out of bed, grabbed the crutches, and wobbled to her office down the hall. The crutches hurt her armpits, and she was incredibly slow and unsteady. She dropped into the chair and called Wilhelm to let him know she would be out of commission for a while.

"I assumed as much," he said, "and I've already reworked the schedule. We'll film around you. Will you be available on Monday of next week?"

She sat back and puffed in relief. Filming around her wouldn't increase the cost, which was all L. B. cared about. "Yes, but I'll have to do some sitting."

"We can work around that, too."

"Thank you, Wilhelm."

"If you're not back by then, we'll cease filming until you return. These things happen."

She bit her lip. She had to get back on the set somehow before that happened. "Not to worry. I'll be there," she said. She'd figure it out somehow. She held onto a thread of hope that L. B. would either renew her contract or give her a temporary extension. If she angered him now, the chance of those options lessened.

When this was over, she'd buy Wilhelm a box of Cuban cigars to thank him.

A minute later, the phone rang. It was the agency supplying the private duty nurse she had hired.

"I'm sorry to tell you, but the nurse we assigned to you quit yesterday," the woman said. "She left to take a job at a hospital."

Billie gritted her teeth. After making the difficult decision to admit she needed help, now she had none. Dorothy had helped her get upstairs to her bedroom last night. Who would help her get back downstairs?

"I'm sorry, but there's a nursing shortage, and the demand for nurses is high," the woman said. "The pay is better at the hospitals."

"Do you have another?" Billie asked.

"Everyone we have is completely booked. I'm sorry. Perhaps you can call another agency?"

"I don't know any other agencies. The hospital gave me yours. Can you suggest one?"

"No, I'm sorry. Maybe you could call the hospital and ask."

To herself, Billie muttered, "Goddamn it." Her ankle was throbbing.

Just as Billie was about to hang up the phone, the woman said, "Wait! We just had a nurse come here from another agency."

Billie sat up straighter. "You mean you have someone you can send?"

"No. But I'm trying to remember the agency's name so you can contact them."

Billie sunk back into the chair.

"I'm trying to remember the name of it," the woman said. "It started with a B." She paused. "Beverly Nurses, that was it. I don't have their number, but you could call the operator."

"Thank you, dear. I'll give them a try."

Hanging up the phone, Billie realized she didn't want to make the call to Beverly Nurses only to be told, "Sorry, we don't have anyone." No, she would figure this out on her own. Besides, learning to manage on her own would prepare her for work next week, not to mention save money.

She grabbed her crutches, pushed herself up, and told herself, "I can do this!"

* * *

By Monday, she was back on the set, thank goodness, and sitting in a chair. She felt tired, but she'd successfully acted her way into appearing full of energy. L. B. would never know she had missed a week. They were filming a scene, and lunch was around the corner, which meant a much-needed break.

"In three," Wilhelm called out.

The set was a re-created paneled hallway in a manor house. With Billie on set were Gene and Virginia, who played Abby, their movie son's fiancée. It was her movie son's wedding day, but the son was missing.

"In one," Wilhelm said.

Billie patted her knees and told her ankle, "This is it. You can do it." She took Gene's arm and stood, putting the weight on her good ankle and her hand on his back. It worked, and a smile spread across her face. Her ankle was a little stiff and sore, but it held.

An assistant removed the chair, causing Billie to hold a fearful breath.

"Action," Wilhelm called.

The character Dr. Grauer entered, a balding man in his sixties with a stiff-upper-lip personality.

"Dr. Grauer," Abby said, slapping her hands on her cheeks. "He's done it again."

"What has he done?" asked Dr. Grauer.

"He jilted me. He was supposed to have been here three hours ago," Abby whined.

Billie's ankle twitched. She turned on mother-tears and dropped her forehead onto the shoulder of her movie husband Cornelius, played by Gene.

"It's Neil," Billie (as Lillian) whined. "He did it again."

"Did what again?" Cornelius said.

"He didn't get married again," Lillian said.

The son character posed a chronic problem of failing to show up for his own weddings. The scene went on for another couple of minutes, and then Wilhelm said, "Cut."

Could there be a more ridiculous script? Billie wondered. And to think she was pushing herself with her injured ankle for such a terrible film.

She needed to make some changes to her career. This script was horrible, and she didn't want to keep doing these B films. She was a much better actress than this.

Chapter Twenty-two

Billie stood leaning on her cane in front of a glass building that looked a bit like a spaceship, ready to enter for her appointment with Myron Selznick. Myron was one of the more successful movie agents in town and the brother of film director David Selznick. Graduating from crutches to a cane was a plus, but she worried it made her look like an old lady. She was determined to enter the building not showing any weakness, hoping to make the cane look like an accessory. In front of her was a tall, lanky porter in his twenties, holding the door open.

"Hello, Miss Burke. You are Miss Billie Burke, aren't you?"

"Yes, I am," she said, with a wide grin, happy that a boy his age knew who she was.

"What happened to you, ma'am?"

She flinched inside. "I missed a step at the studio. I was talking to someone, and I simply missed it. It's just a bad sprain."

"I am so sorry. I had a sprain once. Ouch. I know how it hurts." He removed his hat and bowed. "I love your films. I saw your silent films as a child. You are very funny."

"Thank you."

Her first step inside was onto a floor resembling a sheet of black ice. She'd have to be mindful. Fortunately, the cane had a rubber cap to avoid slippage. She hoped it would work here.

From behind a chrome-plated counter, a pencil-thin receptionist looked up at Billie. "May I help you?"

"I have an appointment with Mr. Selznick. I'm Miss Billie Burke."

"I thought I recognized your face from somewhere. It's a pleasure to meet you." She held up her right hand. "Stay right there. Let me get you some help." She pressed her lips together. "We don't have a wheelchair, but security can help you manage the floor."

"Oh, no, dear. Thank you, but I'm sure I'll be fine."

"Are you sure?"

She wasn't, but she said yes anyway.

The receptionist pressed an intercom button and spoke into the machine. "Mr. Selznick, Miss Burke is here."

The box squeaked back. Billie thought she heard a garbled "Send her in."

"Mr. Selznick's office is the first door on the right, not far." The girl pointed.

Billie made her way carefully down a hallway with frosted glass walls and straightened the jacket of her pea-green suit before knocking.

The door opened to a beaming Myron. He looked different from the last time she'd seen him at a party two years ago. His facial features were rounder, and he seemed ten years older. He'd also developed a paunch.

"Mrs. Ziegfeld," Myron said. "It's so good to see you again. Please come in." He paused. "What in the world happened to you?"

She turned on a determined look. "It's just a sprain. I'll be back to normal soon. I'm still on the set, so I'm fine."

"We could have rescheduled."

"No, no," she said. "As Shakespeare once said, 'Play out the play.'"

He unbuttoned his jacket and sat behind his desk. "I saw your departure from MGM in the paper. I'm glad you're here. I can't believe the fool let you go."

"Yes, well, that's two of us."

"You've come to the right place. Did you know we represent Olive Thomas?" He grinned with pride. Olive was a film actress and model. Early in her career, she had been a *Ziegfeld Follies* girl.

Billie stiffened. Flo had had an affair with Olive; it had been all over the national press, though she supposed Myron was too young to know about it. "Is that so?" she said. It was time to shift the subject. "Who else do you represent?"

"A stable of talent. You'll be impressed." He checked the names off on his fingers. "Constance Bennett, W. C. Fields, Paulette Goddard, Katharine Hepburn, Vivien Leigh, Carole Lombard, Laurence Olivier."

Billie nodded. "That's quite a roster." She meant it.

"It certainly is. Here's what I can do for you, Mrs. Ziegfeld."

"I go by Burke. Miss Billie Burke. Ziegfeld is my married name. I—"

"We'll get you three times your salary at MGM," he interrupted, pounding a fist on his desk.

She jumped in her seat, startled both by the sound of his fist and by his bold statement. "How?"

"I know the secret codes when it comes to mogul decisions. I even have the code to Mr. Mayer's mind."

That was one code Billie could admit she wished she had herself. "Mr. Selznick, I—"

"You can call me Myron."

"What do you mean by *code*?"

He tapped a finger on his forehead. "I know what makes his mind work."

She chuckled. "You must be the only one."

"I am."

"Can you give me an example?"

"I gave Joe Schenck a lot of grief at Twentieth Century. You know Joe?"

"Yes. He's a hard-boiled man." As chairman of the 20th Century Fox, Joe was one of the most powerful and influential people in the film business.

"When he wouldn't give my clients what I demanded, he threw me off the lot."

She missed a breath. Maybe this wasn't going to work out. If she was going to hire an agent, she wanted someone calmer, less aggressive.

"But I kept after him," he said, "and my clients got raises. Guess what happened two months later."

"What?"

"I was back on the lot. He'd violated an agreement, and my client insisted on negotiating through me."

"Lucky for the client."

Myron punched a fist into his palm. Billie flinched.

"Sometimes you have to be tough to get results," he said.

Though she did want results, she didn't want to alienate anybody. On the other hand, this was a tough business. She leaned in. "I've never hired an agent before. How would this work?"

"I'd become your official representative for film and radio. I'd negotiate your agreements and take ten percent of what you make."

She held in a smile. That was five percent less than she had expected. Dorothy had suggested the percentage might be higher.

"I'll get director refusal and story and cast approval."

"Script approval, too?"

"Certainly, and I'll promote you to death."

She felt a sigh of relief move through her, but fought to keep it inside. "What about live theater? I want to get back on the stage."

"I don't do live theater, but if you get a role, you'll owe me five percent of what you earn."

Her eyes widened. "But you wouldn't have done anything."

"Most agents charge five. Besides, I'm promoting you. It's the exposure you get that makes them want to hire you. So, in reality, I *did* do something."

"We may have to disagree on that one."

"We represent you totally. That's how it works, Mrs. Ziegfeld."

"Burke. Miss Billie Burke."

"I'll be knocking on a lot of doors for you, and that work incurs expenses—talent list ads in industry rags, salaries for my press staff. The list is endless. Our efforts are endless."

She pressed her lips together, wondering if the terms were worth it. Obviously, this man got results: He had a strong client list and a reputation for success. She needed work and the money; if he could deliver it, she would be willing to put up with his theatrics. The biggest issue with him was his abrasiveness.

"How is your relationship with L. B.?" she said. "I want roles at MGM when I can get them."

"We go way back, L. B. and me," he said. "I got Katharine Hepburn that swell deal over there."

"He can be combative, and he controls the industry."

He nodded. "I know. Believe me."

"How do you handle him?"

"He listens to me."

She shook her head. "How so?" Myron wasn't listening to her, that was for sure.

"Trust me."

It was the most famous line all men uttered, and the one you should never believe. "I have two more agents to interview," she said. "I'll let you know."

"Who?" he said with narrowed eyes.

She looked away. "Ernie Orsatti and—"

"Ernie and I go way back. He's great, but he doesn't have my zap and zing, or my client base."

She looked at him. "Well, I will think about it and let you know."

He stood. "Wonderful. You think about it."

She pushed herself up. Her ankle was stiff and sore, but she was determined to leave gracefully. "I appreciate your time."

He stood, walked around his desk, and handed her his card. "I want to represent you, Mrs. Ziegfeld."

On to the next agent.

* * *

Later in the week, Billie was second in line at the Brown Derby maître d' stand, holding herself up with the cane.

She was there to meet with Minna Wallace for dinner. She'd been looking forward to meeting this agent. As a woman, Minna would understand Billie's situation, Billie was sure. She also suspected Minna wouldn't insist on calling her "Mrs. Ziegfeld."

A waiter seated the couple in front of her as Billie hobbled forward.

"Miss Burke," said the maître d'. "What happened to you?"

She explained.

He shook his head, then said, "You're here to see Mrs. Wallace, yes. She's in the California Room. Can you follow me? Do you need assistance?"

"I may be a little slow, but I can make it on my own, thank you."

He tucked a menu under his arm. "I am slow myself, so we make a good match."

He led her past several seated tables to an open walnut door at the back of the room. Inside, a woman about ten years younger than Billie rose to greet her. The woman had a warm, open face and wore a sky-blue suit.

"Miss Burke," she called out, extending her hand.

Billie leaned on her cane with one hand and shook the woman's hand with the other.

"I'm Minna Wallace." She looked down at Billie's feet. "What in the world happened to you?"

"I lost a tennis match."

"And you took it out on yourself by breaking a foot?"

Billie laughed. "No, it's just a sprained ankle. I slipped off a step at the studio. It'll be fine in a few days." A few days was a bit of a reality dodge to let Minna know the she was ready and able to work. A couple of weeks had already passed, and the ankle was much better, but it still had a couple more weeks to go before it would be fully healed.

They sat, and launched into an easy conversation about children, the weather, and their hometowns. It felt comfortable.

The waiter entered, took their orders, and left.

Minna smiled. "Miss Burke," she said, unfolding a cloth napkin on her lap. "I'm a businesswoman, so I'll get to the point. What would you like to know about the Collier Agency?"

"Tell me whatever you think I should know," Billie replied. "I've never hired an agent before. My mother used to handle everything, then my husband, and then MGM."

"Mr. Ziegfeld made such a mark on American theater. You both did, and you still will."

"Yes, he did. He was quite a creative force."

"As are you, and we all know you were the force behind him."

"Well, not really, but thank you." Minna's comment was a polite exaggeration. Billie had been influential, but Flo had been quite a force of his own. Regardless, she didn't want to appear big-headed to Minna.

"I'll get to the point. You're a busy woman. Let me introduce what Collier does for its clients," she said, then speedily rattled off a list of things similar to Myron's list. It seemed to Billie almost as if Minna wanted to get it over with quickly.

"Sounds wonderful," Billie said. "Who do you represent?"

"Myrna Loy, Joan Blondell, Errol Flynn, Spring Byington, Greta Garbo, and Dorothy Arzner, whom you know. Young talent, mostly."

Billie bristled at the word *young*. "It was Dorothy who gave me your card."

"We're thrilled to represent her."

Minna's list contained A-list talent, which surprised Billie. Minna was a woman, and women usually got the leftovers in this business.

"Do you do theater?" Billie asked.

Minna sipped her water. "No. We're strictly film, and we don't take a cut if you do live stage work like the other agents do."

After the salads arrived, Minna said, "Miss Burke, may I ask you something?"

"Of course," Billie said, tossing the lettuce with her fork.

"Can you handle long days and weeks?"

That line was what Billie feared the most: being set aside for her age. People wrongfully believed that as soon as you passed forty years old, you declined physically, mentally, and artistically. Billie set down her fork and bit the inside of her cheek to maintain some self-control. "Certainly. I do it all the time. It's part of the job. I love the late hours.

It reminds me of the old days. I sleep well, and I take care of myself."

"It will be hard to find anything but radio if you aren't mobile," Minna said, nodding toward Billie's ankle. "I'm sure you understand."

"It's just a sprain, and it'll heal in a week or two. I'm still working on the set. Nothing has changed. I am in perfect health."

"What happened at MGM? Why aren't they keeping you?"

Billie squeezed her fork. She didn't want to tell Minna the truth, because she might see Billie as baggage she couldn't sell. A public same-sex relationship could kill a career quicker than aging, but she also didn't want to lie.

"It's the end of my contract. Studios are dumping talent left and right given the decline in European sales. L. B. says he has too many of my type in stock."

"MGM is in good shape, and you're a big name. The studio released more films last year than ever, and I don't see any signs of that slowing down."

Was Minna implying that being let go from MGM was Billie's fault?

"That was the reason L. B. gave, and I don't doubt it," Billie replied. "There are probably things going on behind the scenes that I don't know about, but I was just nominated for an Academy Award, so it has nothing to do with my work. All of my films make money, and my reviews are excellent. It's just the way L. B. is. I'm one of five he's letting go."

"Who are the others?"

"I don't know. Regardless, I see this as something positive, a message from heaven telling me it is time to go out on my own. Believe me when I say this: I would love to stay at MGM, but I'm also a realist, or I'm trying to become one, at least."

Minna shook her head. "Miss Burke, you are one of the greatest talents in the industry, but we are a small agency, and we don't take on clients whose careers might be waning."

"I thought it was your job to build careers."

"Yours is already built."

"I'm not finished. A career is never finished."

"We can only build if the career is buildable. We don't have the time to invest otherwise."

"I'm a perfect hire. Every studio needs mothers, aunts, and storekeepers. I'm fit and healthy. My doctor can tell you that. I eat well, do calisthenics every morning, and buy so much yak milk that I have become an honorary Tibetan." She chuckled.

Minna sat straight-faced and leaned forward. "I hope you don't mind me asking your age. I know it's inappropriate, but I need to know what I'm working with."

It was the cane and ankle, making people think she was older than she really was. Billie held back a snarl, and felt her pulse quicken. But she answered calmly, "I'm fifty-two."

She loved the two years MGM shaved off from her real age of fifty-four. It was what the public understood, so why tamper with it?

"You seem younger. I would have guessed you were in your mid-forties."

"I feel thirty-five inside. And I'm playing a thirty-five-year-old in *The Wizard of Oz*. Age is irrelevant if you can do the work, and I can do the work."

Minna sat back. "Mrs. Collier, the agency's owner, focuses on newer talent. She likes to develop it and hold onto the actor. Not that you're old, Miss Burke. You have another ten to fifteen years of work in you."

"More than that, I hope."

"Well, you know what I mean."

Billie wasn't ready for the glue pot. She wanted to bolt.

"You seem younger on the screen. Now, don't get me wrong. You look marvelous in person too, and you're famous. But, well, I hope you understand. I don't want to insult you."

Too late for that.

Minna patted Billie's wrist. Billie yanked away her arm. Minna looked taken aback, but then her face softened. "You are such a talented, big star, and lovely person, but mid-forties is as high as Mrs. Collier will go," she said.

"Then why did you agree to meet with me?" Billie asked.

"We sometimes make an exception."

"You mentioned Spring Byington," Billie said. "She's my age."

"She's a personal friend of Mrs. Collier. They met before she opened the agency. You told me on the phone you were also talking to Mr. Orsatti and Mr. Selznick?"

"Mr. Selznick wants to sign me, but I haven't decided. I see Mr. Orsatti tomorrow," Billie said.

"They're both go-getters. If Mr. Selznick wants to sign you, that's great. He gets results. I know Mr. Orsatti very little. Let me know where you end up."

Billie knew she would do no such thing.

* * *

Two days later, she entered Ernie Orsatti's office to smiles and someone her age.

"Hello, Miss Burke. I'm Mrs. Morgenstein," the receptionist said. "I've seen all your movies and loved them—especially *Peggy*, where you fixed that car wearing overalls. Women don't do that. I can't fix a thing except maybe a broken pie crust."

"We're even, then," Billie said, "because I cannot bake a pie. I'm not the world's greatest cook."

Mrs. Morgenstein slapped her hands to her cheeks. "Oh, my. Since you're such a big star, I suppose people cook for you."

"No. I manage on my own somehow," Billie said.

"Well, it must be working because you look beautiful."

"Thank you."

"Have a seat. Mr. Orsatti will be with you shortly."

Taking a seat, Billie studied the space: beige walls, frosted-glass doors, Waterfall-style furniture. Framed posters of baseball players hung on the walls, with "Cardinals" printed on the jerseys. Did ballplayers have agents, too? Did everyone have agents? Such a new, strange world.

Mr. Orsatti's door flew open. He was a tall man—maybe six feet—in his mid-thirties with broad shoulders and a thick neck. He wore a crisp white shirt and an apricot-colored tie in a way that made him look like he'd prefer to be in jeans and a chambray shirt. He spread his arms across the doorjamb as if to hold it up.

"Miss Billie Burke, is that you?" he bellowed.

She squeezed the chair's arms. His gestures were fast, strong, intentional, and forceful. Yet there was a sweetness to him that made her smile. She could see the little boy in him.

"Yes, I am Miss Burke," she said, reaching for her cane.

"My goodness," he said. "What happened to you?"

Her shoulders tightened. The question brought her back to her meeting with Minna. "Oh, nothing. Just a sprain. Missed a step. I'll be fine in a couple of weeks. It's a pleasure to meet you."

She followed him into his office and took a seat.

Ernie dropped into a swivel chair. "Miss Burke, I love your films. Especially *Topper*. Very funny."

Billie sat up straight and clutched her purse. "Thank you. The series is fun to make."

"More to come?"

"Not that I know of."

He slapped his palms together and rubbed his hands. "Maybe I can get you a few more."

She smiled.

"I'm glad you're here." He pointed at her. "You know, we have Buster Keaton now. Signed him the other day."

"He's such a talented comedian." Buster was king of the silents, but hadn't made the transition to talkies. There were many actors like him. Billie thanked the heavens she had managed the transition without a hitch. Her stage training and experience—things Buster didn't have—had sustained her. Her shoulders relaxed. If Orsatti could place Buster, there was hope for her yet.

"I don't want to waste your time, so I'll get to the point." He pushed a sheet of paper toward her. "I'm going to be honest with you, Miss Burke. Depending on your wants, we will push for everything on this list."

She picked up the paper and read: director approval, project choice, refusal options. In all, there were ten bulleted items.

"No studio will give you everything," he said. "But you have to ask for more than you can get and settle in the middle."

"That makes sense," she said.

"You're an established artist, which makes my job easier. You're a brand—a household name. But everything depends on how you see yourself going into the future. May I ask you a question?"

She nodded.

"What would your ideal work-life be? Where do you want to go from here?"

She tapped a finger to her lips. "I'd like to be a leading lady on Broadway again."

"What else?"

"If you can make that magic happen, I'll sign the contract today."

"We don't do theater. We're film, radio, and television. But we would be supportive of stage work."

"Do you take a cut?"

"No. We don't expect payment if we don't put you there ourselves."

She nodded. Thank goodness he didn't help himself to that trough uninvited.

"What else do you want?" he said.

"For starters, I want a thousand dollars per week, minimum."

He pointed at her. "You should be earning that now."

"I'm getting seven hundred sixty-seven dollars."

"I'll get you more than that."

"I love radio, and I'd like more challenging film roles with better scripts. I'm a trained dramatic actress. I don't mind the occasional flibbertigibbet. They're fun every once in a while, but that's it."

"We can do that. We include television in our contracts."

"You're kidding. I've heard of television, but—"

"No, I mean it. You transitioned from stage to radio and silent films to talkies. Television is the next transition."

"There is no television." She'd read about it in the paper, but it seemed to be decades into the future.

"Actually, they have it in New York and London. It'll be here in Los Angeles sooner than you think. It's like radio, in a way. People won't have to leave their parlors to go to the movie palace."

"Mr. Orsatti."

"Call me Ernie."

"Ernie. What can you get for me now? You mentioned Buster Keaton. If you can get him a contract, you're working miracles. Who else is on your client list?"

"Sonja Henie. And we just signed Judy Garland."

"Oh, thank goodness." She put her hands in a prayer position. "She needs it. The studio runs her life, and her mother is no help."

"So, what do you say? Can we sign you?" He reached into his desk, pulled a file, and set it on the blotter. "I have the contract right here." He patted it twice.

She paused to consider her options. Minna was out of the picture. Myron? Ernie? They each had strengths and weaknesses. She knew Myron could get results, but he was erratic. Ernie was up and coming, but this business was new to him. She preferred someone with experience. Of course, agenting itself was new; perhaps her expectation was unrealistic.

"I need to think about it," she said.

"Well, let me know," he said. "Should I check back with you in a week?"

"No. I'll call you."

Heading home, she made her decision: She would hire an agent as a test, just as she'd done with Tom. A month? Two months? Three months? She wasn't sure for how long, but she would at least try it.

Chapter Twenty-three

Later that night, Billie was home and chatting with Patty on their weekly call. Patty sounded better about the apprenticeship than the last time they'd spoken, but Billie was keeping her fingers crossed, still praying that things would work out.

"How's your ankle?" Patty asked.

"Healing. I've graduated to a cane. What types of things are you working on, dear?"

Patty paused. "You won't believe this."

"Try me."

"Sports," Patty said, with a groan. "Mr. Ellison has me working on sports."

Billie belly-laughed. The girl was like her father, which meant she had no interest at all in athletics. Billie was the family athlete.

Patty continued, sounding excited. "The Baseball Hall of Fame is opening in Cooperstown, and I'm helping to cover it."

"That's wonderful, dear. I'm glad things are working out." Billie sat back and relaxed. Finally, the apprenticeship seemed to be working.

"And I finally got into Yankee Stadium. Mr. Ellison gave me a tour."

"Your daddy tossed around the idea of putting the *Follies* in there. You didn't know that."

"I can't imagine it. It's so big. Daddy would have had trouble filling it."

"Perhaps. He certainly thought otherwise. What else are you working on?"

Patty paused again, so Billie filled the silence herself and said, "Speaking of baseball, I met a famous player today."

"Who?"

"Ernie Orsatti. He played for the St. Louis Cardinals and has a World Series ring."

"Where did you meet him?"

"At his office. He's a movie talent agent now. I was thinking of hiring him."

"That doesn't sound like you. You hate agents almost as much as hospitals."

"It's time to try something new. Money is money, and God knows I could use it. Besides, agents are getting the job done. It's like having a private army, except they only get paid when they win."

"So, are you going to hire Mr. Orsatti?" Patty asked.

"I'm trying to decide between him and another agent." She paused. "I have an idea."

"Mother, I know that sound. The answer is no, whatever it is."

"Agents represent film scenario writers. When you get back, you should make appointments with them. Your aunt Dorothy has an agent."

"She doesn't need one."

"She thinks she does."

"I'm not interested in that kind of writing."

"They do radio."

Patty sighed audibly. "If you bring it up again, I'll hang up."

Billie squeezed the phone cord. "I know you had a bad experience at MGM, but perhaps—"

"One, two, three, four, five—"

"All right, all right," Billie said, winding the phone cord around her wrist. She had to be careful not to push it too hard, because Patty would push back. "But you sound like you are enjoying your work."

"Six, seven, eight . . ."

* * *

Two nights later, Billie was in the kitchen in her robe, sipping tea and reading the *Los Angeles Examiner* when the phone rang, startling her. It was Myron Selznick.

"Got ya something," he blurted out before she could even say hello.

"Already?"

"Of course."

She tingled all over. She'd hired him just yesterday, deciding to put up with his pushiness, at least for a trial period. If he insulted someone, she'd apologize for him. After all, work was work, and she was sure he could get it for her.

"I got you a role in one of my brother's films," he said. Director David Selznick was his brother, which was another reason for hiring him.

"*Gone with the Wind?*" She giggled, feeling giddy. "What am I? One of the horses?"

"No, not *Gone with the Wind*. The film's title—at least for today—is *Come Friday*, and he's distributing it through United Artists. You'll play a funny lady named Aunt Abby."

"How funny?" she said through gritted teeth. Yet another brain-dead character.

"It's not your usual bubbly, nutty character, but still funny. That's what my brother said. You'd be great, and he wants you. You have perfect comedic timing."

"I thought I made it clear: No more roles like that."

"We'll get you better parts, but you're still a lead in the film and in the first five credits. It'll take a while to establish you as a freelancer. We've got to get you out there, get the jobs, show you mean it. After that, work will race in like lead horses to the finish line."

She rubbed her forehead. Maybe he was right. The film was work, and it had come overnight. It was a start.

"Mrs. Ziegfeld, you still with me?"

She'd given up trying to get him to call her by the right name. He wasn't listening. "How about the money?"

"Eight weeks minimum, nine hundred per week, eleven hundred per week after the eighth week."

She pushed up from the chair and paced. That was a solid salary, and a six-week guarantee, not eight, was the norm. Films were like construction projects: They almost always ran over.

"I asked for twelve hundred," Myron said. "But nine hundred was as high as he'd go. We'll get higher salaries as we go along. Keep in mind that filming starts after your MGM contract expires. We won't have to worry about L. B."

"Thank goodness for that," she said.

"And one more thing. You're going to like this one."

"Did you get me a theater role?"

"I spoke with L. B."

She threw her back against the chair and closed her eyes. Her jaw stiffened. "You called him?"

"He wants you for another film. He called me. He must have found out I'm representing you. Maybe he's worried about losing you."

"He fired me, remember?"

"It was a good conversation. I'm meeting with him tomorrow at two to discuss details."

"I'm filming. I can't get out."

"It'll be just him and me."

"No, I have to be there." She couldn't let Myron go alone. He was excessive, and she wanted to be there to keep things calm. Once L. B. got stirred, he stayed stirred.

"You can't be there," Myron said, his voice stern. "That's how it works."

"If it involves him, I have to be there. I'm still under contract with MGM."

"I know what I'm doing, Mrs. Ziegfeld. Trust me."

"It's Miss Burke," she snapped. "Why wouldn't you want me there?"

"For the same reason attorneys want their clients silent in the courtroom. They don't want them opening their mouths and ruining things. This is a game, Mrs. Ziegfeld. That's all it is."

She squeezed the phone. She didn't want someone negotiating her work without her there. What if he negotiated something she didn't want? Would she be stuck with it?

"You need to trust me to do my job."

She tried to remind herself that she'd hired him because he got results. Still, she couldn't help feeling unsettled. She wasn't sure she could trust him, yet she knew she had to try. "What are you going to discuss?"

"Your compensation for the film, how many weeks, things like that. It's what agents do. We negotiate terms. You and L. B. go way back, and he can read your every flinch. He'll try to provoke you to take less, so you absolutely need to be somewhere else at two o'clock tomorrow, anywhere but in that meeting."

His reasoning made sense, and she relaxed. "I'm on the set until four and should be home by quarter after five. Call me at home, no matter what happens."

Chapter Twenty-four

The next day, after filming, Billie hobbled into her dressing room, leaning heavily on the cane. Healing isn't a straight line, she had learned. One day, she could get around with only a little pain. Other days, sharp spikes ran through her ankle, and she felt exhausted at day's end. Today was shaping up to be one of the bad days. She saw a note in her mailbox. It was from The Mount.

Billie entered the dressing room, dropped onto her pink cushy chair, counted to ten, and opened it.

"Call me," it read. "Mr. Mayer would like to see you."

"Oh, good grief," she said, dropping her chin. "When will this end?" After the last time they spoke, she dreaded even bumping into L. B. on the lot. She picked up the receiver and dialed.

"Can you come now?" The Mount said. Her voice sounded urgent.

Billie leaned back and closed her eyes. Was she a good enough actress to hide her feelings and her injury? She looked like an eighty-year-old woman with this cane. Walking in looking like that wouldn't help.

"I'm on my way," Billie said.

She picked up her purse, hobbled outside, and hailed an electric cart, all the while wondering what L. B. wanted. He'd met with Myron earlier, and she had a sinking feeling that the meeting hadn't gone well. She squeezed the life out of her purse.

When she arrived at the building, she pulled out a smile, steadied herself, and entered without much wobbling. Her ankle hurt, but she breathed through the pain. She couldn't do this without the cane, so she'd have to make the best of it.

The Mount waved her into L. B.'s office. He sat behind his desk with a scowl, and said nothing by way of greeting as she took a seat.

"You hired an agent," he said, his jaw tight.

She felt herself relax. If this was the issue, she felt a sense of pride for having some power over him. It gave her a sense of control. "Yes," she said, nodding. "Everyone's doing it these days. You're letting me go, and I have to find work."

"You still work for me. You can't do it."

"Others have agents, and they still work for you. Why not me? It doesn't affect our agreement. He's only lining things up for me for after my contract ends. I can't wait until I'm unemployed to find work."

"I don't like the agent you chose."

She held back a smirk. If L. B. didn't like Myron, then she knew Myron must be good, maybe even better than she thought.

"He has a film for you with his brother?" he said.

She nodded.

"I have another film planned for you, giving you another three weeks. Your contract says I can extend it as I wish. You can't do the other film, because you will still be under contract with me."

"You should have said something earlier," Billie said.

"I don't have to tell you. The contract says I can do it, and I will."

"Too late, I guess," Billie said. "I have this other film to do now. I've already committed. You should have told me."

"Your agent also wants a higher salary for the film I'm adding, and I told him no. You will be paid according to your regular contract rate. He wasn't happy about it."

She folded her hands in her lap, and her ankle suddenly felt better. So *that* was why L. B. was really mad.

"He shouted and told me what he thought of me," L. B. said. He shoved his glasses up his nose and grunted.

Billie felt a little giddy inside. She loved that someone had shouted at L. B. It was a dream fulfilled. "Why don't you find someone else for the role?" she said.

"I don't have anyone else."

"You said I was an extra in my category, which was why you fired me."

"I can do whatever I want as long as you work for me."

She bristled. "I will speak with Myron to sort this out."

"Be my guest, but Myron is banned from the lot after he shouted at me about another client last week. Nobody shouts at me. Nobody," he said, jabbing a finger at her. "After this last film, you're through here forever. You're through everywhere." He juggled papers on his desk. "Now leave. I have work to do."

Billie felt a bit dazed. If L. B. actually did what he was threatening, her career would be finished. She had to do something. She grabbed her cane, pushed up, and wobbled out at a surprisingly fast pace.

* * *

When she got home, she called Myron's office. The receiver shook in her hand: seventh ring, eighth ring. The secretary picked up on the ninth.

"He's in a meeting," the secretary said.

Billie's jaw stiffened. "Get him on the phone, please."

"I can't."

"If you don't, he will lose me as a client."

"Very well."

Billie waited and waited.

"Mrs. Ziegfeld," Myron said, cheerily. "Actually, my phone meeting just ended. I'm glad you called. I—"

"L. B. called me into his office," she said, her voice shaking.

"Don't worry. I'll work it out. Agents get thrown out all the time. It's part of the negotiation process. Unless you're tough, they walk all over you."

"I do not like doing business through fighting."

"Then you'll never make it, Mrs. Ziegfeld."

"It's Miss Billie Burke! And you're fired."

Chapter Twenty-five

Billie had tried to sleep, but tossed in bed for hours. When the alarm finally went off, she groaned as she pulled herself out of bed. She didn't have to be on the set, but she had fan mail to answer and a decision to make about what to do. She didn't want to be controlled by L. B. She wanted out. The past seven years under contract with MGM had provided security, but she deserved better, given her experience and history. She wasn't anybody's slave.

So, what next?

She picked up the cane and hobbled to her office, where she picked up Ernie's business card and drummed it against her hand, mulling the pros and cons. He was new to the business, but he knew L. B. and seemed calmer than Myron. She did have a few conditions, however.

"It's great to hear from you," Ernie's voice beamed into her ear when she called.

"I'm considering hiring you, but I have some conditions," she said.

"Shoot 'em at me."

"You must deal peacefully with everyone in the industry, especially L. B. Mayer. You can be tough, but you can't be argumentative."

"No problem."

"I am in control."

"Absolutely."

"I can cancel our agreement at any time."

"That's standard."

She took a deep breath. "Then let's give it a try." She sat back, feeling relief wash over her.

"Don't worry about L. B.," Ernie said. "He and I are friends, and I don't yell at people. You can terminate the agreement at any time, with or without cause. I can deliver the contract to your MGM bungalow."

"No, drop it off at the Motion Picture Relief Fund. They'll review it for me." The Relief Fund was a nonprofit group of barristers. They didn't charge fees to actors.

"Will do, Miss Burke. Glad to have you on board. You won't regret it."

She smiled. This could work.

* * *

The next day, she was in her dressing room when the phone rang.

"Excellent news," Ernie said in a peppy voice. Times had changed.

"Already?"

"You're going to like this."

She sat on the chaise and leaned back. "Let me guess," she said. "A lifetime contract at Paramount at two thousand a week?" She certainly deserved it, but she meant it as a half-joke. She assumed she'd never such a thing.

"Maybe not that grand." He paused. "I talked to L. B. today."

"Oh, God," Billie said. She closed her eyes. If this agent failed, there was no one left on her list. She'd have to find some more. Who would she ask?

"I'm not Selznick, so don't worry. L. B. and I settle our differences without shouting at each other. I can clean up Selznick's mess."

She opened her eyes and bunched the phone cord in her hand. "How are you going to do that?"

"I'm going to rebuild the bridge first. He knows I represent you, and he's agreed to talk to me about that extra movie."

"He's not mad that I hired another agent?"

"No," he said. "I'd like to get you that extra film at MGM, but as a freelancer with a higher rate. If I can do that, will you consider it?"

She stopped twisting the cord. "Yes, but good luck."

"Good luck to both of us. You're coming with me."

Her pulse raced. Her shoulders tensed. "I need to go. I understand that. But facing that man is stressful after everything that's happened."

"It's fine if you'd rather not go, Miss Burke. I just wanted to make sure you felt you had control. It might actually be smoother without you there. Nothing personal. It's just often easier without the actress in the room. I'm asking for a thousand a week, with twelve hundred for weeks beyond six. How does that sound?"

That was a switch. "Better," she said with an ounce of skepticism.

"And I have some more news you'll like," Ernie said.

"There cannot be enough of that."

"I may have a film for you at another studio."

Billie's shoulders relaxed, and a grin spread across her face. If she got one film at another studio, they could sign her for more, or even for a long-term contract.

"It's a Walter Wanger picture," he said.

She shook her head. "He is at Columbia. I'm not working for them." Columbia's pictures were among the worst in the business, a factory of B films. It was bad enough she was in MGM B films. But MGM was an A-level studio, so an occasional B film at MGM didn't hurt her.

"They're on their way up," he said.

She scoffed.

"Besides, United Artists is distributing it," Ernie said, "and you know its reputation. It's careful about everything."

She sat and crossed her legs. "Okay, well, maybe if UA is involved. Who's the director?"

"Tay Garnett."

She smiled. She'd never met Tay, nor seen his films, but she'd heard he'd done miracles with Clark Gable and Jean Harlow for *China Seas*.

"*Eternally Yours* is the working title," Ernie said. "You'd play a funny woman named Aunt Clair. But—"

Billie sighed. "Funny in what way?" she said, fighting not to grimace.

"She's funny, not crazy. It's a comedy, but not slapstick. I told him your concern, and he said it was smart and funny."

"It had better be. How much will they pay?"

"It's a six-week guarantee at twelve hundred per week, then thirteen hundred per week after six weeks."

Her jaw dropped. It was more than she was earning now. This agent thing was working. "Yes, yes. You have my blessing."

"I have to get it past L. B. first."

She closed her eyes. She wished L. B. didn't have to be involved. He controlled a lot of the industry outside of MGM, and he could be unpredictable.

"But I will," Ernie said when she didn't reply. "The Columbia picture will be after the extra weeks at MGM, but I want to know L. B.'s plans down the road. I'm doing it as a courtesy. He always appreciates that."

"Thank you," she said. She couldn't help feeling relieved she had hired Ernie. It all seemed to be working out.

"And one more thing," he said.

"What?"

"Television."

"There is no television."

"It's up and coming."

"But I need work now."

"And we're getting it. But we need to plan ahead and plant those seeds. I think you should read up on it."

"I have enough to read. I have seventy-two fan letters on my desk to read, and I also like to answer them."

"Your daughter is in New York. Have her sniff around. There must be articles in the New York papers. Have her clip some and mail them to you. I'd love to set up a meeting between you and the DuMont Network in New York."

"It would be an excuse to go home, at least." She'd check on Patty's work, stop by the Empire Theatre for old times' sake, do some shopping . . .

"You have a couple of decades ahead of you at least, and I'm going to see to it that they're full of work."

* * *

That night, Billie called Patty from the kitchen phone. The connection was weak and scratchy.

"Speak up, dear," Billie said.

"How is your ankle?" Patty said.

"I'm done with the cane, finally. The ankle is still a little sore, and it's stiff in the morning, but I'm getting there. I no longer look like an invalid."

"Terrific news."

"How is the apprenticeship going?"

"They're doing a couple of scripts I approved," Patty said. She'd been assigned to the slush pile.

"See? I told you the future Shakespeare might be in that stack."

"Why are you yelling?" Patty asked.

"Bad connection."

"It's all right on my end. I can hear you just fine."

"I have a ridiculous question for you."

"Oh, ta gu."

"Speak louder, dear," Billie said, squeezing the receiver.

"So, what's new?" Patty said.

"Do you read much about television?"

"It's in the paper all the time," Patty said. "You should do it."

"Do what?"

"Television. Daddy would have loved it. You remember how he ate up radio?"

"Yes."

"My agent thinks I should try it."

"So, you hired one, finally?" Patty asked.

"Yes, dear. Mr. Orsatti, the former baseball player."

"Smart move. Many of our radio actors have them. It's the thing to do these days. It makes you modern."

"I am already modern," Billie insisted.

"Ha!"

Billie sighed. "Well, anyway, could you collect some articles about television and send them to me? Send them by airmail. I'll wire the money."

"Prepare for a huge package," Patty said. "I'll have to buy a trunk to ship them."

"Oh, and dear? Mr. Orsatti is sending me to New York to talk to someone at the DuMont television network. He's to DuMont is paying for the whole thing, roundtrip. We'll need to discuss dates so I know your schedule."

"Terrific."

"I'm looking forward to returning to the radio station to see how it has changed. And to see you at work."

There was a long silence from Patty, worrying Billie. She crossed her fingers that her daughter would hang in there.

Chapter Twenty-six

Billie was seated in Dorothy's classically decorated home. It looked like a museum: a statue in every parlor corner—Athena, Aphrodite, the Charities, Phoebe. Above the fireplace mantle was a replica of the painting *The Muses*, the inspirational goddesses of literature, science, and the arts. The room smelled like pine, reminding Billie of New York.

A woman stepped in wearing a mocha-colored cotton dress over a pencil-thin frame. Billie recognized her as Zoë an umlaut Akins, a friend of Dorothy's and a writer. Zoë's hand felt cold when Billie shook it by way of greeting.

"Marion let me in," Zoë said, her voice light and airy.

Dorothy looked left and right, as if wondering where Marion had gone.

"You just missed her," Zoë said. "She left for rehearsal."

Dorothy's face slackened. "She said she'd be home for dinner and not to worry. So much for that! Why don't the two of you talk while I get us some merlot?"

"I could use some," Zoë said.

Dorothy left for the kitchen as Zoë sat in a chair next to Billie's.

"It's been a while," Billie said.

"Six years since *Christopher Strong*."

"You did such a beautiful job on the script."

"Thank you." Zoë paused. "I actually have a project for you. I'm writing a play for you."

"Oh, how lovely."

"I think you'll like it."

For twenty-two years, playwrights had written plays wanting Billie for the lead role, but not one playwright had done that since she moved to Los Angeles. Having Zoë eager to put her in a role felt like old times. Billie felt important again. "What's it called?"

"*Bright Shadows*. It's about a woman who married several times, inherited money, and is being hounded by her ex-husbands for pieces of it."

Billie's body tingled. "Oh, I like that. It sounds intriguing."

"I want you to play the divorcée. It's the lead role. She disposes of her men like Glinda does the Wicked Witch."

"Oh, you know about Glinda?"

"I read the script."

"My character would kill them off?"

"Not murder them, if that's what you mean. No, you'd destroy them with attitude."

Billie sat up straight, smiling.

"It's a comedy, but don't worry. I know you're trying to get away from playing the flibbertigibbets. Dorothy told me. The character isn't a scatterbrain, just a strong, funny woman, much like you are in real life."

Billie chuckled. "You don't know me well. I'm not the least bit funny in real life. It's all an act."

"Well, then, it's a good act."

Dorothy returned with three long-stemmed glasses of wine. Billie took one sip, and that would end it. Wine went right to her head, and she had to navigate the narrow, winding streets of the Hills to get home.

"You're on board?" Dorothy asked Billie. "This is what you wanted."

"She doesn't know everything yet," Zoë said.

"Know what?" Billie asked suspiciously.

Dorothy set her glass down and leaned back. "I'm going to direct the play."

"What?! You've never directed a play."

"I'd never directed a film before my first one, either."

"Plays are different," Billie said.

Dorothy sat back and crossed her legs. "Not really."

Billie threw her head back, bristled, and then clicked off a list on her fingers. "Plays are more realistic, for one thing. They are in real time without the stops and starts. Second, there is a bigger picture going on, not just a series of snippets. And third, you have to think about everything going on across the stage and how the audience will react."

"I know of all that. I go to plays, and I live with Marion. Believe me, I've heard it all."

"Dance is different."

"Not really. It's just a play without words. You're using movement and music to tell the story."

"Plays are complicated, that's all." An inexperienced theatrical director could ruin even the best work. Dorothy was her friend, and Billie appreciated the offer, but if it didn't go well, it could hurt Billie's career in the long run.

"Perhaps so, but you could teach me."

Billie set her glass down and crossed her legs. It was useless to argue. "Who's going to produce it?" Producers usually picked directors, not the other way around.

"That's where you come in," Dorothy said, pointing at her.

"Uh-oh." Billie shook her head. "I don't produce. Flo was the producer. I merely helped and nagged."

"I'm not asking you to produce," Dorothy said. "I want you to ask Terry Duffy to produce it."

Terry owned a chain of theaters across California. Seven years ago, he'd hired Billie for the lead in *The Marquise*. Billie had planned on asking him for parts again; she didn't want to clutter that possibility by making a script pitch. She shook her head. "No, I can't do that. I hardly know him."

"You know him better than we do," Dorothy said, pointing back and forth between herself and Zoë. "I've never even met him."

"Nor have I," Zoë said. "All my plays have been produced in New York."

Repeating the word *no* to Dorothy never worked. Billie paused, took a breath, and tucked in her chin, beginning to feel resigned to having to do it, she said, "How long will the play be?"

"Full length, but I'm only on page four," Zoë said.

Good grief. She couldn't approach Terry about an unfinished script. "When will it be finished?"

Zoë shrugged. "I don't know. When I'm finished."

"You can't rush art," Dorothy said.

"Flo sure did, and look at his success." Billie stiffened her back. "Look, I can't talk to someone about an unfinished script. Producers only accept unfinished work from writers they've worked with before and trust."

"Sell her name, then," Dorothy said. "She won a Pulitzer. He must know that. It's not like you're starting from scratch."

"Who says I am going to sell it at all?" Billie said.

Dorothy sat back and smirked. "Oh, I think you will."

Billie turned to Zoë. "I'm sure he knows who you are, but has he ever asked you for a script?"

"No."

"Maybe he's seen the movies," Dorothy said.

"If he has, and he liked them, he'd have called her."

"Mr. Duffy trusts you," Zoë said. "You were powerful in *The Marquise*. He'll remember that."

"That was seven years ago," Billie said.

"I can write a description of the play for you, so you have something to show him," Zoë said.

Dorothy pushed herself up and motioned to Billie. "Follow me."

"Where are we going?"

"Into the kitchen for a second. C'mon."

Billie shoved herself up with a groan.

They entered an entertainer's kitchen with two white-enameled Frigidaires, a Wedgewood double-oven stove, and white cupboards surrounding them. Billie smelled oregano.

Dorothy closed the door behind them. Billie folded her arms across her chest and leaned against the cold aluminum counter's edge.

"I know you don't want to do this," Dorothy said. "I understand that, but I need it, and I'm asking for your help." She paused. "You know that RKO hasn't offered me another film. I thought it would be a good idea to branch out and do theater, too. You're looking for theater roles, so it helps us both. I know that pitching to Terry when the play is incomplete will be difficult, but—"

"The problem for me is Zoë," Billie whispered. "She's a terrific writer, but Terry doesn't know her work. He's the type of producer who, if he knows and likes someone's work, he contacts them to create something for him. What if I pitch this to him and he likes it, and then Zoë doesn't deliver? She admits she's only on page four and can't provide a completion date. I've worked with lots of writers, and many never finish, and even if they do, it can be terrible. I want to help you and I'm willing to take a risk, but this could damage us both."

"Zoë is Zoë. She's a leaf in the wind that always manages to land gracefully. She came through on *Christopher Strong*; she will come through on this."

Billie looked away. She'd encountered many artists like this. It was hard to pin them down, and they often didn't finish the work by the time it was needed.

"When this is successful," Dorothy said, "we will both be in demand."

Billie looked at Dorothy and saw a tear in her eye. It was the first time she'd seen Dorothy cry in years. Dorothy had always been a loyal friend, casting Billie in a string of movies that helped build her film career. Billie owed her.

Billie sighed. "I will figure out a way to present this to Terry." She pulled Dorothy into a hug.

"Thank you," Dorothy said, sniffling.

They let go, and Billie wiped her tears. "I have three conditions, however."

Dorothy smiled like she was expecting that. "I'm listening."

"I need a finished script or at least a projected completion date. I won't do this without one or the other."

Dorothy nodded.

"I'll need a summary budget and a fact sheet."

Dorothy's face brightened. "I can create those."

"And I'll need that story summary. Can you get it from her?"

"Done," Dorothy said.

"Then I'm in."

Chapter Twenty-seven

A week later, Billie opened the door to Terry Duffy's office in the El Capital Theatre. He was just inside the door, startling her. He looked like a kid anticipating Santa Claus. Had he been standing there the entire time?

"Come in, come in, Miss Burke." He motioned her inside. Terry looked the same: a short man Billie's height with orangey-red hair, ocean-blue eyes, and an Irish pug nose.

Billie turned on her smile. "It's good to see you. It's been what? Three years?"

"Yes. I think so."

They walked into a nearby conference room and sat. Through the window was a view of the Hollywood Hotel, a large wooden structure that reminded her of the set from *The Thief of Baghdad*. Sitting here gave her an adrenaline rush. It felt like the old days she missed. It felt like home.

Billie said, "I called because I have an idea for you." She patted the folder on the table.

"So you said on the phone. What is it?"

"I have a playwright friend with a play to propose. Have you heard of Zoë Akins?"

"Yes, of course," he said. "She's a talented writer. What's the play?"

"*Bright Shadows.*"

"Based on the novel?"

Her heart lost a beat. There was a novel? "No. I think it just shares a similar title. It's an original work."

"Do you have a copy?" he asked, motioning to the folder.

Her shoulders tightened as she pulled out the sheet Zoë had prepared. "It's almost finished, but I have a summary here."

He put on wire-rimmed glasses and took the sheet. "When can I see the full play?"

"Four months?"

He rolled his eyes and set the paper down. "Oh, geez. Another one of those."

She had known that was coming.

"It's quite funny," Billie said.

"You've read it, or what there is of it?"

"When we spoke, Zoë summarized if for me. It's about a woman getting back at her former husbands. They all want pieces of her inheritance."

"How does she do that?"

"Miss Akins has several ideas, but hasn't landed on a final one yet."

He groaned.

"Divorce is such a big issue, and this infuses it with humor," she said.

"Divorce isn't funny."

"The play pokes fun at it, which makes it funny. Women will flock to this play, and they're the ones who decide what gets seen."

"Their husbands will hate it."

Billie faked a laugh. "No, I'm sure they'll laugh, too."

"Well, it doesn't matter. I won't consider it without a script."

Billie's neck stiffened. "I understand your concern, but consider this: Miss Dorothy Arzner wants to direct. Do you know who she is?"

He squinted.

"She's a film director at RKO," Billie clarified.

"A woman?!" he said, sounding surprised.

"Yes. She's directed at MGM, too, so she knows what she's doing. She launched the careers of Katharine Hepburn and Rosalind Russell. You've heard of them, I suppose?"

"You'd have to be dead not to know who they are."

"Did you see *Christopher Strong* or *The Bride Wore Red*? They were two of her films."

"No. I don't see many films. Has she ever directed theater?"

"Not in so many words, but directing a film is much the same."

He shook his head.

Billie put her hands on the folder and leaned forward. "Well, she's quite good." Billie pulled out the fact sheet and budget and handed them to him. "As you can see, Miss Arzner estimates the budget at five thousand dollars for a three-month run here and in San Francisco. That's very economical."

"Miss Burke, I—"

"These are two very accomplished professionals. I know it seems like a risk, but you could think about it, and when the play is finished in the next couple of months, we can revisit the idea."

He picked up the budget and studied it. "When I see a script and a cost estimate that makes sense, I'll review it. Five thousand dollars sounds impossibly low. Travel will eat up a thousand on its own."

"The budget is preliminary, of course, but it provides a bit of a range."

He paused and put a finger to his chin. "Now that you mention it, I did hear about *Christopher Strong*. My wife loved the film and said you were terrific in it." He sighed. "I suppose I can at least talk to Mrs. Arzner."

She cleared her throat. "It is Miss Arzner." She needed to check her excitement. This was a business deal, and she needed to give herself a firm upper hand.

"Have her call me."

"I certainly will," she said in a businesslike voice. Billie sat back and smiled. "Thank you."

He pointed to the paper. "I see you are suggested for the lead."

"It's being written for me, yes."

"Nice coincidence because you were on my call list for a role." He rose, picked up an accordion folder from his desk, and returned to his seat. "I've been thinking about you since the Academy nomination. I saw *Merrily*. My wife dragged me—no offense. I didn't know you were in it until I arrived at the theater. I found it very funny. You're a talented actress."

"Thank you." Her neck relaxed.

"I want you for the lead in a new musical comedy titled, so far, *Here We Go*. Ralph Spence and Fred Schiller are writing the script. You interested?"

She clutched the question like a trophy. "Yes, and I know Mr. Spence," she said, talking a little faster, telling herself to slow down. "He used to work for my husband. I've never heard of Mr. Schiller. Who is doing the songs?"

"Frederick Loewe and Earle Crooker."

She felt giddy. "I've heard of Crooker."

"They're both brilliant," Terry said. "You're going to like them. Loewe wrote *The Great Lady*. You've heard of it?"

She was embarrassed to say no. Her theatrical knowledge had atrophied after so many years focused on film. She used to know every serious artist and producer in New

York and had entertained them at Burkeley Crest. She'd have to catch up.

"The show will open here at the El Capitan next February," he said, "and will move from here to San Francisco. You'll be tied up for at least four months, maybe longer. What are your commitments?"

She squeezed her purse. "I have to check with my agent."

"Should I be speaking with him?"

"No," she said quickly. "He handles film and radio. I'm on my own for theater. He only needs to know for scheduling reasons."

"Who is he? Your agent?"

"Ernie Orsatti."

"I don't know him. Well, anyway, here's the package." He lifted a paper from the accordion file. "It's eleven hundred per week with a three-month guarantee, plus six weeks of rehearsals. If we head to San Francisco, it'll be twelve-fifty weekly for a one-month run. After that, we'll move the show to New York for a run there."

Her hands flew to her mouth, and her tiptoes bounced against the floor. "New York? Wonderful." She wanted to shout hallelujah, and the salary was terrific. She resisted reaching out to hug him.

"What's the New York rate?" she said.

"The same as San Francisco."

She bit her lip. The money was low for New York.

"Well, Miss Burke?"

She wanted to say yes, but she didn't want to come in cheap. If she did that, she'd have trouble getting better offers later.

"Terry," she said as she adjusted herself in the chair. "I appreciate your considering me for the role. I'm flattered, and that is a reasonable salary, but I was hoping it would be possible to get eight percent of the gross in New York." Profit sharing had been growing as an option.

He rose and strolled to the window, scratching his chin.

Every bone in her body vibrated. She opened her mouth to take it back, but stopped herself. She wanted the part, and didn't want to scare him off, but she also didn't want to cheat herself. She'd never done this before, and it made her nervous.

He looked out the window, put his hands behind his back, and rocked on his feet.

She wrung her hands and gritted her teeth, trying not to say anything. But she couldn't hold it in. "I'm sorry," she said. "I don't mean to upset you, but perhaps you don't know that Actors' Equity requires a profit percentage to the lead performer. Before you open, they will look into the production and study performer compensation. Noncompliance in New York often results in fines and other troubles."

He turned to face her.

Sweat formed on her upper lip. "I am suggesting this for your security when the show lands in New York. Things have changed since Flo produced there, that's for sure."

"I know about the New York percentage, but they have special arrangements for nonregional production companies."

"It's starting to happen in film, too. Norma Shearer gets ten percent at MGM. Miriam Hopkins, too. I am suggesting eight, and just for the New York run. That's the New York rate."

Terry looked away again, fumbling his fingers through his hair. Then he exhaled. "Moving a production from Los Angeles to New York is quite expensive, and I must consider the costs. If I were a New York producer, I wouldn't have those costs, and I think Equity would understand that." He paused, turned, and looked at her. "I can offer three percent of the net in New York if we get there."

What if the play doesn't make money? She squeezed her purse. "Equity will make you take from the gross. I don't think they'll compromise on that."

He looked at the ceiling, paused, sighed, then said, "Three percent of the gross. I can't do eight. The risk is too high."

Billie relaxed in her chill as the weight lifted. She couldn't believe he'd come around so quickly.

He pointed at her. "And you ask for nothing more."

She wanted to cheer but forced herself to remain reserved. The New York stage—she was back.

"Deal," she said with a nod.

"As soon as I have everything in line, I'll draw up the contracts," he said.

* * *

Later in the day, Billie was in Ernie's office to sign two film contracts: the extra film for MGM and the Columbia picture. She was surprised at how easily this was flowing. It gave her hope.

"Until the end of the added film," Ernie said, "they'll pay you extra to attend the *Oz* opening."

She tilted her head and smiled at the word *extra*. Her smile suddenly dropped at a realization: Would she get to keep her dressing room at MGM? She dreaded moving out of the bungalow she'd decorated like a second home. Studios put contract actors into tents for dressing rooms, which would feel degrading at this stage in her career.

"Miss Burke. You with me?" he said.

A tear rolled down her cheek as she realized that when she signed the contract for MGM, her tenure there would come to an end. It would be official. She closed her eyes, reopened them, and said, "I'm sorry. I was in another world for a bit. Thank you for doing all of this." She took a breath, removed her gloves, picked up the fountain pen, and signed both contracts quickly.

"You'll be busy for the next six to eight months, and this is just the beginning. Don't worry."

"I know," she said, biting her lip. "It's just . . ."

Ernie leaned forward and said, his voice soft, "Do you want me to work on a seven-year?"

Her shoulders relaxed. That's what she'd wanted all along, and getting that would provide security. "Yes."

"You'd be MGM property again."

"I know," she said with a sigh. "But . . ." She scratched her head.

"Let me see what I can do, but I wouldn't bet on it. I know L. B., and there's no way to go back. It's nothing personal."

She sat back, suddenly exhausted.

"The Wanger film won't start until July first," he said, "but Columbia agreed to delay shooting your scenes if the MGM picture went over eight weeks. L. B. said it shouldn't exceed six, but you know how things go."

"Oh, yes. I do."

"The Wanger film isn't in color, and it isn't a musical. It's a simple film, so keeping on schedule should be easier."

"I appreciate Mr. Wanger's flexibility, and Columbia's."

"I'm working on more films," Ernie said, "but keep in mind that your work schedule may only be booked six to nine months in advance, maybe a year."

"I expected that."

She sat up straight, her energy returning from weeks of draining. Work was streaming in. "Terry Duffy offered me a play."

"Terrific. When does it begin rehearsals?"

"Truthfully, the script and music aren't finished, so I wouldn't worry about it. It's more important that I'm working and earning a living than waiting for a theater schedule. Once the thing is written, we can begin negotiating a schedule. He produces out of Los Angeles, so he understands how to work around the movie industry."

"You understand that you're committed once you sign a film contract."

She nodded. "Yes, of course. I always follow through on my commitments."

Ernie sat back and smiled. "New York's a go for television, by the way. Dr. DuMont wants to see you. I negotiated with The Mount for you. She's giving you nine days off in three weeks. Dr. DuMont is eager to talk to you."

Billie grinned ear to ear. Television seemed so far-fetched, but at worst, it was giving her the chance to go home on somebody else's dime, spend time with her daughter, network, learn something, and maybe—just maybe—get some new work.

Ernie's eyes were sparkling. "He's planning a nationwide network. If you get in now, you can carve a place for yourself, and he will pay for the whole trip: flight, meals, hotel, ground transportation. He wants you. It's also good for me, I have to admit, because our agency could get in the door as the first one in the country handling television talent. We think television is going to be huge." He extended his arms wide. "Just huge."

She shook her head. He was so young.

Chapter Twenty-eight

Three weeks later, Billie was in New York at the Greenwich Village Brevoort, waiting in the lobby for a taxi to DuMont Television. She'd squeezed a box of Partaga cigars under her arm for Dr. DuMont. Ernie had suggested it.

The eighty-five-year-old Brevoort had long reminded her of Paris: marble pillars, Oriental carpets, rosewood paneling, brocatelle wallpaper. Its lobby had fast-moving people, cigar smells, and fine clothes.

"That's Miss Billie Burke," a woman said from behind her. "My stars! I've seen all of her pictures."

Billie lifted her chest and smiled as she turned.

"May I have your autograph? My name is Bernice," the woman said.

"Certainly," Billie said, nodding. She still mattered in New York City, the entertainment and creativity capital.

The woman dug through her purse for a pad as a gentleman walked up. "You're Miss Billie Burke."

The woman pointed to him. "My husband."

"I loved the *Follies*," he said. "I miss them. Will there be others?"

"I hope so," Billie said, smiling inside. "The Shuberts own them now."

Billie signed the notepad and returned it to Bernice.

"Are you in a play here?" the husband asked. "We'll buy tickets."

"Not this trip. I'm here on other business," Billie said.

"A new movie?" the woman asked.

"No, television."

"Oh," the couple said together, trying to sound polite, then they nodded cordially and strolled away.

Billie took that to mean they didn't quite understand what she was saying or how television worked, which was to be expected, given that it was so new. She squeezed the box again under her arm. She could only hope this was the right move.

* * *

As her taxi pulled away from the curb, the driver asked, "When was the last time you were here, Miss Burke?"

"Nineteen thirty-one."

"Well, then! You don't want to miss Rockefeller Center. It'll be on the right from Forty-eighth to Fifty-first. It's new, and it's really something."

They approached Sixth Avenue. When she was a child, they'd lived a couple of blocks from the intersection. Something was missing, and it felt disorienting. She checked the street signs; yes, it was Sixth and Eighth. "What happened to the El train?" she asked.

"Been gone a year. They're putting the trains underground in Manhattan. Isn't it wonderful?"

Her jaw dropped. Wonderful? More like unnerving. She hadn't been gone that long, and already, the city was dramatically changing. Feeling and being "at home" was important. It provided structure and continuity to her life. If New York had changed this much in such a short time, it wouldn't feel like home anymore. It felt like a piece of her life was being pulled out from underneath her.

"I used to live just down the street, and the train used to rumble past our windows."

They turned right on Sixth, and things looked the same for several blocks. When they reached Fortieth, she saw that Bryant Park was still on the right, with the Beaux-Arts New York Public Library as the backdrop. But where did the reservoir go? It used to be in the middle of the park.

After a bit, the driver said, "The new Rockefeller Center is coming up soon. I heard on the radio that it's the largest private building project ever built." As they reached Forty-eighth Street, he pointed to the right. "There it is. Isn't it a beauty?"

Billie tried to remember what had been there before but couldn't. Now, there were Art Deco limestone skyscrapers. Everything had a crisp, clean, expensive feel to it.

Seeing a sign for West Fifty-first Street, she closed her eyes and clutched her purse, her body tense. "Let me know when we get there."

After what felt like no time, Billie heard the driver announce, "This is it, Miss Burke."

She opened her eyes.

"On the right."

The Radio City tower was another Art Deco beauty, a wedding cake–towered building. When she last lived here, the towers were all in Lower Manhattan, below Canal. The whole island was bursting with them now.

"A masterpiece, isn't it?" Just a few blocks later was a newer, smaller tower on the right. The driver got out of the car and opened her door. "I'll wait here for you. When you're done, I'll take you anywhere you want to go."

* * *

A receptionist showed her to DuMont's office, got her seated, and said he would be right with her. She heard a noise from the hallway. A cluster of employees had gathered outside the open door: men in dark suits, women in pastel dresses, a mail boy with a cart. They pointed, smiled, and whispered. They were so cute, like a group of schoolchildren.

"You're Miss Billie Burke," a man about her age said, waving his hand.

"Who's that?" the mail boy asked.

The man smacked him on the back of the head. "What's wrong with you?"

Billie stood and smiled. Some of the people pulled pencils from shirt pockets, hoping for autographs, but they scattered at the same time she heard a man's voice from behind her.

"Miss Burke?"

Startled, she jumped, turned around, and put a hand over her heart. He must have entered through reception.

The man was in his early forties, wearing a charcoal-colored suit and a crisp white shirt. He made her think of Woodrow Wilson.

"Dr. Allen DuMont," he said as he took her gloved hand. He seemed genuine and open, like a farm boy in the big city. "I'm sorry if I frightened you."

Billie waved the comment away. "I startle easily. Don't worry. It is a pleasure to meet you, Dr. DuMont."

"I'm sorry I wasn't here when you stepped in. I was called to the labs for an emergency, or so I was told."

"Is everything all right?" she said.

"It was a birthday party for one of our scientists. Can I offer you a piece of cake?"

She shook her head. "No, thank you. Actresses never eat cake unless it's made of one hundred percent carrots."

He chuckled and pointed to a cushioned chair across from his desk. "Please sit."

"Thank you for bringing me out here," she said as she sat. "It's so good to be home, and the Brevoort is my favorite hotel."

He sat behind his desk. "My pleasure. And what is this?" He picked up the gift—the box of cigars—she had left on his blotter.

"I heard you smoked them. A token of my appreciation. After all, you did pay for the trip. It's the least I could do."

He opened the lid, lifted a cigar, closed his eyes, and sniffed. "Aah. Thank you." He sat back and folded his hands on his lap. "Mr. Orsatti said you're interested in television."

She chuckled. "He's interested, that's for sure. But yes, I'm always interested in new platforms for performance. I started on stage, then I added radio, and then film. Now television, it seems. I hear you're planning a network."

"We are, but it will be three years until we spread it nationwide. We're working on it, though."

"I know it's hard to put together a network. It was for radio. Piecemeal at first, then it builds."

"Orsatti says you have ideas for programming. You're a tremendous comedienne, by the way."

"Thank you, and yes, I do have ideas."

Ernie had suggested coming up with a list, and he had helped her prepare it. It included producing Shakespeare and a talk show featuring Billie.

DuMont leaned forward and put his hands on his desk. "Before you present your ideas, let me tell you what we're doing. We have a local market of about three hundred television users and nightly broadcasts for an hour. We'll add another hundred users this year, I hope, maybe more. Most programs are educational."

"Lectures?"

"Yes, mini-lectures of fifteen minutes each, but we do other things, too. We're trying to lift public sensibilities. Last night, for example, Jascha Heifetz performed. The violinist?"

Billie crossed her legs at the knee. "I think I may have heard of him." Actually, she hadn't. But hearing about a musician made her think of Francis. They hadn't spoken since the divorce disaster. She should give him a call when she got home. "It sounds a bit like newsreels for television."

"Yes, in a way, though we see ourselves more like teachers than news people."

She nodded. "Some of my ideas bridge entertainment and education, but others are pure entertainment. Entertainment draws audiences to the station, and then you can teach them. If the movie business is any indication, people want to be entertained, and they're willing to pay for it. I have a couple of things that might interest you."

He leaned forward and motioned for her to continue.

"I suggest doing one of my husband's musicals, like *Show Boat*."

"A bit expensive and long."

"You could break it into parts. Make it a series. It's extremely popular with the public but hasn't been on a New York stage since nineteen thirty-two."

"I remember it. My wife and I loved it."

"It's time to bring it out again."

He twirled a cigar in his fingers. "We do weekly shows and need variety from week to week. To see *Show Boat* would take weeks. People's attention spans are getting shorter."

"What about an abridged version of *Romeo and Juliet*? There's one that can fit into an hour. You could even divide it into two parts. Shakespeare is both educational and entertaining."

"Maybe eventually, but any theater production is probably too expensive to produce for television. Right now, I need short, simple programs." He stopped spinning the cigar.

"What about a talk show, with a hostess? You could schedule guest artists, authors, or whomever, and they would be interviewed. I would love to host something."

He unfolded his hands and nodded. A smile spread across his face, and Billie felt her shoulders relax.

"Like *Vox Populi*?" he asked, referring to a popular radio program of interviews, quizzes, and human-interest features.

"Somewhat, but I would be interviewing guests in a studio about their work and ideas. Maybe a movie actress, a painter, a judge. The movie star would draw one audience, the painter another, and the judge a third. Radio does this already, but now people could see them instead of just hearing them."

"And you would broadcast from here, in New York?"

Her back tensed. She had no intention of moving back to New York. Southern California was now home. Her work and her friends were there, and soon enough, her daughter would be, too. "I know you prefer live broadcasts, but I live in Los Angeles, and most of my work is in film. I'd want to do it from there if I could. It could be filmed in Los Angeles and shipped to New York like a movie or a newsreel."

He sat back. "I love the idea, but all national television production is here, and our operations are here. Maybe, when we grow, we can add the West Coast, but we aren't ready for it yet."

"When do you think you might expand? Los Angeles could be your second location. The talent is equal in both cities. That's what radio did—set up in the east and then the west."

"We plan to expand here in the east over the next few years. We don't have a plan for the west yet. I do love your idea for a talk show, though. It fits with our programming."

She had come here not sure she wanted to do television, but seeing the technology around her, and the enthusiasm of this man, she realized that she'd forgotten how much she enjoyed being part of modern and upcoming performance opportunities. That's how she felt when she did radio for the first time, and then film. They'd both started like television—primitive, small, grappling at ideas to make things work. Being a part of new technology could keep her image fresh. She sat up straight and felt an energy surge. "Perhaps you could contract a studio to produce it and agree to profit-sharing."

"Maybe someday," he said. "But for now, everything is here in New York. The studio is here in the building, fully equipped."

"Perhaps I could fly here periodically, film it, and return to Los Angeles."

"At this point, we're committed to live television, but I'll think about it."

"Perhaps we could stay in touch," she said. "You never know what the future may bring."

"You are absolutely right, Miss Burke." He sat back. "What are you planning to do with your daughter while you are here?"

"For now. She's apprenticing here, then she'll move back to Los Angeles. I want to take her to that new Rockefeller Center and see some theater."

He smiled. "I hope you added a few days to see how much the city has changed."

"Oh, I have seen quite a bit of that already. This is the capital of change," she said. Too much change for her. New York was feeling less and less familiar.

Chapter Twenty-nine

Satisfied that she'd done her best in the meeting and that all was not lost, Billie decided she wanted to visit some of her old haunts. Tipping her driver fifty cents, she asked him to take her to the Ziegfeld Theatre. Upon their arrival, he told her, "Enjoy the movie, ma'am."

She knew it had been converted from live theater to movies, but hearing the word *movie* still punched her gut.

Stepping out of the car, she shook her head and felt a tear come to her eye. The marquee read "Lowe's Ziegfeld," making the place look like a casino. *Mr. Chips* was playing. She looked at the cornerstone where she and Patty had once inserted an iron time capsule filled with production programs, family photos, and a stone from the world's oldest theater, in Greece. She stepped closer, removed her glove, and caressed the stone. Tears began to stream as she softly sang "Old Man River" from *Show Boat*, the theater's second show. She couldn't believe that this wasn't hers anymore. It had all happened so fast.

She took a pink handkerchief from her purse, dotted the corners of her eyes, and got back into the car.

* * *

Twenty minutes later, she was in front of her next destination: the Empire Theatre in Herald Square. This was where she had started in 1907. She had continued on stage here for almost two decades.

She smiled and let out a huge breath. It was still a theater. Its gray-stone, gingerbread-decorated Victorian facade was grimier than she remembered, but intact. She tucked her purse under her arm and walked toward the building. The marquis announced a play and not a movie: *Life with Father.*

She'd performed here when she married Flo, when Patty was born, and while she triple-timed herself on radio and in film. It had paid for Burkeley Crest.

"Hello. Lovely day, isn't it?" she said to a woman walking by, her voice chipper. The woman nodded back and smiled.

Billie lifted her shoulders and walked inside. A grin spread across her face, and chills ran through her. There they were: the copper-colored marble, the sweeping staircase to the mezzanine. The life-sized portraits of leading performers—Mr. Gillette, Miss Barrymore, Billie herself—were still there.

She lingered in front of her portrait and then headed for the auditorium doors, grabbing a brass handle and turning. It was locked. She tried the other doors. All locked. Her shoulders dropped.

"Can I help you, ma'am?" said a young woman in the ticket booth to the left.

"I am sorry to bother you, dear." Billie pointed toward the auditorium doors. "But they seem to be locked." They were open all the time when she worked here.

"Yes. The management keeps them locked until an hour before the performance. Do I know you? You look familiar."

Billie turned and pointed to her portrait. "That's me. Miss Billie Burke. I performed here for twenty years. I do movies now."

"Oh, my," the girl said, putting her hands to her face. "It's wonderful to meet you. Which movies?"

"Perhaps you saw *Topper*?"

The girl's face lit up. "Oh, yes. I remember you! You were funny."

"Thank you. May I go into the auditorium? Can you let me in?"

The girl's cheeks fell. "Sorry, ma'am, but I don't have a key."

"Perhaps you can call someone to let me in?"

"Let me try the janitor." She put the phone receiver up to her ear. There was a long pause. "I'm sorry. Nobody's answering."

"Who owns the theater these days?" Billie asked. She'd lost track. Perhaps she knew the owner and could get inside that way.

"Don't know, ma'am. I just started working here."

"Is Mrs. Ringman still working in the office?"

The girl shook her head. "Sorry, ma'am. I've never heard of her."

The theater was the same, but the times were not. Nonetheless, Billie wanted to see the show. It would nice to be inside the theater once again. "I would like to purchase two tickets for tonight's performance of *Life with Father*, please. In the orchestra section, please."

* * *

She wondered what to do next. She'd planned to visit more of her old haunts, but her energy was drained. Instead of more sightseeing, she thought she'd make a surprise visit to Patty's workplace.

The taxi dropped her at Patty's office building, and Billie stepped inside. The lobby was long and narrow, the marble walls cracked and stained. The elevator took her to the sixth floor. Along both sides of the hall were office doors with frosted glass panels and company names painted on them in black. When she got to the door where WCCD Radio should have been, the sign on the door instead said, "McGarvey, O'Toole, and Hammond, Esq." She shook her head. Had she forgotten the station's location? Did they move, and she didn't know it? According to the listing she'd seen in the lobby, they were still on this floor.

She returned to the elevator and pushed the button. When it rumbled up, the attendant opened the door.

"Billie Burke," he blurted out, his eyes big. "You're Miss Billie Burke. I knew you looked familiar on the ride up."

She smiled, but felt embarrassed. "Yes, that's me. Can you help me? I'm trying to find my daughter. She works for WCCD Radio."

"You're on the wrong floor. They moved to five. I'll take you down. Get in."

As the elevator moved downward, the attendant dug through his pockets. "I have a pencil and a piece of paper here somewhere if you wouldn't mind giving me an autograph."

She signed as the elevator came to a stop, then she walked down the hall, seeing the sign for WCCD painted on a door to the left. She heaved a sigh of relief, then straightened her skirt and smiled. She wanted Patty to see her looking cheerful and relaxed. She turned the knob, stepped in, and the bells on the door jingled. Her insides bubbled.

The reception area was the size of a projection room but with two dirty windows at the rear facing an alley. Dust tickled her nose. She sneezed.

"Bless you," the receptionist said without glancing up from her work.

"Thank you," Billie said. She recognized the voice. It was Mrs. O'Brandon. She'd been the receptionist here for years and years. She looked the same but had a few more wrinkles, a smaller smile, and grayer hair.

The steam pipes hissed and clanked.

Mrs. O'Brandon looked up. "Why, Miss Burke! What a surprise." She rose and stepped out from behind her desk. "I'm thrilled to see you."

The two shared a hug.

"You're as lovely as ever," the receptionist said. "Patty said you were in town, but I didn't know you were coming to the office. That girl is full of secrets."

"She knew I was coming to New York, but she didn't know I was coming here now. I'd planned this for later. And yes, she is full of secrets."

"She went out to get coffee for Mr. Ellison, but she'll be right back. Please, have a seat." She motioned to a chair in the waiting area. "I wish I had something to offer you."

"I'm fine, thank you. And thank you for having Patty. I hope she's been behaving."

Mrs. O'Brandon waved off the comment. "She's wonderful. I'll be sad when she leaves, and it was so good to have a Ziegfeld here again. She reminds me so much of her father."

The phone rang and Mrs. O'Brandon gave Billie an apologetic smile as she reached to answer it. "WCCD Radio, may I help you?"

Just as Billie picked up a copy of *Ladies' Home Journal*, the office door squealed open and Patty walked in, carrying two cups of coffee. She walked past Billie without seeing her.

Still on the telephone, Mrs. O'Brandon took the coffee, smiled, and nodded toward Billie.

Patty turned around, and her jaw dropped. "Mother. What are you doing here?!"

Billie stood, opened her arms, and wrapped them around her daughter. It felt so good, she didn't want to let go. She stepped back, smiled, and held the girl's shoulders. "Are you disappointed that I came right now?"

"Don't be silly. I'm glad you're here."

Billie pointed outside. "My meeting at DuMont television was only a few blocks that way. I thought I'd drop by."

"I'll give you the tour. Things have changed quite a bit."

Billie sighed. "It seems just about everything has changed."

* * *

In the hall, Billie took Patty's hand and squeezed.

"You wanted to go to a play tonight, yes?" Patty asked.

"Yes, and dinner. How about *Life with Father* at The Empire?"

"That sounds fine."

"Good. I was there this morning and bought us tickets." Billie pulled back and studied Patty's dress. "Are you planning on going home to change first? I need to go back to the hotel."

Patty looked down at her dress. "This dress is fine, Mother. People don't wear formal gowns and tuxedos to the theater in New York anymore. To the opera, yes. But not theater."

Billie pursed her lips. It was the same in Los Angeles, but California was less formal in general, so she had learned to accept it. She had hoped that informality hadn't reached New York yet. Back in the day, theater attendance was a big deal, an opportunity to be seen. Dressing down for a play seemed sacrilegious, almost as if doing so cheapened the whole experience.

"I don't have a gown," Patty said. "I can't change unless you want to buy me one."

"Yes," Billie said. "We can go over to that new Rockefeller Center."

"Really, Mother, what I'm wearing is fine. I don't want to be overdressed." Patty paused and looked around the hallway. "I want to give you the whole tour. Are you in a hurry?"

"I'm feeling suddenly exhausted. Can we just sit and talk for a few minutes? Maybe we can take the tour later."

"I suppose," Patty said, pointing to a door at the end of the hall. "There's a conference room down there."

"Good."

They passed the recording studio. The red light was on above the door.

"I'd like to say hello to John Ellison before I leave," Billie said.

"He's going to be in there for a while. He does just about everything around here these days."

Inside the conference room was a wooden table and chairs, the same furniture Billie remembered from when she'd visited the office back on the sixth floor. Billie took a seat at the head of the table. Patty poured two glasses of water, set them down, and sat beside her mother.

Billie sipped the water and waited. Mother's intuition told her that Patty had something to say. Billie hoped it was something like, "I got a job here as a script writer or a journalist." She'd prefer to have Patty with her in Los Angeles, but starting a real career was more important—though Billie had a sneaking suspicion she was about to be told, again, that Patty wanted to come home.

"I'd planned to discuss this with you sometime during your visit," Patty said. "We might as well do it now." She took a deep breath and looked directly at her mother. "I want to come home with you. I don't want to do this anymore." Patty's voice had an air of finality to it.

"We had an agreement."

"The work is boring. I get coffee, read unsolicited scripts, run errands. I'm not doing any writing. I'm not learning anything except how to fetch things. The people are wonderful and they're nice to me, but I'm not writing, and writing is the whole point."

"But you're almost finished."

"I know, but I want to come home."

"How are you going to become a writer? You have to build a network."

"A network fetching coffee? Besides, I don't want to be a full-time writer. I don't want a career as a writer. I'm not a career person."

Billie squeezed the glass, hoping it wouldn't break. She didn't know what else to do to move her daughter into a career. It was so frustrating. "When did that change?"

"I never wanted it. *You* wanted it. I've tried to tell you." Patty looked aside.

Billie took a chest-raising breath. "You have to have a career in something, even if you get married," she said. "Things happen. You need an emergency backup system to stay afloat."

"You've said that a hundred times."

"Because it's true."

"I want a husband and a family. I'm placing my trust there."

She looked her daughter in the eye, but Patty looked away.

"I'm a woman, and I know about life's tornados," Billie said. "A man can be gone just like that." She snapped her fingers. "They die. They get sick. They leave. You never know. If you have children, you'll be left with them, and they are expensive to raise. How will you pay for all of that?"

Patty looked at her mother. "You love what you do, and you're talented. You could never stop working. You'll die on the stage. I don't love writing. I like it, but I don't love it like you love acting."

"Then do something else."

Patty white-knuckled the table's edge. "I don't want to do anything else. You can't plan life to the end. Sometimes, you just have to trust things to work out independently."

Billie opened her mouth, shut it, and pressed her lips together.

"This is the modern era," Patty continued, "and I want to make my own decisions. You made yours."

"Your grandmother and your father made them for me, although he often believed otherwise. It only looked like I made them."

"I never heard you complain."

"Because I'm your mother. Mothers don't complain about those things to their children."

"I'm going back home with you, even if I have to pay for the ticket myself."

"Where are you going to get the money for it?"

"I have some money of my own."

"That much?"

"Yes. I'm homesick. I miss you, and I miss William. I don't want to delay my life for two more weeks."

Billie sat back and looked out the dirt-caked window. What would Flo say if he were here? He'd say, "Let her alone. It's her life." Billie's mother would have said the same thing, a lesson she'd learned from parenting her own daughter.

"Trust me, Mother," Patty said.

Billie's eyes teared up. Here was her daughter, a rational, smart, sophisticated, capable girl, and more mature than Billie had been at that age. Billie had tried to steer Patty toward the stage, but that hadn't worked. Later, when the girl showed a gift for writing, Billie capitalized on it as a career path. But alas, perhaps that wasn't the right choice, either.

Billie sighed, threw up her arms, and looked at the water glass on the table, now sitting in a puddle. "Fine."

"Fine what?"

"You can come home, but you have to be the one to tell Mr. Ellison. I don't want to be in the room. If you want to take charge of your career, you have to do the hard things."

Patty's eyes sparkled and gleamed. "Thank you, Mother."

"But we're stopping at that Rockefeller Center and getting you something to wear," Billie said. "You are *not* going to the theater in that dress."

Chapter Thirty

After shopping, Billie and Patty were in the hotel room for Billie's afternoon phone appointment with Ernie.

"So, how's New York?" Ernie asked in a chipper voice.

Billie put a hand to her forehead. "Don't ask."

"I have fantastic news," he said. "Wanna hear?"

She sat up straight. "I could use some."

"I spoke with DuMont; he loved your idea about the talk show."

"Did he change his mind? He wants to hire me?"

"He's considering your idea of filming in Los Angeles and shipping it east. If I were you, I'd start planning that show, at least in your head."

She smiled. Since arriving in New York, she'd become more enthusiastic about television and had been hoping for this. She'd sent a thank-you note and some show ideas to Dr. DuMont. "Did he say when he would air it?"

"No, but he wants to do it. He loved it. And I have more. Are you sitting down?"

"Yes. I don't have the energy to stand. Why?"

"You remember saying you wanted seven more years at MGM?"

She jumped up. "Yes."

"I got you three."

Terrific news. She paced as she wrapped the phone cord around her arm. "That's wonderful news. Thank you."

"You're welcome."

"Can I do other work outside of MGM?"

"Absolutely."

"And do I have script approval?"

"You got it. And those loan-outs," he said.

"How much money do I keep on each?" MGM usually kept a hundred percent.

"We're still negotiating, but don't expect much. Those loan-outs make them money. MGM still owns you, and you're a tool for income generation. But I did get you a thousand dollars per week with annual fifteen percent raises."

She'd wanted twelve hundred, but it was still a jump above what she'd been making before, not to mention it was job security.

"There's one small thing," he said.

She sat on the edge of her chair.

"L B. wants to meet with you before he signs."

She put her hand to her forehead. She didn't want to face L. B. after all that had happened. "What for? Can't you handle it?"

"I'll be there, but he wants you there, too." He paused. "I thought you wanted to be a part of it?"

"I did, but . . ."

"You have to be there, or there's no contract. Don't worry. I'll get you through it. This is a good thing. You should celebrate."

Yes, it was a good thing, but L. B. had a reputation for wrapping ropes around the necks of talents during contract negotiations, pulling hard, and dragging them around the around until they said, "Stop, I'll do whatever you want." She hoped she could avoid that fate.

Chapter Thirty-one

The plane's engines roared over Chicago. Billie was glad to be heading home. Funny, she thought; up to now, she'd almost never assigned that word, *home*, to Los Angeles. She'd longed for New York for the past seven years, but New York wasn't home anymore. It had become almost foreign to her. Now, she longed for the warm sun and palm trees.

Billie glanced at the cover of *Photoplay* in her lap. A snippet mentioned the group Women Associated, which Billie knew met at the Beverly Hotel. Billie had thought about joining.

"You know, dear," Billie said to Patty, sitting beside her. "You should go to a meeting of Women Associated when you get back. We could go together."

"What's that?"

"It helps professional women find jobs."

Patty turned to the aisle and opened her book, clearly disinterested. "We'll see."

"Adrian, the designer, is getting married this summer," Billie said, trying again with another topic.

Patty snapped her head around with a surprised look.

Billie chuckled. "He's marrying Janet Gaynor."

"What!?" Patty leaned toward Billie and whispered, "But he's a twilight."

"You know that. I know that. He knows that. Miss Gaynor knows that. In the real world, that doesn't matter to many women. They just want a man, any man, and a twilight is safe. Although I've heard that the two of them actually love each other."

"I don't understand it." Patty shook her head.

"Neither do I. But then, most women marry without love. They do it to appear normal or because they want children. Many want to be cared for and protected. Adrian and Janet have the advantage of loving each other, at least as friends." Billie paused and put a finger to her lips. "Do you see William that way? As your best friend?"

"I'm starting to, yes."

"Is he courting you exclusively?"

Patty closed the book on her finger, put her head back, and closed her eyes. "Yes, Mother," she said through gritted teeth.

"What do you know about his parents?" Billie said.

"Plenty," Patty said. "They're good people. I even talked to them on the phone. Mother, where is this going?"

"I haven't spent much time with him, dear. Are you hiding him from me? You never provide much detail."

"You'll get to know him in good time. Just don't ask him too many questions when he picks us up at the airport."

"Me? No, never." Actually, she had a two-mile list of questions for him.

Patty snorted.

* * *

Two days after returning from New York, Patty came home from an afternoon with William. Billie was on the couch in the front parlor reading the *Los Angeles Examiner*. Patty walked in and cleared her throat.

Billie looked up.

"Now, don't say no," Patty said, wagging a finger at her mother.

"Oh, dear."

"William wants to take us to the Ballet Russe de Monte Carlo at the Hollywood Bowl. He'll pay for everything. He thought you'd enjoy it."

Billie's shoulders relaxed. She loved the Hollywood Bowl. It felt so "ancient Greece" to her. She and Flo had been to Greece and appreciated the hillside outdoor amphitheaters. They were smaller than the Bowl, but it was the same idea.

"I told him I didn't think you'd like it," Patty said, "and he didn't believe me."

Billie tilted her head. "Why would you tell him that?"

"When was the last time you went to the ballet?"

"I've been a time or two."

"Not in my lifetime," Patty said. "Daddy never went, either."

"True, although he certainly created them on stage."

"Anyway, William said, 'A woman of her refinement? Impossible.'"

Billie opened her mouth and shut it.

"And no, he's not a twilight," Patty hastened to add.

"I never said that."

"I saw it on your face."

Billie had to admit, the thought had occurred to her, but Patty had been around twilights; they were hard to miss in theater and film. Patty would know one if she saw one.

"There's a lot you don't know about me," Billie said. "I saw the Royal Ballet in London."

Patty's eyes narrowed. "When?"

"Before you were born. With a friend, back in England."

That "friend" had been Stanley. It seemed like yesterday. Of course, Patty didn't know about him and didn't need to know now.

"I hope the seats are good," Billie said. "That place seats over fifteen thousand people." A concert at the Bowl was one thing; you went to listen. A ballet was another thing; you went to look.

"William likes ballet, so I think he'll get good seats. You'll need to read up on it, though."

"You, too, dear."

"He already knows I don't know anything about it. He plans to teach me, and I intend to let him."

Billie hung her head. She didn't even have a library card. She was still the daughter of a circus clown inside, trying to be sophisticated.

* * *

"Thank you for inviting me here and paying for the tickets," she said to William as they took their seats the night of the ballet.

"You're welcome."

"Patty tells me you love ballet. What got you interested?"

"I saw a French company touring in New York City when I lived there. I really enjoyed it."

"I can't say I've seen a lot of ballet," she said, "but what I've seen I've enjoyed."

"What have you seen?"

Patty smirked.

"*Swan Lake*, in London," Billie said.

"A classic," he said.

"The Royal Ballet performed it. Have you seen the San Francisco Ballet? I hear it's new." She'd read about it in the *Los Angeles Times*.

His eyes smiled. "Actually, it's been around for a few years as a school, but now it's staging works. It hasn't toured yet, but I've read about it. They just performed *Coppélia*."

She didn't know enough to comment.

"You'd like it," he said. "It's a comedy. And you're a comedienne."

She scoffed. "I perform as one. The truth is, I'm not really that funny."

"That's true," Patty quipped.

"Well, you're good at it," William said.

The orchestra tuned.

"I hear you may have an apprenticeship starting soon," Billie said.

"Yes, I got an apprenticeship with the Lloyd Wright architects the other day," William said. He sounded like he thought he had to prove his worthiness.

"I hear a lot of impressive things about you from Patty. You sound like an accomplished young man. Is this apprenticeship with Frank Lloyd Wright?"

"The son," he said. "He has an office in Santa Monica."

"He starts tomorrow," Patty said, sounding proud.

"When do you get your license?" Billie asked him.

"Two years or so," he said.

"What are your plans after that?"

Patty and William shared a glance.

"To become an architect," he said.

"What kind of architect?"

"Residential," he said. "You know, designing people's homes."

There were about ten minutes left until show time, and Billie wanted to learn as much as possible about William before curtain. There might not be time later.

"William," she said. "Where do you see yourself ten years from now?"

William stiffened. Patty's eyes narrowed.

Billie fingered her pearl necklace, wondering why they both seemed so uncomfortable with a question that any mother would feel she had a right to ask. Was he planning to move and take her daughter away from Los Angeles? Patty was Billie's only close family, and Billie couldn't follow Patty around like Billie's mother had followed Billie. The film industry was in Los Angeles, period.

William took a deep breath and straightened his back. "I have no plans beyond finishing this apprenticeship, getting a license, and getting a job as an architect. That's as far ahead as I can think. I'm a planner, but not that far in advance. I always assume things will work out in the end, and they usually do."

Three of her questions had been answered: No, he wasn't a twilight; her intuition had informed her of that. Yes, he was a nice, safe young man. And yes, he would become a professional who could support her daughter. If Patty wouldn't have a stable career of her own, then her husband would need one.

But Billie had other questions: What were his intentions for Patty? How did he feel about children? She wanted grandchildren.

As the ballet began, she decided she would get the answers the next time he saw him. Besides, more questions would arise. As long as they were answered before William asked Patty to marry him, everything would be fine. And if he didn't propose, Billie wouldn't be worse off for knowing more about the young man.

Chapter Thirty-two

Billie and Ernie were in the hall outside L. B.'s office, and she felt sick. Nothing she was trying seemed to be able to calm her: deep breathing, self-demands, outright orders.

"Relax," Ernie said. "I've got this. It's all theater. Pretend you're a character in a play, and this is the climax scene. None of it's real. It's all play-acting on stage."

He meant well, but he had no idea what he was talking about. On stage, Billie *was* the character. It was never "make-believe." Before the curtain, the character inhabited her and stayed with her. Sometimes, it was hard to come out of the role when the play was over.

"Maybe you should do this alone," she said.

"We discussed this."

"What if we upset him? He's angry enough as it is."

"He's always angry. Anger is fuel for him." Ernie shoved his hands into his pockets. "My granddaddy once said, 'Like a stone thrown into a lake, the surface returns to neutral.' Don't worry. This'll work out. Let him throw the stone. Let the waves spread. Then sit back and let me handle it. It may get a bit wild—"

"Oh, dear."

"But he needs you, and I know him. He'll bluster, but in the end, it'll be a business decision, and he's already decided what he wants to do. In some ways, it was decided for him. That Academy nomination and your calm response to losing boosted you."

"I wish I could trust that."

"Just follow my lead."

The Mount popped her head out of the door. "You can go in now."

Ernie buttoned his gray suit jacket as Billie took a big, audible breath and straightened her back.

Ernie reached for the door, pausing only to say, "Remember, stick to what we rehearsed."

Her gloved hands were shaking. She closed her eyes and whispered, "Rabbits, rabbits, rabbits."

* * *

L. B. rose from his desk. "Ernie, come in, come in." He approached them and shook Ernie's hand like a water pump, ignoring Billie entirely.

She stiffened her posture and tucked in her chin. She would be a businesswoman about this, mature to the end—the adult in the room.

L. B. crossed his arms over his potbelly and tapped a finger to his chin. "What do you think of that Lou Gehrig?" he asked Ernie. "Two thousand one hundred and thirty consecutive games played."

"Pretty amazing that he retired," Ernie said. "The Yankees are going to miss him. Wish I'd made it that far."

L. B. punched him on the shoulder. Inside, Billie rolled her eyes. Why did men do that? Didn't it hurt?

L. B. pushed his glasses up his nose. "Well, now you're in the pit with the rest of us."

"Perhaps so."

"Sit, sit." L. B. motioned to two chairs in front of his desk, and went around to his own seat.

"You look lovely today, Billie," L. B. said.

Billie breathed in and out slowly. She knew that he often began friendly but finished angrily. "Thank you."

"I've seen some of the early *Oz* scenes," L. B. said. "I'm quite pleased."

"Thank you," she said again.

"Shall we get started?" L. B. picked up a brown folder from his desk and pulled out a document.

Ernie reached into his leather briefcase and pulled out his own copy.

"I discussed this with Ernie over the phone," L. B. said. "He told me you agreed to the financial terms but had other concerns." He folded his hands on his desk. His eyes narrowed.

After a second review of the agreement, Billie had noticed that the contract would allow L. B. to control too much of her independent work, and that had to be changed. There was no point in agreeing to this contract if she couldn't develop other opportunities as well. What if he dumped her again?

"I can present those concerns," Ernie said.

L. B. leaned back. "I want to hear them from her."

Billie pushed her knees together to stop the knocking. She pointed to the agreement. "On page two, the 'We Control' section. Item two-one-three-A. Where it says, 'Metro Goldwyn Mayer controls all loan-outs to other studios. No additional compensation to ACTRESS.' I would like to share compensation. And in the second clause, it says you control all of my work as an actress, but I need to be free to do records, theater, and radio."

L. B. put his hands behind his head. "Nothing is stopping you from doing those things. You'll need my permission, that's all, and I'll control the compensation."

Ernie leaned forward. "She appreciates the renewal, L. B., but she wants to be free to do other things. Stretching her talents will make her an even better actress, and you won't lose any money. In fact, you'll be making money."

"How is that?" L. B. asked, leaning forward.

"The contract says she'll do seven films per year."

"Yes."

Ernie patted the contract. "She'll be doing twice as many because I'll be getting them for her. You'll get a cut without expelling any effort. Plus, the more work she does, the more people will see and love her, which benefits your films."

Billie tried to hold in a smile. She liked that argument.

"If she's busier, she will make more mistakes," L. B. said. "And she made a doozy when it came to that newsreel. You wouldn't believe the things these actors do."

"My behavior? Again?" Billie said, her voice almost a growl.

L. B. cracked a smile and Billie cursed herself. She told herself to shut up.

Ernie touched her wrist. "That sort of thing won't happen again, so you needn't worry."

"I can't control what she does for others unless I make her behavior a contractual contingency. MGM is the world's leading studio. We set the example for all of the others. I have to control her if she's going to work for me."

A flash of rage ran through Billie. She was tired of men controlling her, telling her what to do and not do. She'd been in this business for decades. Hadn't she earned some freedom? "When have I ever done anything horrible?" she blurted.

Ernie held a finger to his lips to hush her.

L. B. patted the contract. "Everyone signs the standard contract. Sign it, or walk."

"Then I'll walk," she said.

"Billie!" Ernie snapped, reaching for her hand again. "Let me handle this."

She shoved his hand aside.

"She's lined up a play with Terry Duffy," Ernie said to L. B. "She's also been talking to DuMont about television."

L. B. threw his head back and laughed. "Television? There's nothing out there, and she's not moving to New York if she signs my agreement."

"Television is on the way up. She already negotiated a talk show."

"I've told you there is *no* work outside of MGM, and that's final. If you work for us, you're mine."

"I refuse to belong to anyone anymore," Billie snapped.

Ernie leaned over and whispered to Billie, "Let me handle this."

"I'm the one who decides if you're trouble for us or not," L. B. said, pointing to the contract on his desk. "You sign this or you leave."

Ernie looked at her with pleading eyes.

Yes, the contract gave her other options, but those options were new to her. MGM provided security, and she knew the people around here. It was a home for her, and she wasn't ready to completely jump into a new home. Maybe she should sign. This contract was a guaranteed job with some freedom, which was more than she had before. She stood, reached for the pen with a shaking hand, and flipped to the signature page. She paused and looked up.

"You know I need this money," she said to L. B. "You know my situation. The least you could do is—"

"I don't care about your situation. They don't pay me to care about your situation. Besides, your husband got you into this mess, not me. It's not my problem."

"The stock market crashed! That's why he lost the theater."

"The Shuberts survived. Frohman made it through."

"Why, you . . ." She studied L. B.'s desk, searching for something to throw. The nameplate? The pen? The inkwell? The paperweight? Then she looked at the closed door. L. B. had a button under his desk to summon security guards. She felt her shoulders sink. She picked up the contract, tore it in half, and threw it at L. B, but the papers didn't reach him. They just fluttered harmlessly to the desk.

She turned and stormed out of the office.

"Billie, please wait for me in the hall," she heard Ernie saying as she strode away.

The Mount leapt to her feet. "Miss Burke? May I—"

Billie kept going, closing the hallway door behind her. Leaning against it for a moment, she tried to calm herself. Her chest heaved; her pulse raced.

She should have let Ernie handle things. That was clear, now. It was the comment about Flo that sent her over the edge. Yes, L. B. was right that Flo shouldn't have put all of his money into stocks for a single company, but he was new at investing, and he was hardly the only person who'd made that mistake. What killed Flo was that people didn't have money to buy tickets, and that had nothing to do with her husband.

"Count your blessings when you're sad," her grandmother Flood had always said. Oma had been so patient and wise. "Do it even when you're mad. You'll feel better. Focus on the good things, and you will have more of them." Of course, Oma had never known L. B.

Billie took a deep breath. She'd at least try counting her blessings.

Blessing number one: She had Patty.

Number two: She had an agent. Few people had agents.

Number three: She had two films lined up.

Number four: She had a musical to do with Terry.

Number five: If she would be willing to move to New York, she would have a television show to do. And maybe, she could do it from here someday.

Billie felt calmer for a minute, but realized that none of the new work was for certain. Promises didn't always materialize. Oh God, what had she done? Nine months of work versus three years? She should have taken the three. She should walk back in there right now and say, "Have it your way. Do what you want with me." At least she'd have a job.

She straightened her skirt, walked to the door, and reached for the knob, but before she could turn it, the door creaked open and Ernie emerged, hands on his hips, the corners of his mouth down-turned.

"I'm going to throw myself to the lion," she told Ernie.

"Don't be ridiculous," he said.

"But I need the work."

He led her to the end of the corridor and stopped. He looked her in the eye. "Next time, listen to me," he said, his voice snippy.

"I'm sorry," she said.

He nodded his forgiveness. "Okay, here's the deal," he said. "You get the same weekly salary and increases in the agreement."

"Okay," she said, her pulse slowing, relieved her outburst hadn't ruined everything.

"You maintain top billing in your films, but have no control over the parts."

Top billing was good. No control was not good. But Ernie had a smile creeping across his face. Something good was coming, she could tell.

"L. B. sees no changes from the usual roles," Ernie said, "so at least you won't have to worry about playing old maids and fishwives. You keep the revenue from theater, radio, television, and books."

Her shoulders relaxed.

"But you share the fees on films I line up fifty-fifty. I'll negotiate higher salaries to make up the difference. It only applies to films, not television, radio, or theater."

"But he has nothing to do with those films."

"Studio contracts are ownership agreements, and agenting is new. Nobody knows the rules because there aren't any. We're all shooting in the dark. This deal is for three years, not forever, and you'll still be making a lot more money than you are right now. Let's take this inch by inch." He paused. "Do we have a deal?"

"When I do other things, will I still earn my MGM salary?"

"Yes. Radio and the other projects are on top of that salary, so nothing changes. However, you'll still have to present yourself as an MGM actress, and scheduling will be tricky because we'll have to work around the MGM films." He took a breath. "And you'll have to live and work by the studio's moral conditions, which haven't changed."

She bristled and asked from the side of her mouth, "Does L. B. live by those standards?"

"Like or not, he still owns you, but at least your boat will be stronger while it floats on this steady cash river."

She sighed. She'd gotten much of what she wanted: more money, some stability, and the right to do other things. Ernie was right. It was a start.

"I told you I'd do this," Ernie said, "and I did."

"Why did L. B. act like that?"

"Because he can be a jerk, and he wanted to see the great Mrs. Ziegfeld suffer before he gave in. L. B. sees himself as the Flo Ziegfeld of the movies, and he doesn't think he gets enough credit for it."

Her jaw dropped. "He said that?"

"No, but I know him. Your husband was a powerful man in entertainment."

"So, what made him change his mind? It certainly wasn't anything I did or said."

"Two things: First, he needs you because you are a big name. And second, there was Beatrice."

Her jaw dropped open. "You mean *the* Beatrice? L. B.'s girlfriend?"

"Yes."

"What about her?"

"She liked you," he said. "You had a chat with her at a function?"

Billie nodded. "The Jewish Home Benefit."

"Smart move. She thinks you're a kind person, which you are, and when she saw the notice in the paper about your being let go, she said something to L. B."

Her eyes popped wide. "He told you that?"

He shook his head. "No. Beatrice told me that." He paused. "I represent her. She signed with me the other day. And don't forget." He pointed at Billie. "I'll be taking ten percent of your television earnings. Three years, maybe less, and you're on. Now, go home and celebrate, and next time, follow the script."

Billie bounced on her toes. She'd been wrong about agents, and was happy with this one. She felt a sense of ease again, like in the old days. She ran through a list of things she wanted to buy, including a home. Renting felt temporary, so unstable, and transitional. Those days were ending.

Chapter Thirty-three

It was the night of *Oz*'s opening, and the black Packard limousine headed north on Highland Avenue with Billie, Patty, William, and Francis inside. She'd learned through the grapevine that Francis's divorce was final, and she felt both sorry and relieved for him. They'd had tea and talked, mending their quarrel, and Billie thought he'd appreciate being her escort to the opening. He grabbed at the chance. He'd never been to an opening like this one.

The car rounded the corner at Highland, with Grauman's Chinese Theater coming up on the right.

"Oh, my God," Patty said as she pointed out the window. Bleachers lined the street, filled with cheering young people waving sweaters and scarves. Mounted police strode up and down. Klieg spotlights lit the sky. The energy was solid and throbbing. Billie had never seen such a spectacle for an opening. Goosebumps broke out all over her.

"I could get used to this," William said.

"There'll be plenty more to attend," Billie said. "Perhaps none this big, and but more nonetheless."

Francis's eyes opened wide. "Oh my God," he said. "Look at that." He pointed to the theater, the curved hip-and-gable roof of the Chinese Theater glowing in the distance.

William started to roll down the curbside window.

"Don't do that," Billie quickly said.

"We just need to be careful, that's all," Patty told him, in a gentler tone.

"Crowds like this can get out of control quickly," Billie said. "I'm sorry for snapping. We're like zoo animals in a cage. They'll reach inside the car or toss things through the window."

"Good grief," William said. He rolled the window up.

"This business can be exciting, but it comes with dangers. Enjoy it, work with it, but be careful," Billie said. "It's not all that it seems."

Francis took a breath and stretched his neck to look out the window. He shook his head. "It was nothing like this for my first film."

"B films don't get as much attention," Billie said.

The car stopped at the theater forecourt as the band outside played "The Merry Old Land of Oz." Billie tapped her toes to the rhythm of the tune she'd come to know so well.

"The entrance looks like a film set," Francis said.

The car rolled to a stop in front of the entrance. The red carpet was actually golden, the same color as the film's

Yellow Brick Road. The Munchkinland Mayor opened the door.

"You and I are going to get out first," Billie told Francis. Next, she addressed William. "Dear, once we're out, I'll give you a signal, and then you step out, hold your hand for Patty, and let her step out with you. She is your princess for the evening. Think of her that way."

"I love this," William said as he straightened the lapel of his tuxedo.

The car door opened, and Francis stepped out with a Hollywood smile and held his hand out for Billie. She took it, lifted her skirt, and stepped onto the carpet in her pearl-colored chiffon gown. The street crowd roared in approval.

Every bone inside of her was vibrating. Billie turned on her biggest smile and waved at the crowd. Francis did the same.

A man called out, "I love you, Miss Burke!"

She blew him a kiss and took Francis's arm. He escorted her down the carpet, which was edged with corn stalks. Scattered Munchkins danced to the music.

Flash, flash, flash went the cameras. "Miss Burke, over here," yelled a cameraman to the right. A brimmed hat shielded his eyes.

She paused, posed, smiled, and waved.

Flash, flash, flash.

A reporter called out, "Miss Burke? You getting married?"

She waved off the remark. Let them print what they wanted. She didn't give a codswallop. Let the whole world see Billie and Francis together. Let the whole world see her. Miss Billie Burke was never going away. She had the power within herself to do whatever she wanted. She had her own pair of ruby slippers, and they'd been on her feet the entire time.

Chapter Thirty-four

Epilogue

September 1952

Billie was relaxing in the backyard until she had to work later. She was lying back on a chaise-longue, eyes closed, with a wide-brimmed hat over her face.

She had just returned from taping an NBC television episode of *Doc Corkle*. She played Melinda, a flibbertigibbet, a role she didn't mind so much because she had other, more serious parts.

The gate to Patty's backyard, next door, banged open. Both her home and Billie's, here in Brentwood, had been designed by William. Billie loved having her family next door. She got to see her grandchildren daily without having them underfoot.

Billie sat up and opened her eyes, pushing the hat brim off her face. The intruder was her ten-year-old granddaughter, Gayle—whose presence was more than welcome.

"He took it," Gayle said, running to Billie. Gayle had Billie's mother's personality: strong-willed, direct, unrelenting, but quick to be kind. She also had Flo's flair for drama. Each of the grandchildren had inherited personality chunks from family members, and it was fun to parse them out. When Billie was a child, her mother had often told her, "You have so-and-so's personality, so-and-so's red hair, so-and so's temper." Billie had shrugged it off as adult-speak. Now, she understood.

Billie stood and kissed Gayle on the forehead. The child's hair smelled like shampoo.

"What are you saying? What's wrong?" Billie said.

"Gary," the girl said in disgust. "He took my *Gauntlet* book." Gary was Gayle's six-year-old brother. "I was almost finished, too."

Billie made a sad face. "I'm sure we'll find it. It must be somewhere."

Gayle was competing in the Fifth Annual Reading Competition sponsored at her school and was determined to read the most books by tomorrow's deadline to win a trophy. *The Gauntlet* was her tenth and final book. She was three books ahead of her classmates.

"I looked everywhere," Gayle said, "but I couldn't find it. He said he didn't do it, but I know he did because you know how he is."

Gayle was right: That's how he was, because little boys did those kinds of things. Gary wasn't a devious child. He was sweet like his father. It was just that he was six years old.

Having grandchildren taught Billie a few new things about love. She'd loved Flo, but when she had Patty, she felt a deeper attachment to her daughter. She didn't think there could be a deeper love until the grandchildren came along. The feelings she had for her grandchildren couldn't be put into words.

"What did your mother say about it, dear?" Billie said.

Gayle gesticulated. "She was busy, so I came here. I think he buried it somewhere. He plays back here sometimes."

"Well, it's not in the pool," Billie said with a laugh. "Do you want me to help you look for it?"

"Yes," Gayle said.

The gate's hinges squealed, and Patty walked in with her two-year-old daughter, Pamela, on her hip. She had a book in her other hand.

"Gayle, come home, please," Patty said. "Oma has to work later. Give her some time to rest."

"Good grief," Billie scoffed. "I'm not that old." Billie was in good health. Her figure was trim, her life good. She worked like a horse because she wanted to; it kept her alive. Sometimes she even had to turn work down.

"I have the book," Patty said as she lifted it. "Pamela had it."

Gayle grabbed it.

Patty waved a finger at the girl. "The next time something like this happens, you come to me first."

Gayle's chin dropped. "Yes, Mother." She turned to Billie with a question in her face.

"Yes, dear?" Billie asked her.

"Um, may I have another book, Oma? Please?"

"Ten is enough," Patty said. "And Oma is busy."

"But what if it's not enough?" Gayle asked. "What if the other kids catch up tonight?"

Patty sighed. "It's up to you, Mother," she said to Billie.

"I'll get my purse," Billie said. She had plenty of time before she had to go to work, and nothing would please her more than to spend some extra time with her granddaughter.

Inside the house, the phone rang. Billie held up a finger to tell Gayle to wait, then jogged inside to answer. Ernie was on the other end.

"We got it!" he said.

"Got what?"

"That talk show you always wanted. DuMont is on board. He suggests calling it *At Home with Billie Burke*."

She felt an adrenaline rush. "How many years has it been?"

"It doesn't matter now. It's finally happening. He's committing to ten episodes to see how it goes."

Billie smiled as she thought back to the way L. B. had mocked television. How wrong he had been! In fact, he'd been wrong about the future so often that he was pushed out at MGM last year. Everyone on the lot breathed easier these days.

"Guess how much money?" he said.

"I have no idea."

"C'mon. Guess."

"Okay. Two hundred dollars per episode."

"Higher."

She paced quicker. "Five hundred dollars per episode?"

"Higher."

Her insides felt like they were bubbling. "Tell me."

"A thousand dollars per episode, and you have full control over guests, script, everything."

Her jaw dropped. She didn't know what to say.

"We'll discuss details when you come to the office tomorrow. But for tonight, enjoy," Ernie said.

Hanging up the phone, Billie hustled outside, only to find Gayle was gone.

"She's changing her clothes," Patty said. Frowning, she wagged a finger at Billie. "Just one book, Mother. One. And dinner is at six, so no ice cream."

Billie was planning to treat the child to a Coke, and a Coke wasn't ice cream. Patty would never have to know. "Fine. And I have good news. You remember years ago when I visited you at the radio station in New York? I was in town meeting about the possibility of a talk show on television?"

"Oh, God. Those horrible days," Patty moaned.

Billie raised her arms. "Well, it happened."

"What happened?"

"That was Ernie on the phone. He heard from DuMont. I got it. The talk show—the one I pitched back then."

Patty clapped her hands. "You're kidding?! I'd forgotten all about that. Finally! What a wonderful surprise."

"I'm already making a list of guests in my head."

"Who?"

"Artists. Francis, for one." He was in Texas teaching music. He didn't tour anymore.

"William will be glued to the set." There was a long pause, then Patty put a finger to her lip.

Something was wrong. Billie felt the tingling inside her stop in an instant.

"Mother, while I'm here, I have something to discuss with you."

"You look serious."

"Perhaps you should sit." Patty motioned to the chaise.

"I'll stand." Patty and her family were moving. Billie was sure of it. William had been traveling to San Francisco for work. Perhaps they were moving there.

"This is William's last trip north, if that's what you're thinking," Patty said.

Oh, thank goodness, Billie thought. "Then what is it?"

Suddenly, Patty's entire face changed, and she grinned ear to ear. "You're going to have a new grandchild."

Billie's hands flew to her face, and tears flooded her eyes. Patty had always wanted a big family. Being an only child had been lonely for her at times, but with a career,

Billie could only handle one child. She opened her arms and wrapped them around her daughter.

All these years, all the hard work, but Billie finally had it all: a career, a family, a house of her own that she loved. The tornado had ended, and there was no place like home.

Author's Note

Glinda's Ruby Slippers, set in 1939 Los Angeles, puts us on the set of *The Wizard of Oz* and in the middle of the Golden Age of Hollywood. The journey is from the perspective of Billie Burke, the actress who played Glinda. The story unfolds during Billie's life when she faced a contract renewal at MGM. The renewal was in jeopardy, which tested her ability to remake herself at the age of fifty-four. She had to relearn how to build a career during the Great Depression, in an era when the only talent that mattered was under age thirty-five.

The public knows Billie as Glinda the Good Witch in *The Wizard of Oz* and as Mrs. Topper in the *Topper* film series. However, from 1906 through the 1930s, she was the Queen of Entertainment, much like a combination of Bette Midler, Angelina Jolie, and Emma Watson today.

Glinda's Ruby Slippers began in 2002 as a postdoctoral biography of Billie Burke. After seven years of research,

I ran into a problem: Someone had published another version first. The book was *Mrs. Ziegfeld: The Public and Private Lives of Billie Burke*, by Grant Hayter-Menzies (2009). Seeing that made my heart sink: I'd just finished reading hundreds of books and articles and had traveled coast-to-coast sifting through archival materials, including Billie's letters, spending a lot of my own money to get the job done. Resigned, I bought a copy and read the book, hoping it would be horrible and that I could write a better one. But the book was good, and I couldn't improve on it. I didn't know what to do next, and I didn't want to waste my work and money.

For the next couple of months, I journaled and brainstormed until it came to me: I'd write a historical novel, staying as true to the history as I could. The idea excited me, but I'd never written fiction, and I didn't know where to begin, so I simply got started. When I finished with the first version, I gave it to a friend to read.

"Nobody cares who Billie Burke is," my friend said. "What they care about is the film. Center it on that. And by the way, this reads like a textbook."

His view was discouraging to hear, yet it motivated me to try a new approach. I refused to give up. Billie's story was important and had a message for everyone today.

At the time, I lived in New York City, a great place to be when you have a problem like this, given that New York is the center of the American literary world. For help, I turned to Gotham Writer's Workshop and enrolled in its novel-writing workshop. Novelist Diana Spechler led the workshop, and she had this to say: "Pick an episode in her life and make a story around it. You can build a backstory into it. Oh, and this reads like a biography."

Biography, textbook—pretty much the same thing. I hope I fixed the problem.

On Tuesday nights for three years, I worked with Gotham in a critique group of peers to narrow the story and learn to write fiction. I listened to those around the table make suggestions to improve the work. Early on, I chose the episode: Billie's contract renewal during *Oz* filming. The renewal webbed through her past, present, and future. It also incorporated the beloved film and Hollywood's Golden Era, two things that would pull in the reader. I based the episode choice on a collection of Billie's letters housed at Boston University, communications not referenced in *Mrs. Ziegfeld*. The letters showed her emotional desperation about finding work and love.

Glinda's Ruby Slippers re-creates the life and times of Billie Burke—actor, mother, daughter, and wife. The book is technically fiction, but it is based on historical research and real-life events. It takes the reader behind the scenes and shows Billie Burke fighting back to keep her career alive in an industry obsessed with youth and beauty.

Everything in *Glinda* is true, likely true, or possibly true given the time, the personalities, and Hollywood's culture. I had to bend things here and there to create a story and fill in some blanks. What historians find left behind is never the complete picture. For example, I set *Oz*'s premiere two months earlier than it really was and gave fictitious names to a few real-life characters because my portrayals had less historical detail than the others.

Rumors did exist about Billie being a lesbian in a relationship with Dorothy Arzner, but it was more likely a close friendship. Changes like this don't matter because I focused on the emotional journey. Based on primary and secondary sources, I tried to portray every real-life character in an honest, thoughtful way. I relied heavily on primary-source materials, including Billie's communications, media quotes, radio and television shows, and Patty's book on the family.

Acknowledgments

First, I want to thank my editor at Blydyn Square Books, Tara Tomczyk, for her thoughtful and meticulous edits and questions. She read the book all the way through at least twice, maybe three times. She deserves a special medal of some kind.

I want to thank Diana Spechler (*Who by Fire*, 2008; *Skinny*, 2011) for supporting the book. Diana helped transform *Glinda* from something reading like an encyclopedia to a novel based on a true story.

I also want to thank the other brave friends and groups who read and commented on the manuscript along the way. They demonstrated considerable patience, especially the first two on this list who read the entire thing twice: Mick Landaiche, Rebecca Taber-Conover, Mario Meallot, Randall Freeman, Scott Morrow, Stephen Fleming, Kevin Grail, and Dawn Wojcik. The book also went through a critiquing process with the Northeast Los Angeles Writer's Group.

I owe so much to the following libraries, archives, and museums that gave me access to their collections and answered my many questions: Academy of Motion Pictures, Margaret Herrick Library; American Film Institute, Louis B. Mayer Library; Beverly Hills Public Library Historical Archives; Boston University Library, Nancy Hamilton Collection; Circus Historical Society; Cleveland Playhouse Archives; Cleveland Public Library, Cleveland Press Collection; Eddie Brandt's Saturday Matinee; Forest Lawn Memorial Park; Glendale Public Library, Special Collections; Hollywood Forever Cemetery, Los Angeles; Hastings-on-Hudson Historical Society, New York; Hollywood Bowl Museum; Hollywood History Museum; Huntington Library, Selma Akins Papers; Kensico Cemetery, New York; Lasky-DeMille Barn; Library of Congress, Motion Picture and Television Reading Room, Recorded Sound Reference Collection; Los Angeles County, Norwalk, Birth, Marriage and Death Records, Real Estate Records; Los Angeles Public Library; Lower Eastside Tenement Museum; Lyceum Theater, New York City; Museum of the City of New York, Theater Collection; Museum of the Moving Image; New York Public Library, Billy Rose Theatre Collection (William Baral Papers, Robinson Locke Collection, Margaret Hamilton Papers, Anna Held Papers, Flo Ziegfeld–Billie Burke Papers); New York Public Library, Schwarzman Building, Manuscripts and Archives Collection (Charles Frohman Letterpress Books); Ohio Historical Society; Paley Center for Media, Beverly Hills; Paramount Studios; Lemberg Archives; Sony Pictures; Southern Western Law School (Former Bullocks Wilshire Department Store); UCLA Charles E. Young Research Library; UCLA Film and Television Archive; University of Washington, Seattle, Wesley C. Wehr Collection; USC Cinematic Arts Collection, Dorothy Arzner Collection; Los Angeles County Library, West Hollywood; Western Reserve Historical Society, Cleveland, Ohio; and Will Rogers State Historical Park.

I would also like to thank those who let me interview them about the movie, its players, and the period. I list them in alphabetical order by last name: Dr. Andrew Davis, California State Polytechnic University, Pomona (William Burke, circus and vaudeville history); Richard Halverson, actor, Minneapolis, Minnesota (Margaret Hamilton); Lora Martinolich, Glendale Public Library Special Collections (Glendale "Grand Central" Airport); Marc Wannamaker, Beverly Hills historian (Beverly Hills, Billie Burke); Wesley C. Wehr, University of Washington, Seattle, Washington (Margaret Hamilton).

I also want to thank Javista Organic Coffee in Hollywood, where I wrote the final editions.

I want to thank my mother, JoAnn Radice, and my grandmothers, Elizabeth Ann Vetter and Mary Grace Radice, for instilling a love of history in me.

About the Author

Mike Radice has a Ph.D. in Public History focusing on theater history. He was the former assistant director of the Skyscraper Museum (NYC) and director of education of the Harriet Beecher Stowe Center, a historic site. He has published more than thirty articles and short stories, and two nonfiction books: *Professional Money-Raising for Schools* (2014) and *Spiritual Nutrition* (2024). He lives in Los Angeles, California.

Thank You

FOR READING

Glinda's Ruby Slippers!

WE HOPE YOU'VE ENJOYED IT! HERE AT BLYDYN SQUARE BOOKS, WE TAKE SPECIAL CARE IN PRODUCING BOOKS OF THE HIGHEST QUALITY FOR YOUR ENTERTAINMENT AND EDUCATION. WE DO OUR BEST TO CREATE "BOOKS THAT MAKE YOU THINK!"

TO FIND OUT MORE ABOUT US OR TO SEE WHAT OTHER TITLES WE OFFER, PLEASE VISIT BLYDYNSQUAREBOOKS.COM.

STAY UP TO DATE WITH OUR LATEST NEWS (AND BE ELIGIBLE TO WIN PRIZES) BY SUBSCRIBING TO OUR NEWSLETTER: